SUSAN WIGGS

is a bestselling mainstream author with more than one million copies of her books in print. Wiggs, a former teacher, believes that love can create a world in which all wounds are healed, and her award-winning tales of adventure and romance bear this out. Noted for their scenes of emotional truth, evoking both tears and laughter, her novels regularly appear on national bestseller lists. Susan lives with her family on an island in the Pacific Northwest, where she is working on her next book.

KATE HOFFMANN

started reading romance when she was an elementary school music teacher. She started writing romance when she was an advertising copywriter. And in 1993, the year her first Temptation novel was published, she quit the nine-to-five world and became a full-time romance writer. Since then, Kate has published more than thirty stories with Harlequin, including Temptation, Duets, continuity series and anthologies. Kate's first single-title release, *Reunited,* will be published in 2002. Kate lives in Wisconsin with her three cats and her computer. When she's not writing, she enjoys gardening, golfing and genealogy.

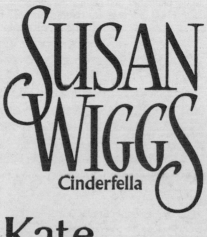

SUSAN WIGGS
Cinderfella

Kate Hoffmann
Lady of the Night

HARLEQUIN®

TORONTO • NEW YORK • LONDON
AMSTERDAM • PARIS • SYDNEY • HAMBURG
STOCKHOLM • ATHENS • TOKYO • MILAN • MADRID
PRAGUE • WARSAW • BUDAPEST • AUCKLAND

ISBN 0-373-83523-X

HARLEQUIN SPECIAL Vol. 3

CONTENTS

Cinderfella

Susan Wiggs

Chapter One

"Hey, Riley! You going to the ball?"

"Come on, Brad," Derek said. "Riley thinks a ball has to say 'Wilson' on it to be any good."

Jack Riley looked up from a Zenlike contemplation of his aged high-top sneakers, which he had propped on a stack of files on his desk. The world's smallest Christmas tree, hung with decorations made by kids at the shelter, perched atop his computer monitor.

For all Jack cared, the cluttered newsroom, the ringing phones, the glaring fluorescent lights and the two yammering preppies could vanish in a puff of smoke.

"Look at the boy, Brad. Like, old Riley's got nothing to wear." Derek Crenshaw took nauseating pride in his cashmere sweaters from Brooks Brothers—supplied by overindulgent parents.

"Gimme a break," Riley said, scratching his gray CUNY sweatshirt. "I got a clean set of sweats in my gym bag."

Guffaws burst from his companions. The preppies, playing at being ace reporters, were so easily amused, Jack thought, folding his long legs under his desk and snatching a pencil from behind his ear. He pushed his thick-lensed glasses up on his nose. For a moment, his gaze rested on the engraved invitation that lay atop the rubble on his desk. Somewhere, a mile under, lay a brand-new ink blotter purchased with scraped-together pennies by a grateful young boy he had once helped.

Jack squinted through his horn-rims at the cream stock card. "Miss Madeleine Langston requests the pleasure of your company.... Nine o'clock...at the Dakota... Black tie only..."

"Black tie," Jack muttered, lowering the bill of his Yankees cap. Miss Madeleine Langston was no doubt praying Mr. Jack Riley would drop off the face of the earth. Why the hell had she invited him, anyway? Pity? Guilt? Or did the young heiress have a yen for slumming with nobodies from Brooklyn?

"Hey, Riley!" Derek said, advancing on him with a Sharpie marker. "Maybe I could, like, you know, draw a black tie on the front of your shirt."

"Hey, Derek," Jack said, effortlessly mimicking his co-worker's southern California accent. "Maybe I could, like, break your kneecaps and toss you in a shallow grave."

Brad and a few of the mailroom boys again burst into laughter.

"Working hard, gentlemen?" The blade-sharp question knifed through the merriment.

Jack looked across the newsroom, and there she was.

The ice maiden. The crystal goddess. The bane of his existence.

His publisher.

"Er, Jack was just finishing up," Derek said hastily, capping the marker and dropping a manila legal file on the danger zone of Jack's desk.

Madeleine Langston effortlessly negotiated a path

through the maze of desks. She moved as if the layout of the bright glass-walled newsroom was imprinted on her brain like circuits on a computer chip.

After her father's death six months before, she had inherited the *Courier*. Everyone had expected her to retire gracefully to the Hamptons and let the income roll in. For a while, she had. Then, just three weeks ago, she had fired the inept managing editor and appointed herself publisher. Apparently she was having trouble finding someone to reflect her standards of perfection, so for the time being, and to the dismay of all the staff, she had taken on the duties herself.

Until last week, she had stayed off the city-room turf, preferring her sterile corner office one floor up. This was only the second time Jack had seen her up close. She was terrifyingly gorgeous. He liked her much better as a brittle voice on the telephone.

Because he knew it would annoy her, he put his feet back up on his desk, crossed his ankles and linked his fingers behind his head. He peered at her from beneath the brim of his cap.

Madeleine Langston advanced like a guided missile. She was, Jack decided, the only woman in Manhattan who could wear an ivory wool suit all day and not get a single wrinkle in it. Probably because she had no body heat. None at all.

What she did have was looks, brains and money. In deadly excess. She made him want to cross his fingers to ward off evil. Worse, she made him want to make love to her until she cried out for mercy—or for more.

She stopped in front of his desk. He had a perfect view of her face: dainty cheekbones and a nose that was probably used as a model at plastic-surgery conventions; eyes as blue as the bottom of a swimming pool; pale blond hair done into some sort of painfully neat macramé arrangement.

She brought a French-manicured fingernail to her full lower lip and held it there just for a moment in case of the unlikely event that she had not gotten his attention. She eyed the lopsided miniature Christmas tree; clearly it was as alien to her as moon rock.

If she was waiting for him to stand and remove his cap, she would miss her party tonight.

"The waste-management finance scandal?" she inquired. Her upper-crust East Coast accent rang with the tones of generations of selective breeding and years at Marymount and Vassar.

Jack gave her his most crooked, irritating smile and stroked the week-old bristle on his chin. "Why don't you hurry up and hire a managing editor to ride herd over us wayward boys?"

"This is my paper, Mr. Riley, and I'll 'ride herd' over whomever I please."

"Sounds kinky, Miz Langston," he muttered. Leaning forward, he jerked a file from the stack under his feet and held it out to her.

Platinum-and-pearl rings flashed as she opened the file. An empty potato-chip bag drifted to the floor. She made an admirable effort to ignore it. Her gaze snapped over the typed copy.

She gave the barest of nods, then said, "And the school, er, health controversy?"

Jack chuckled. "You mean the debate about whether or not we should hand out rubbers to high schoolers?" He savored the delicate coral blush on her cheeks. "Yeah, it's ready." Keeping his gaze trained on the boss lady, he tapped on his keyboard. The printer beside his desk ejected a copy of the story.

Her refined nostrils flared subtly. "Mr. Riley, how has such a charming man managed to live so long without sustaining serious bodily injury?"

He grinned and toyed with the short, curly ponytail at the nape of his neck. "Guess I'm just quick on my feet, sweetheart."

Her look of disdain would have done Katharine Hepburn proud. "I see." She took the hard copy, still warm from the printer, and added it to her stack.

To his relief, she turned her ice-dagger gaze on Brad and Derek. "What about you gentlemen? Have you made your deadlines, for a change?"

They stared at her like a pair of dieters eyeing a box of Godiva chocolates. Idiots, thought Jack. He knew they had a standing bet to see who could get her into bed first. As if either one had a chance. Who would want to, except maybe a polar explorer with a suit that could withstand subzero temperatures?

Jack Riley, that's who, he thought in self-disgust. She was everything he should despise in a woman, but perversely, he found her the sexiest thing he had ever seen. He wanted her. Bad. Wanted to melt the ice around her with his own heat.

"Sure thing, Miss Langston," Brad said, looking like the soul of efficiency.

"Yep," Derek agreed.

"Excellent." Madeleine turned to go. Before Jack could get comfortable again, she pivoted back, her three-hundred-dollar shoes clicking on the linoleum floor. "Oh, and gentlemen? Will I see you at the Dakota tonight?"

"Of course," Derek and Brad said in unison. Their cashmere sweaters and Top-Siders personified the ersatz newsroom-clone look. They would be swell in their tuxes. Just swell.

Madeleine Langston's gaze fixed on Jack. Damn, she was a good-looking woman. What a waste of a great set of j—

"Well?" she asked, interrupting his thought. "Are you coming?"

Jack decided it was too easy to take advantage of her choice of words, so he relented. "Naw," he said, laughing with his eyes at her look of relief. "I've got a date with the Urban Animals."

She raised a pruned eyebrow. "Urban Animals?"

"A group of punked-up ice skaters in Central Park."

"Oh. You'll be missed."

Jack could contain his laughter no longer. God, she was a pain in the ass. Only their second face-to-face meeting and they were already in hate. He loved to razz her. "You know," he said, "I might just be able to tear myself away...."

Her wide, beautiful eyes flashed a message of distress. For an ice goddess, she was a damned poor liar, and her habit of blushing made her seem almost human.

"Don't worry, Princess," he said consolingly, dropping the invitation into the overflowing wastebasket beside his desk. "Prince Charming has other plans."

Chapter Two

Wearing the perfect dress, Madeleine Langston stood in the perfect suite in the Dakota. In the center of the room stood a perfect designer Christmas tree. She heard the perfect strains of the swing band, watched the perfect poise of the guests and nibbled one of the perfect hors d'oeuvres.

"Madeleine, darling!" William Wornich, the gossip columnist of the *Courier,* leaned forward to kiss the air beside her cheek. "Wonderful party. It's perfect, a perfect fairy-tale ball."

"Thank you, William. Isn't it just?"

Acrid smoke from his cigar made her eyes smart. Damn. She would have to take her contacts out, and she was practically blind without them.

Unrepentant, Wornich stood back and held her at arm's length. "And that dress! Too cunning. Wherever did you get it?"

She gave him a practiced smile. "Darling, you'd never believe it if I told you." It had been her grandmother's: a vintage 1940s affair of black silk taffeta set off with cascades of bugle beads at the shoulders and hem. The perfect dancing dress. The problem was, there was no one here with whom she wanted to dance.

Oh, Daddy. The thought of him came unbidden, as evocative as the spice of wassail or the scent of pine boughs. The lavish apartment in the Dakota had belonged to him, and next week it would be sold. It was strange being back here, strange seeing the people he had known. He himself had planned the party, months in advance, never knowing he wouldn't be around to play the host.

There was one advantage to being back at the apartment that was full of achingly sweet memories. Having the party here meant she could leave. She could escape.

"Madeleine, dear," Wornich said with a sly wink and a fresh puff of smoke, "I must ask you. I know you're hosting this in memory of your father, but what's the real purpose of the party? Husband hunting?"

She was so inured to the question that she didn't bother to take offense. After Daddy's death, everyone had expected her to find a husband who could take over the helm of the *Courier*. Or a tycoon who would buy her out.

Madeleine had chosen a completely different route. She had demanded that the board of trustees appoint her publisher. Lately she had worked herself into exhaustion as managing editor. No one could figure out why.

Madeleine Langston knew why. She had to find a way to define herself, to look in the mirror and see a person who did things. Important things. Useful things. Things that made her human.

"Don't be foolish, William," she said breezily, blinking away smoke. "All the men I meet are either after my money, my status, or they're scared to death of me."

"All of them, darling?"

"All of them."

As William flitted off to alight amongst a group of

book critics, Madeleine ducked into the powder room to remove her contacts. The cigar smoke had made them unbearable. No matter. Her nearsightedness would just serve to blur the dullness of the company.

She stared into the mirror and thought about her exchange with William Wornich.

"All of them, darling?"

"All of them."

She finally admitted to herself that there was one exception—Jack Riley.

The thought of him brought a shiver of disgust to Madeleine. Although she barely knew him, she was already certain that Jack Riley was everything she detested in a man. He was crude, unkempt, irreverent and arrogant.

He was also the most talented and dependable writer on her staff.

She knew she shouldn't let him irritate her, but he had an annoying way of getting under her skin. That horrible half-grown beard and ponytail, those sly taunts designed to make her feel like a fraud, that cocky, go-to-hell attitude. He had the air of a man who bit off life in great, sloppy chunks and had no patience with those who were cautious and timid.

Like her.

Her visit to the city room earlier had been a disaster. She had gone down to mingle with the writers, perhaps become one of the gang. What a joke, thinking she could mingle. She came off like a cold fish every time. None of them seemed to realize she was simply shy. Least of all the insufferable Mr. Riley, who was anything *but* shy. He didn't even know her. Had only seen her on one other occasion. So why did he seem to have it in for her?

Trying to dismiss thoughts of him, she removed her contact lenses and put them in her beaded evening bag, then leaned forward to peer at her slightly hazy image in the pink-tinted mirror. She should have fixed her lipstick before taking out the lenses.

Exhaling a sigh, she decided the world would have to face Madeleine Langston without fresh lipstick. She stepped from the powder room and into the white-lightning glare of a camera flash. Her smile was automatic as someone snapped her picture for the society pages; her conversation was fluent as she discussed her father's legacy in publishing. None of the elegant company would ever guess how utterly awkward she felt.

Or how unbearably lonely. It was nearly Christmas, and she would be spending the holiday with her cat. It was too pathetic.

Once again, her errant thoughts wandered to Jack Riley. He wasn't bored. At this moment, he was probably dressed in something scandalously tight, made of black leather, and careening on ice skates around the pond in Central Park.

Bored, that's what he was.

Jack glared at the files on his desk. Derek and Brad owed him big this time. He had finished proofing their work for them. Their boring, pedestrian work. He himself hadn't done a juicy story in weeks. What was wrong with Manhattan these days? Where was all the murder and mayhem when a guy needed it?

Jack locked his desk, turned off his computer and left the office, ducking under a dried-up sprig of mistletoe. In the long, gleaming corridor, he encountered one of the cleaning ladies.

"Working late again, Jack?" she called out.

He grinned and looked down at his well-lived-in

sweats. "You won't see me turning into a pumpkin yet, Cora."

"Yeah, but have you checked your car lately?"

"A car? On my salary?" he asked. He'd long since sold his over-the-hill Mercury Marquis. Six years ago, he'd driven it to Manhattan from Muleshoe, Texas. He'd had nothing but a journalism degree from UT and a pocketful of dreams. "I'm taking the subway, sweetheart."

"Be careful, Jack."

He had cause to remember her admonition when, five minutes later, he turned down Lexington and saw two large thugs in the process of mugging a small, rotund man.

You're a New Yorker now, pal, he told himself, even as he broke into a run toward the shadowy figures. *You're supposed to look the other way.* But deep inside his Texas-born-and-bred chest beat the heart of a man who despised violence and injustice.

His size-twelve feet carried him swiftly over the littered, frozen street. One lowlife had the little man shoved up against the rough brick wall of a building. The other groped inside the victim's pockets.

Jack launched himself into a body slam. Stringy hair slapped him in the face. The breath left his target in a whoosh. Curling his fist into the back of a leather collar, Jack sent the man sprawling into a mound of midwinter slush. He fell easily—probably weak from being strung out on drugs—and crashed into a heap of damp cardboard boxes.

A fist smashed into Jack's stomach. His mercilessly conditioned muscles tightened at the contact. Even as he grunted, more in annoyance than pain, he clipped his assailant on the jaw with a lightning uppercut. The man howled and fled, clutching his face. His oily companion dragged himself up.

Jack stood ready, his feet planted, his body taut and his nerves alive with the dark hum of adrenaline. The mugger sized him up for about three seconds, then stumbled off after his companion.

Jack started to pursue them. But one glance at the pale, sweating face of the victim stopped him.

He was a munchkin man, impeccably dressed in a topcoat, holding a brass-headed cane. He had a neatly clipped mustache and goatee. His hands, clutching the cane, shook.

"Are you hurt?" Jack asked. He stooped and retrieved an expensive-looking hat, handing it to the man.

"N-no. Just shaken." The man produced a silk handkerchief, using it to mop his forehead. He put the hat on. "Thanks."

In the foggy glow of a streetlamp, Jack inspected the ashen, heavily jowled face. "You sure? You want me to call a doctor or something?"

"No. I'll just go back to the shop and call a cab. I've got a truck, but I don't feel like driving tonight." The man looked at Jack and suddenly seemed to remember himself. "Listen to me. The man saves my life and I don't even introduce myself." He stuck out a gloved hand. "Harry Fodgother."

"John Patrick Riley. Call me Jack." He instantly placed the little man. Back when he was first starting out at the paper, he'd done a stint as a copy editor. Fodgother's name had appeared frequently in the society column: The Donald Dazzled the Dames in His Exclusive Harry Fodgother Tux.... "You're the tailor, right?"

Harry's features pinched with mock disdain. "Gentlemen's clothier, if you please." He laughed. "I call myself that, I get to charge double."

He extracted a wad of keys from his pocket and opened a heavy steel door marked Deliveries. Jack followed him, passing through a large room filled with bolts of fabric, sewing machines, dress dummies and drafting tables. The walls boasted photos of Who's Who types sporting Fodgother's creations.

When they entered the shop, Jack's feet sank two inches into the plush carpet. The showroom was done in leather, brass and hunter green, like a gentlemen's English bar, complete with hunting scenes on the walls. There wasn't a stitch of clothing in sight. He suspected the ready-to-wears were tucked into the antique armoires, chests and highboys.

"Nice place," he remarked.

"Indeed." Harry switched on a green-shaded banker's lamp on a desk and picked up the phone. "There's an icebox under the counter there. Have a beer."

Jack opened a beer for himself and one for Harry while Fodgother called for a cab. When he hung up, Jack asked, "Aren't you going to report this to the police?"

Fodgother shook his head. "They were just a couple of dopers. I didn't really get a look at them. You came along before they took anything except my pride. Police would take all night and…" His voice trailed off as Jack drew something out of his pocket.

"Damn," Jack said, frowning. "I thought I threw this away." Actually, he *had* thrown the invitation away, but on impulse he had rescued the card. Maybe to show his mother, who always wanted to hear about his high-falutin' New York City friends. She never could get it into her head that he didn't hobnob with John F. Kennedy, Jr., on a regular basis.

He came out from behind the counter and handed Harry a beer.

"You were working late," Jack observed. "Cheers."

"I work all through the season." He lifted his beer bottle. "Mazel tov."

Jack grinned and took a sip. "Same to you."

"You're not from around here."

"Texas, but my accent's fading fast unless I think about it."

Harry picked up the cream stock card. He read it quickly, then slapped his forehead. "An invitation from Madeleine Langston! How on earth did you come by this?"

Jack took another slug of beer. "She's my boss. Otherwise known as the bitch goddess."

"Gorgeous, though. She used to go out with one of my 46-Regulars."

Jack chuckled, picturing Madeleine Langston accompanied by an empty suit. Then his amusement faded as the empty suit changed into an image of himself. Sheesh. He was losing his mind. He was one sick puppy. He *wanted* her.

"Don't tell me you aren't smitten with her." Harry pointed his cane at Jack. "I was young once, too."

"She's a snow queen," Jack protested. "Cruella De Vil. I'd have better luck with an ice sculpture."

"Methinks the gentleman doth protest too much."

"I don't even know her. Met her once, maybe twice. And believe me, the earth did *not* move."

"The Dakota," Harry murmured. "That's her late father's annual party." He shook his head sadly. "It'll be her first year without him. Her last year for the party. Just think how that must make her feel."

Jack nearly gagged on his beer. Harry made him actually think of Madeleine as a person—someone with feelings, someone who could be hurt. He shouldn't care. But he did.

"She's probably dancing holes in the rug," he said.

"She's probably drinking too much and smiling too hard and wishing someone would rescue her."

"How would you know?" Jack asked, taking a swallow of beer.

Harry pointed the tip of his cane at Jack's chest. "I know. Trust me."

Pushy little squirt, Jack thought. Harry just kept staring at him. His scrutiny was so drawn out and intense that Jack's ears heated. "I guess I don't look much like your usual clients, right?"

"I like a challenge. Maybe there's a prince beneath those rags." Twirling his cane, Harry walked in a slow circle around Jack, muttering numbers under his breath. "Jack Riley, I'm going to outfit you like you never dreamed. It'll be like magic. You won't know yourself."

"Er, I'm not really into clothes, Harry."

"Come on, haven't you ever wanted to walk into a roomful of people and knock 'em dead?"

"Only if they're Republicans."

"Bah. You joke when you could go to this ball and meet the woman of your dreams."

Jack couldn't help himself. He laughed out loud.

Harry pointed the cane again. "Let me do this for you. You saved my life."

"Actually, I'm more the down-home, beer-and-TV type, Harry."

"Miracles happen, my boy."

Jack shoved his hands into the pockets of his Yankees jacket. "She's not my type—"

"I think you're the type who likes to have fun. Who

can't stand the thought of a lonely lady at a party where everyone wants something from her.'' Harry eyed the card meaningfully. He reached up and removed Jack's glasses. ''Drink your beer, cowboy. We've got work to do—and fast.''

Hell, Jack decided in amused resignation, had no fury like a tailor—er, gentleman clothier—in the throes of gratitude.

Chapter Three

Madeleine caught herself squinting at the clock again. Ten-thirty. Two whole minutes had passed since she had last checked. She had smiled a hundred plastic smiles, murmured a hundred lame greetings and taken a hundred sips of her now lukewarm Dom Pérignon. The bubbly was starting to take its toll.

She was, as always, graceful and cautious when tipsy. Objects took on a rather pleasant warm fuzziness. Watching a model in a dress that appeared to be constructed entirely of soda-can pull tabs, Madeleine repressed a tiny urge to giggle.

The urge died when Britt Beckworth III started across the room toward her. Like a human Ken doll, he had a square jaw, comb-furrowed hair and an empty head.

Madeleine sought shelter in the shadow of a stoneware Thorleifsson sculpture in the foyer. What was it about her, she wondered, that made her a virtual magnet for boring, self-seeking men? And catty, competitive women? Couldn't she, for God's sake, just have a friend?

She saw no likely candidate in the room. Derek and Brad from the city room kept looking at her with gazes of hopeful lust—not quite the sentiment she wanted to inspire in men.

She glanced longingly at the door. Her feet moved toward it without volition. Her thoughts were focused on the small red car made by an Italian manufacturer with an unpronounceable name. It was in the garage, gassed up and gleaming. She wished she hadn't drunk so much champagne and ditched her contacts for the night, because she really wanted to get in the car and just drive. Fast and far. Until she came to a place where the name Madeleine Langston meant nothing.

She wanted to do something wild and totally out of character. To lose control, for once in her life. Or even more intriguing, to surrender control to someone else, someone she could trust. Someone who would sweep her off her feet.

I wish, she thought. *I wish...* She closed her eyes and tried to will away the yearning, but she couldn't. She knew such things didn't happen in real life, but still...

Her hand closed around the doorknob. She was surprised to feel it turn from without, and she stepped back, marshaling her excuses. *Too glad to see you, darling, but I simply must run,* she rehearsed silently. *We'll do lunch....*

The door opened.

The excuses died in Madeleine's throat. She stepped back and stared, suddenly certain beyond any doubt that she had died and gone to heaven.

He stood well over six feet tall, even after he removed his black Stetson to reveal a wealth of glossy dark hair. "Hi, darlin'," he said easily, handing her a familiar card. "This got me past the doorman. Will it get me past you?"

"Not if I can help it," Madeleine murmured before

she could stop herself. Her awed gaze took in his beautifully groomed hair. Candlelight created russet highlights in the waves that spilled over the starched collar of his snowy shirt and sleekly cut jacket. The garment made a dark, enticing sculpture of his broad shoulders. He wore it open to reveal Florentine buttons down the minutely pleated front of his shirt and black dress slacks that hugged his narrow waist and hips. The toes of his black cowboy boots were narrow enough to stomp a roach in a corner of the Flatiron Building.

Studying his rugged, freshly shaven face, she felt a flicker of recognition. On the one hand, he looked startlingly familiar. Yet on the other hand, when he gave her a lazy, long-lipped smile, she was certain she had never seen that face before—except in the most pleasant of dreams.

"Darlin'," he said, "if we stand here much longer, somebody's going to hang a hat on one of us."

"Of course," she said, stepping back and setting his invitation on the hall table. "Come in, Mr...."

"Uh, Patrick. John...Patrick. But call me John, Miss..."

"Madeleine," she said quickly. But she liked it better when he called her "darlin'."

"Dance with me, darlin'." He put his hat on the table.

The swing band was playing a languorous tune from the forties. The bluesy strains invaded her, making it almost impossible not to sway. Feeling suddenly breezy, as if all the bubbles in the champagne she'd drunk had taken flight, Madeleine put her hand in his and let him sweep her into heaven.

To his utter amazement, Jack Riley found himself in the middle of a parquet floor, swaying slowly to a haunting, old-fashioned melody, with Madeleine Langston in his arms.

His senses hummed in disbelief. Either she was part of the game or she honestly didn't recognize him. Could Harry Fodgother's magic have changed him so much?

Catching a glimpse of himself in an antique mirror, he began to think it was possible. The horn-rims were gone. The upscale tux and boots and the shave and hairstyle had turned him from a Brooklyn slob into an urban cowboy. That, coupled with his exaggerated Texas drawl, made the perfect disguise.

Maybe.

Almost unconsciously, he tightened his hold on her waist and felt an unexpected jolt of attraction. The ice princess was different up close. She was warm. Soft. Touchable.

He'd taken ballroom dancing for a PE credit in college, and for the first time in his life he put the lessons to use. Her hand pressed softly against his arm. Bitch goddess? No way. At the moment she was as sweet and responsive as a kitten. And that smell! It was like holding a bouquet of freshly cut lilies in his arms.

"Enjoying the party?" he asked, watching the way his breath stirred her hair. Little wispy locks fell around her temples and neck. She had it all caught up in a strand of crystal beads.

"Mmm. I am now. I'd been dreading this party for weeks." She sent him a sweet-sad smile that he felt all the way to his fingertips. "It's my father's apartment. He passed away, but I felt obligated to put on his annual party one last time."

"I'm sorry for your loss," he said.

"I'm coping." Her thigh brushed his as they changed

direction on the dance floor. Her smile took on a mischievous light. "It's a great way to pick up men."

He swallowed painfully, his throat suddenly dry. "You do this often?"

She laughed. "You're my first. And I think you're worth waiting for."

Her easy admission took him aback. She knew. She had to. She was playing games with him. Yet a doubt took root in his mind. Madeleine Langston was incapable of lying. Jack had seen her try when she'd pretended she wanted him at her party. He'd seen her slender body stiffen, her face flush to the roots of her blonder-than-blond hair. She was a terrible liar.

Moving to the edge of the dance floor, he backed her against a marble pillar and stopped. He braced his hand on the wall and stared down into her face. Lord, she was beautiful. A cool, ivory Botticelli rising up out of her ocean kingdom, her eyes alight with—Jesus—admiration.

"Madeleine."

She touched his narrow silk bow tie. "I love the way you say my name."

Jack's collar suddenly felt uncomfortably tight. This was insane. "Have...have we met before?" He watched her intently for a reaction.

Her face was very close. She lifted one slender finger and touched his chin lightly, like an inquisitive child. His clean-shaven chin, which Harry Fodgother had splashed with something hideously expensive. "Impossible," she whispered, lowering her hand to trail it down his chest. "If I'd met you before, I never would have forgotten it."

Too late. She would kill him now if she found out.

Panicked, he grabbed her wrist and pulled her hand away. "Madeleine, don't do this," he said. "Don't pretend you don't know—"

"Oh, God." She rose on tiptoe to look past him. Her eyes held a wild, hunted look. "Here they come."

Jack glanced around to see William Wornich surrounded by a gaggle of bold-faced types easing toward them. In a heartbeat, he understood. Madeleine lived like a bug under a magnifying glass, regularly getting burned by the intensified rays of public attention. He could see tomorrow's headlines: Publishing Heiress Two-Steps with Mystery Cowboy.

"Come on." Ramming on his new Stetson, he slid his arm around her and bent to whisper in her ear, "Let's get out of here."

A flash blinded him, and he heard the whir of a camera's motor drive. He saw Brad and Derek on the far side of the room. Needing no more prodding, he drew Madeleine swiftly to the door. They ignored the voices calling after them and plunged into the elevator. For an endless moment, the doors stood open, framing the advancing curiosity seekers, Brad and Derek included.

Jack tugged the brim of his hat lower and jammed his thumb on the Close button. The elevator doors slid shut with an electronic sigh.

Madeleine pressed herself back against the wall as they glided downward. A slow smile curved her lips. "Thank you."

"You're welcome, ma'am."

"I forgot my coat."

"Would you like me to go back for it?"

"No. Absolutely not."

In a fraudulently chivalrous gesture, he whipped off his tux jacket and settled it around her. She was lost in the huge black folds, and when she smiled up at him, he felt a tingle of pure magic.

"Where are we going?" she asked.

He glanced at the panel of elevator buttons. "The parking garage?"

Her laughter chimed like silver bells. "After that, I mean."

"Er, where would you like to go?"

As the doors opened and she preceded him out, she asked, "You're driving?"

"Yes." Was he ever. A grateful Harry Fodgother had lent his truck to him for the night. Over Jack's protests, Harry had handed him a set of keys and an access card to a garage where one parking space cost more than Jack's Brooklyn flat. The truck was a middle-aged tailor's boyhood fantasy: huge, black and outfitted with every gadget GM could imagine, including a horn that gobbled and mooed. "Are you?" Jack asked.

Peering at the truck, she hesitated and caught her lower lip with her teeth. "Not tonight. I overdid it a bit on the champagne. Where are you staying?"

"Staying?" Holding open the passenger door, Jack broke out in a sweat. He hadn't anticipated getting this far. "Er, with...friends in White Plains."

"Oh." She settled into the high bucket seat; her stockinged legs folded with a whisper of silk. The seams at the back were perfect, leading up the most extraordinary pair of calves he had ever seen.

Jack Riley's not-so-secret vice was admiring women's bodies. He loved them, pure and simple. The softness. The curves. The textures and scents.

Disappointment was written on her face. She looked so forlorn that he blurted, "I could take you to a club or something."

She stared at him for a long moment. "Home," she whispered, laying her hand lightly on his sleeve. "I want you to take me home."

Chapter Four

Madeleine's hand trembled slightly as she touched the code on the keypad of the elevator to her Park Avenue apartment. They rode up in silence, surrounded by dim amber lights and bronze-tinted mirrors. She had resolved to do something reckless and out of character. This certainly fit the bill.

She thought about the last time she'd brought a man home. An unmitigated disaster. He'd spent the first hour cataloging the Monet paintings, Calder mobiles and Baccarat fixtures, the second hour trying to maneuver her into the bedroom, and the third trying to figure out why she had pleaded a sudden headache and sent him on his way.

She stole a glance at the tall man beside her. His posture was easy. His hands were linked loosely in front of him. His gaze held a genuine warmth and friendliness she desperately wanted to trust.

Please be different, she pleaded silently. *I need you to be different.*

The doors slipped open. Her hand was a little steadier as she inserted her key card and opened the door.

A few fluted lamps lent discreet, indirect lighting to the corners of the front hall and living room. He removed his hat and set it on the umbrella stand. She shrugged out of his jacket and slung it over a chair. For a moment, his attention was caught by the lighted Monet garden scene over the hall table.

Madeleine held her breath. With a sinking sense of disappointment, she waited for the inevitable discourse on the value of Impressionist art.

"Pretty," he said simply, turning to her.

Madeleine let out a sigh of relief.

"Can I get you something to drink?"

He hesitated. "A beer, maybe?"

She laughed. "You've managed to request the one thing I don't keep on hand." She walked to the bar, studying the array of crystal bottles of Rémy Martin and Glenmorangie and Frangelico.

"It's okay," he said. "What about champagne? Really bad champagne tastes like beer."

"I don't *ever* keep bad champagne."

He leaned his elbow on the bar, indicating the Krups. "Then let's make coffee."

Just what her nerves needed. "I make the world's worst coffee."

"I make the world's best Irish coffee. You'll think you've died and gone to heaven." He loosened his bow tie and plucked at his studs. The dress shirt opened in a vee, and she caught a glimpse of curling russet chest hair. Warmth coiled tightly inside her, surprising her with the pleasurable force of it.

"Ma'am," he said, "watch a master at work." His hands deftly managed the filter and gourmet roast. "The trick is, you use twice as much coffee and twice as much whiskey."

"Ah. That way we'll be too wired to care how it tastes." She opened a bottle of Evian and filled the reservoir of the Krups. While the coffee brewed, Madeleine got a small carton of cream from the kitchen. Returning to the bar, she paused to study him as he opened a bottle of Irish whiskey. Suddenly her apartment, which had seemed so pathetically sterile and lonely, glowed with a cozy ambience.

He glanced up and grinned, taking the cream from her. "Do you live alone here?"

"I live with Blake."

She thought she saw a gratifying blaze of possessiveness in his eyes, but without her contacts, she couldn't be sure. She laughed and admitted, "William Blake is my cat. Sometimes my mother visits, but since my father died, she prefers really long cruises to really warm places."

He gazed at her for a moment. His hand lifted, and she thought he might touch her. She wanted him to. Then he lowered his hand and concentrated on fixing the Irish coffee.

They went into the living room. Madeleine reached for a light switch, but a gentle hand on her wrist stopped her. "I like it dim," he said quietly, "so we can see the city lights."

She glanced at the view out the front window. On the crystal-clear winter night, New York City glittered with its own special magic. "Of course," she said with a smile. "I keep forgetting you're a tourist."

They sat together on a white Italian-leather sofa facing the broad window. Touching the heel of her black satin pump, she asked, "Do you mind?"

"No. God, no. Go ahead, Madeleine."

He was charmingly flustered, and she laughed again, sliding out of her shoes with a grateful sigh.

"Dance your feet off, did you?" he asked.

"Uh-huh." Before she knew what was happening, he had drawn her feet into his lap and begun massaging them. A small, startled gasp escaped her.

His hands stilled. "Am I being presumptuous?"

"Yes."

"Would you like me to stop?"

"No."

His smile unfurled slowly, languidly, matching the motion of his hands as they traveled over the arch of her foot, gently pressing, creating a tiny center of warmth and ease that flowed through her. There was something shockingly sweet about it, too, and she wasn't used to sweetness in a man.

She wondered how far they would go tonight, how long it would take for him to reveal himself as friend or fortune hunter, lover or liar.

"Oh, no, you don't," he whispered, leaning forward to put his mouth very close to her ear.

She shivered with pleasure. "Don't what?"

"Don't start thinking, Madeleine. You'll ruin it."

"Ruin what?"

"This," he said and, cupping her cheek in his large, warm hand, he touched his lips to hers.

She caught her breath, surprised by the cool softness of his mouth. Never before had she known a man who— *No. Don't think.* He was right about that. She was too adept at talking herself out of things.

She pressed closer, letting the shape of her lips fit the shape of his. The taste and texture of him intoxicated her. A peculiar enchantment seemed to be moving through her, leaving a trail of fire in its wake. Yet even now, while hidden flames engulfed her, he seemed to be holding back. Aloof. Waiting. But why? She had all but thrown herself at him.

A possibility struck her like an icy slap. She tore herself away from him and scrambled back into a corner of the sofa. "You fraud!"

Jack felt the blood drain from his face. The jig was up. She'd probably known from the first instant, but he'd proved a convenient escape from a boring party. Now that things were heating up, her ice-goddess persona was kicking in.

"Madeleine, I can explain. I—"

"Oh, I'd like to hear that one, mister." She reached for her coffee and took a sip, then winced as if her throat were on fire.

"Look, Madeleine, I never planned on letting it go this far, but you—"

"You're married!"

"Never!" he said, relief mingling with untimely amusement. "Is that what you thought? Swear to God, Maddy, I'm not."

"Then you have a—a disease or something."

"Not that, either. Honest."

"A fugitive?" she guessed.

"Okay," he said, still amazed by his narrow escape. "I fled Texas to find myself."

"And did you?" She eyed him warily.

"Maybe. I found you. That's something." His gaze swept the showcase apartment. Did she know she lived in the glossy pages of *Architectural Digest?* It was sort of sad, in a way. Empty, somehow. Like the large potted pine tree in the corner. It bore no ornament except a single red bow at the base of the pot.

Madeleine's gaze followed his to the barren tree. "I'm Christmas challenged," she admitted somewhat sheepishly.

"I'm not," said Jack. "Where are the lights and ornaments?"

As soon as the words were out of his mouth, he wanted to reel them back in. Damn, he was an idiot. He had been *this close* to seducing Madeleine Langston and here he was offering to decorate a Christmas tree for her. He was losing it.

She took another sip of her Irish coffee, her eyes bottomless and blue as she peered at him over the rim of the cup. "I might cry," she said softly.

He felt a jolt of unexpected tenderness. "Why?"

"Daddy always made a big deal of Christmas."

He slipped his hand around hers. "I get it. If you'd rather not—"

"I didn't say that," she interrupted. "I was just telling you—if we do the tree, I might cry. I wanted to see if you'd mind."

"Mind!" This woman was a surprise a minute. "Sweetheart, believe me, there are worse things in life than having a pleasantly tipsy, gorgeous woman cry on my shoulder."

She tilted her head to one side. "You've got nice big shoulders. Maybe I won't cry, after all."

But in the end, she did, of course, as they had both known she would. It happened in the wake of laughter, just after they had finished untangling the string of lights and draping them artfully around the odd-looking, skinny tree.

Jack had hit a wall switch, bringing the lights and treetop star to twinkling life. Madeleine stood in front of the glittering tree, bathed in the reflective glow. The colored lights flashed in the beads that ornamented her black dress. She stood very still, looking curiously bereft, her eyes wide and sparkling with tears, her hair nicely mussed, more blond wisps escaping to curl around her face and neck.

"Maddy?" Jack asked softly, as if speaking louder would make her shatter like a crystal goblet on a Memorex commercial.

She wept silently, giant tears rolling down her flawless cheeks. Finally she whispered, "Your shoulders are too far away."

Flooded by a rush of tenderness, he took her in his arms and pressed her cheek into his chest. Her tears soaked the front of his Harry Fodgother original. "Shh," Jack said. "It's okay." He grimaced. For someone who worked with words all day, he wasn't being very eloquent.

After a while, she drew back and said, "It *is* all right. I mean, I miss Daddy. Sometimes it feels like I can't even take the next breath. And then, somehow, I take that breath, and the next and the next, and the world keeps turning, and I know I'll go on."

Jack couldn't help himself. He pressed a kiss to her brow. It was almost reverent, the way his lips touched her, felt the heat and flavor of her skin. The last thing he'd expected of this evening was that Madeleine Langston would turn out to be sweet and vulnerable and wise.

One of the kids at the shelter where Jack volunteered most of his free time had just lost her mother. He would tell her what Madeleine said about breathing. That might help.

He handed her a Kleenex from a box on the table and stood back while she dried her face. She swayed a little, then gave a wobbly laugh. "I'd better lay off the Irish coffee."

He got them each a bottle of mineral water from the

bar. Blake the cat made an appearance, looking haughty and sleek as he batted his paws at the Christmas ornaments. They clinked bottles and drank, looking with absurd pride at the clumsily decorated tree and chuckling at the antics of the cat.

Madeleine leaned back against Jack, and he trailed his free hand up her bare arm. She turned, taking both bottles and setting them aside. Her arms slid up his chest and around his neck, and she bent his head down to hers. "Thank you," she whispered. "Thank you for being with me tonight."

What was she, crazy? Thanking *him* for being with *her?* "Yeah," he said with a soft laugh. "It's been sheer torture, forcing myself to hold a beautiful woman in my arms."

She laughed, too, and stood on tiptoe. Their mouths brushed together and then melded, clinging, the subtle taste of sexual yearning filling Jack until he nearly lost control.

She glided her hands down his chest, opening his shirt. Fancy silver studs dropped to the floor. So did the fancy belt—Harry called it a cummerbund, and Jack had refrained from making a rude remark.

Somewhere, a clock chimed midnight, reminding Jack that he was a fraud. He half expected his tux to turn into a sweat suit and Harry's truck to change into a pumpkin. But he didn't dwell on that for long. Madeleine wouldn't let him.

He felt her soft palms against his bare chest and nearly lost it. *Tell her,* urged the commonsense fairy inside his head. *Hurry up and tell her the truth.*

"Maddy," he murmured against her mouth.

"Mmm?" She nipped at his lower lip, and he hissed in a breath, forgetting what he was going to say.

"I think tonight was meant to be," she whispered.

Lady, you don't know the half of it.

"What do you mean?" he asked, tracing his tongue along her full mouth.

"Right before I met you, I told myself to do something wild. Unexpected. Unlike myself. Then—poof!—you showed up. So…" She took his hand and led him slowly, deliberately, down a dimly lit hallway.

Her bedroom was an interior decorator's wet dream, he supposed. It was dominated by an antique four-poster bed that should have been marked Napoleon Slept Here.

She pulled the tails of his shirt out of his trousers and ran her hands over his bare skin. Every muscle drew taut.

Tell her. Hurry.

Yeah, right, he thought as he found a fancy comb in her hair and pulled it loose. Tell her what? That she's seducing Jack Riley? That she's just confessed all her personal secrets to a guy she despises? That the slob who makes her life hell at work is about to take her to heaven?

It's still not too late. Tell her.

"Maddy." He forced it out.

"Mmm?" she said again, feathering her lips along his collarbone.

"Uh, why are you doing this, Madeleine?"

Her butter-colored hair cascaded down her back. He had never seen it loose before.

"Because I need it," she said. "Do you ever feel like you'll die if you don't touch someone human and warm?"

God, she *would* die if she learned she'd just said that to Jack Riley.

"Sometimes I feel like that," he admitted. And his hands, which had no self-discipline whatsoever, slid down the zipper at the back of her dress.

He made a discovery that drove all but the last crumb of decency from him—the seamed stockings he had admired earlier were attached to a black silk garter belt.

A *garter belt.*

Garter belts drove him insane. He was a sexist pig when it came to garter belts.

He tried one more time to tell her the truth, but he couldn't even manage to get her name out.

"Ahh," Madeleine whispered. "This is crazy. I don't know who you are, or where you came from, but I think I'm falling in love with you."

And on hearing those words, John Patrick Riley of Muleshoe, Texas, knew two things for certain. First, that this would be the most incredible night of his life.

And second, that it would never be repeated.

Chapter Five

"Damn, Madeleine," he said, dropping his shirt to the floor. "You *did* have too much to drink."

Feeling curiously bold, she stepped out of her dress. "Drinking just makes me more honest. I've never told a man what I've just told you. I trust you. Call it instinct, whatever. With you, I feel safe saying anything."

He ducked his head, looking endearingly bashful in the dimness as he removed first one shiny black cowboy boot and then the other. She was faintly amused to see that he wore white athletic socks.

But when he removed his trousers, her amusement changed to sheer, unadulterated lust. She stared at him in the faint glow of the lithophane nightlight near the bed. This man was U.S. Grade-A beefcake. He ought to have a ratings sticker on him.

"You're staring, ma'am," he said.

She swallowed past the dryness in her throat. "The last time I saw a body like that," she admitted, "I was in a museum in Italy."

He laughed and drew her close, so that she could feel the silky-warm firmness of his muscles and inhale the expensive scent of his cologne and the unique essence of him—a thousand times more evocative than the cologne.

"You're not half-bad yourself, ma'am," he said, releasing the hook of her strapless bra. He groaned, a compliment more eloquent than words. He skimmed his hands down to caress her, and she had never felt so cherished or secure.

He seemed to take particular interest in her garter belt. She'd bought it on a whim to go with the vintage dress, never dreaming that anyone would actually see it on her.

He didn't just look; he seemed to inhale her through his eyes. Being the object of such rapt, undivided attention was heady indeed. His total being, every inkling of concentration, was centered entirely on her—her pleasure, her sensibilities, her needs, her desires.

And that, she realized, was why she was going to love this man. He couldn't care less who she was, where she lived, what she owned. He seemed to anticipate her needs before she did, knowing just where she ached for him, just how she wanted to be touched.

He lingered over her stockings; he went down on one knee like a modern-day Prince Charming as he rolled the sheer silk down first one leg and then the other. Then he rose to kiss her, his mouth as tender and sweet as his hands were wicked. He eased her down on the bed, and there was a dreamlike quality to the moment. She had a strange sense of déjà vu, and she knew exactly why. She had experienced a moment like this in her dreams. She had never dared to imagine it could actually happen.

She sighed and arched toward him, winding her arms around his neck and kissing him boldly, using her tongue as he had used his. Her hands went wandering, seeking, even teasing; discovering the shape of him, the way he was made. His was not a physique sculpted by trainers at a gym; he had a sleek, big-bodied healthiness that seemed to come naturally.

Of course, she didn't know. There was so little she knew about him. That mysterious edge added to the deliciousness of loving him this way. He showed her kaleidoscope colors and shooting stars; he gave her the sensation of soaring, reaching. Their joining was a beautiful dance, its rhythms as frank and necessary as a heartbeat. She was stunned by the simple joy of it, of feeling his long body covering hers, of hearing her name on his lips, of crying out in abandon and then sinking into the warm bliss of the aftermath.

A quietness fell over them like settling snowflakes. They lay side by side, holding each other, listening to each other breathe and wondering at the suddenness and the intensity of what had just happened.

After a long time, Madeleine shifted, propping her chin on his chest and looking up at his night-shadowed face. "I want you to know something."

He brushed a wisp of hair from her cheek. "What's that, darlin'?"

"I don't do this very often." She was glad for the darkness; she had begun to blush furiously.

"Do what?" he asked, a smile in his voice.

"This…everything." She felt awkward and tongue-tied, but also exhilarated, and for the first time in her life, able to laugh at herself. "I've never done this on a first date."

"Sweetheart, I hate to burst your bubble, but we never even *had* a date. You picked me up at a party, remember?"

"Oh. Shameless of me." She touched her tongue to his chest, just to see. His groan of pleasure made her smile. "What I mean is, I've never participated in a one-night stand before. I want you to know I'm not that sort of person.''

''You're not.'' The smile still lingered in his voice. ''Then what's so different about tonight?''

''You,'' she said without hesitating. ''*You* make it different. You make me want...'' Her voice trailed off as she slid her hand down the length of him.

''Want what?'' Now his tone sounded strangled, with no trace of a smile.

''More than just one night,'' she whispered. ''Lots more.''

He muttered something that sounded like a curse and surged up. With one swift movement, he turned her on her back and plunged into her, and the rapid rise of his passion took her breath away.

He loved her into a dazed state of drowsiness, until she was replete with exhaustion, and when she finally pillowed her head against his shoulder and drifted happily toward sleep, she made a discovery she had never dared to contemplate before.

Sometimes dreams really did come true.

The electronic burble of a high-tech phone plowed through Jack's consciousness, rousing him from the best sleep he'd had in months.

Between the first and second rings, he remembered exactly where he was.

In the bedroom of Madeleine Langston. With Miz Maddy herself, naked and tousled in his arms.

Holy shit.

Between the second and third rings, he managed to extract himself from the bed. She moaned and sighed, pulling a fluffy pillow over her head.

Perfect, he thought, plunging his legs into his trousers,

his arms into shirt and jacket sleeves. *Sleep on, babe,* he silently pleaded with her. *Give your dream lover a chance to go poof.*

By the fourth ring, he was dressed and on his hands and knees, groping for his second cowboy boot. Where the hell had it gone—?

"Hi, this is Madeleine...."

The sound of her voice nearly brought Jack out of his skin. Then he realized it was an answering machine.

"Oh, Maddy," said William Wornich's tattling voice, "I'm positively *chartreuse* with curiosity. Who *was* he, Maddy? John Wayne, for goodness' sake?"

She muttered something from beneath the pillow.

Oh, shit. She was waking up.

Jack faced an agonizing choice. He could make a run for it and leave her with fond memories of her mystery man or he could do the honorable thing—confess what he had done and suffer the consequences.

It took him exactly half a second to agonize over his choice between hero and coward.

Leaving a size-twelve cowboy boot somewhere in the boudoir, John Patrick Riley raced out of Madeleine's designer apartment—and out of her fairy-tale life.

Chapter Six

"**Y**ou call that a Santa Claus?" Jack asked, looking Derek up and down. They were at the Santiago Youth Center in Brooklyn. Teenage boys loitered outside on the snow-bordered basketball court. From the room next door to Jack's cramped and cluttered office came the low murmur of female voices speaking Spanish. A workshop for girls was in session.

Derek plucked at the moth-eaten red jacket. "I didn't realize you were expecting a miracle on Thirty-fourth Street," he grumbled. "I don't know why I let you talk me into this, Riley."

"Maybe," said Jack, adjusting his thick glasses, "it's your innate sense of human decency, Derek. Your firm conviction that helping underprivileged kids is the right thing to do." Jack rolled up a stick of Juicy Fruit and stuffed it into his mouth. "Not to mention the Knicks tickets you extorted from me."

"Or maybe it's because you keep threatening to break my kneecaps. Why do you waste time in this dump, anyway?"

Because of Annie. The thought awakened a six-year-old ache in Jack. He had loved her with all his heart, but love wasn't enough to save her. In a way, this center was a monument to his first love. Every kid who stayed out of trouble embodied the promise that had been wasted when Annie had died.

"Well?" Derek prompted.

Jack rubbed his hand along his jaw. "I once lost a good friend to drugs and gang wars."

"Man, I'm sorry—"

"It was a long time ago."

Derek picked up the Santa hat, and the pom-pom fell off. "I won't fool anyone in this getup."

"Sure, you will." Jack felt a perverse shiver course over his skin. He took off his cap and ran a hand through his hair. "People see what they want to see."

Derek propped one elbow on a file cabinet and fingered a macramé plant hanger. The macramé had been done by Maria, one of the center's borderline cases. Jack wondered where Maria had gotten to lately.

"What'd you do to yourself, Riley?" Derek asked, pulling Jack from his thoughts. "Something's different."

Jack's ears caught fire with a guilty flush. He put his cap back on and tugged down the brim. "What do you mean?"

"I don't know. Something…" Derek peered closer. "Hey, you shaved for a change. Wonders never cease."

Jack held his breath while trying to look casual. "A latent sense of decency."

"Uh-huh. So how'd it go last night? How'd you make out?"

Jack felt the blood drain from his face. *Damn.* Derek *knew.*

"Well?" Derek prompted, unbuttoning the disreputable Santa suit. "Spill."

"Spill?" Jack almost choked on his gum.

"What was she like? Wild and sweet? Cruel to be kind?"

"Jesus, Derek, quit with the third degree."

"I always wanted to make it with an Urban Animal," Derek said wistfully.

Jack barely managed to conceal his sigh of relief. "Yeah, well, it won't happen if you don't take a chance every now and then."

"I guess." Derek shrugged out of the bright red jacket. He held it up and peered at a hole that looked as if it had been made by a bullet. "This is hopeless. Looks like Santa's been living in Tompkins Square Park instead of the North Pole."

"Maybe it's you," Jack said. "Maybe you're hungover."

"Me?" Derek snorted. "You don't get hungover after a Madeleine Langston party. No one drinks too much at those things. Too dangerous, what with all the society gossips sniffing around." He paused and frowned. "Well, that's almost right."

Jack looked at him sharply. "What's that supposed to mean?"

"Funniest thing." Derek shed the rest of the Santa suit and put it in a battered Macy's bag. "One person overdid it last night. Last person you'd expect."

"Yeah?" Jack pretended benign interest.

"Madeleine Langston. Not too many people noticed, but Brad and I did. You didn't see the paper this morning? Wornich's column?"

"I never read Wornich. What's to read?" Jack suppressed a shudder at the memory of the knowing, teasing voice on Madeleine's answering machine.

Derek grabbed the folded newspaper from a table where a battered coffee urn stood. He shook it open to the society pages. "Check it out," he said, shoving the paper under Jack's nose.

Jack stared. He felt a slow red burn creep up his face. There they were, Madeleine Langston and her Prince Charming, spit-polished and posed as if for the cover of a romance novel. She gazed up at him, her Grace Kelly profile limned by candlelight. The man, his face in shadow, bent slightly to whisper in her ear. His *GQ*-style tux and valet grooming screamed wealth and breeding.

Yet despite the posed look of the picture, he sensed a strange warmth in the shot. The way her slim hand rested in the crook of his arm, the way his entire attention was riveted on her... The overall impression was that the man and woman were fascinated by each other. Somehow it was all there—the yearning, the hesitation, the part-bashful, part-eager sense of inevitability that these people were going to fall in love.

"A picture's worth a thousand words, eh?" Derek asked.

"Yeah, right." Jack dropped the paper negligently on the desk and picked up the Macy's bag. "I know just the guy to fix this." He left the room with Derek in tow. "Best tailor in Manhattan. A gentleman's clothier, as a matter of fact. He'll make you look like a million bucks."

"Sure, Riley."

"I mean it." Jack thought ruefully of the photo in the *Courier*. "The guy makes magic."

Before going into the city, Jack showed Derek around the youth center. It wasn't much to look at, but it had a heart as big as the Dakota. A rambling converted tenement, it had housed the Santiago Center for the past five years.

Five years of triumph and failure. Jack supposed it would always be that way. For every kid they kept out of trouble and in school, another slipped through the cracks.

"I just don't get enough time to spend with them," he said to Derek, opening the metal door to the courtyard.

"I can't figure you out, Riley," Derek declared, trotting out onto the basketball court.

Jack went out, too, smoothly stealing the ball from a lanky boy called André, then passing it to Derek, who made a decent layup and scored. They fooled around for another few minutes, their laughter chasing away the cold.

"You're with the pros now, me lads," Derek declared only seconds before a boy knocked him on his butt and stole a rebound. Laughing, Jack left them playing and squabbling. He sobered instantly when he crossed the yard and entered the director's office.

A girl sat alone there on a metal chair, a crumpled handkerchief crushed in her hand and her unseeing gaze fixed on a wall map of the boroughs. A livid bruise stood out on her right cheekbone, and her lower lip was swollen.

She was so pregnant she looked as if she would give birth any minute.

"Uh," Jack said, clearing his throat, "is someone helping you?"

The girl turned her gaze up to him and blinked slowly, twice. "Hi, Mr. Riley."

His heart flopped over in his chest. They were the biggest, brownest eyes he had ever seen—and he hadn't seen them in months. "Maria," he said. He knelt beside her and took her hands in his. "Where've you been, girl?"

"I never should have stopped coming here." Her swollen lip trembled. "I'm in trouble, Mr. Riley."

"Ah, Maria." He squeezed her hand. "It'll be okay.

Promise. Everything will be fine. Tell me what happened.''

''Nothing will ever be fine again,'' she said softly, with the sense of drama Jack had noticed about her right from the start. ''But I thought it would be. José said he'd get a steady job and a place to live, but he went off and never came back.''

Jack knew the boy; liked him, even. José had been a decent student, a hard worker, more down-to-earth than most. He'd finished school the summer before. Jack touched Maria's bruised cheek, very lightly. ''What about your family?''

The girl's eyes flashed with anger. ''I'm not going home again,'' she said simply. ''That's not my home anymore.''

Jack didn't pry. He knew Maria's mother had remarried. ''So when's the last time you saw José?''

Her eyes teared at the mention of his name. ''A few weeks ago.''

''Tell you what. You go to the kitchen and make yourself a cup of tea, and I'll see about tracking down José for you.''

''Okay.'' She sniffled, then levered herself up and lumbered toward the kitchen. ''Thanks, Mr. Riley.''

''We'll work things out, Maria.'' He watched her go, feeling an odd yearning in his gut. Barely a woman herself, she was going to have a baby. *A baby.* Jack Riley's secret vice was an unadulterated love of babies. ''It's going to be all right,'' he said, even though Maria was already gone.

''We can always hope,'' said a female voice behind him.

He turned to see Sister Doyle, the director, looking uncharacteristically grave as she stood in the doorway of her office. Broad-shouldered and open-faced, she wore jeans and a denim work-shirt; a pair of reading glasses balanced precariously on her nose. Her red hair was cropped short. The only indication of her vocation was the large silver crucifix she always wore on a chain around her neck.

She held a letter in her hand. "Our funding's been cut, Jack. We're fifty grand in the hole. The Langston Trust cut off funds, effective immediately. We're history, Jack. The center will have to close the day after Christmas."

On Monday morning, Madeleine sat at her desk and surreptitiously put her right hand over her heart. Funny. It didn't *feel* any different. But it was. Broken, possibly beyond repair.

Her heart had ached when she had lost her father, but at least there had been a sense of closure about the loss. She missed him, but the grief had mellowed with the passing of time. She had loved him, he had loved her, and she had gathered the cherished memories into her heart, a treasure and a comfort.

John's abandonment, on the other hand, had shattered the very foundations of her beliefs. In retrospect, she realized it had been stupid to pin all her hopes and dreams on one night with a man she had just met; stupid of her to give a man that sort of power over her.

For the ten-thousandth time since Saturday morning, she looked at the color photo of herself and John that had run in the society pages. Ah, but what a man. No one would blame her for falling head over heels for the guy.

"Mystery Cowboy Lassoes Publishing Heiress," the caption read.

Yes, he had lassoed her, all right. Heart and soul. And

body. Even now, in spite of everything, she felt a hot twinge of desire. She had dared to touch him in ways she had never touched a man. With him, she had felt true passion for the first time, and it was like being reborn, like Dorothy walking out of her black-and-white existence into the Technicolor world of Oz.

Madeleine's single foray into casual flings had left her vulnerable, shaken to the foundations of her well-ordered life. She wasn't cut out for this, she decided.

She just cared too damned much.

Against her will, she closed her eyes and remembered the gallant way he'd cloaked her in his tux jacket. The delicious Irish coffee. The foot massage. Decorating the Christmas tree and being held while she wept. Making love until she wept for a totally different reason.

In that one night she'd lived and felt more deeply than she had in a whole lifetime.

Now she had nothing to show for it but a broken heart and a size-twelve Lucchese cowboy boot made, according to the inside label, of European goat. *Goat.* She shuddered.

She shook her head. It was too ironic. Not quite as dainty as a glass slipper but every bit as ridiculous, the boot had been the only clue he had left. The housekeeper had found it under the bed on Saturday and was still giggling about it when Madeleine had left for work this morning.

She glanced down at the photo again and in spite of herself couldn't suppress a smile. It *was* funny, thinking of him dashing down to the parking garage wearing only one shoe in the middle of winter.

She hoped he froze to death.

She prayed he would come back to her.

"Working hard, Miz Langston?" asked a sarcastic voice.

That voice. In it, she heard an echo of— Then she looked up and the bubble burst. Agitated, she regarded Jack Riley in all his disreputable splendor. Battered Yankees cap. Five o'clock shadow at ten in the morning. Eyes piercing from behind thick lenses. A sweatshirt with the slogan I Put the FUN in DysFUNctional.

For no apparent reason, she felt her face flush scarlet. "I didn't hear you knock, Mr. Riley."

"I didn't knock." One side of his mouth lifted in a taunting smile as his attention wandered to the desk. "Didn't know there was anything to interrupt."

Mortified, she moved to snatch the society-page photo from her desk. He slapped his hand down on the paper.

He stood close to the desk, his weather-beaten blue jeans snaring her unwilling attention for a moment before she forced herself to glare up at him. Against her will, she felt a primal pulse of excitement. He did, she conceded, exude a certain caveman charm.

"Madeleine," he said in a voice as rich and suggestive as a proposition.

"Yes?" She was flustered. He had teased her on Friday, but this felt more like a come-on. He had never called her Madeleine before.

He leaned forward, his posture aggressive and suggestive all at once. She braced herself. "What is it, Mr. Riley?"

"I want you—" he moistened his lips, and she gasped "—to take me off the sewage bribery story and give it to Derek or Brad."

"No," she said, plummeting to earth, hating him for his manner. "You're the best reporter for that story." *You're the best I have, damn you.*

"I'm sorry," he said, putting his other hand on the surface of the desk and leaning closer still. "I guess I didn't make myself clear. I'm not doing the sewage story."

"And perhaps I didn't make myself clear, either," she snapped. "You're doing the story. It's not optional."

"Wanna bet?"

"You'd lose."

"Oh, I'm shaking," he said. "What, you're going to fire me?"

She hesitated. She knew the *Trib* or the *Times* would snap him up in a minute. She wondered why he hadn't defected to a larger paper long before.

Hating herself for playing his game, she said, "Suppose you tell me exactly why you're refusing that story."

"I don't have time. I've got another story to write." He straightened, folding his arms across his chest. His eyes seemed to grow harder and colder behind the lenses. "It's about the Santiago Youth Center in Brooklyn. The place is being closed down because its funding got yanked."

He watched her so closely that she wondered if the revelation was supposed to mean something to her. "We're a Manhattan paper," she said simply. Idiotically.

"You," he said with quiet conviction, "are one hell of a piece of work, Miz Langston." He glanced down at the paper on the desk. "But what can I expect from a woman who turns to mush over a guy in a tux and cowboy boots?"

She shot to her feet. "Maybe you could learn a few things about personal grooming and manners, Mr. Riley."

He threw back his head and guffawed so loudly that people in the outer offices craned their necks to stare. And then he simply left.

Chapter Seven

It was nearing quitting time when Madeleine finally screwed up enough courage to go down to the city room. She ducked into the ladies' room and stood there alone for a long time, staring at herself in the mirror.

She looked the same as she always had. Every hair in place. Subtle makeup, a faint sheen of gloss on her lips. Small, trim figure. Suit by Armani, soft angora sweater, understated pearls.

And, as always, something was missing.

That was why she loved the photo of her and John. She had been *more* when she was with him, and it was plain on her face. She'd had "soul," or "fire," or whatever it could be termed.

The only thing that heated her now was her temper as she moved through the city room. Many of the staff had already left for the day. Derek and Brad and Jack sat around drinking sodas and chatting.

As she approached them, her gaze wandered to their feet. Their *feet,* God help her. She was obsessed. She was losing it, checking to see if any of them had size-twelve feet.

And one of them did.

"Is this something new?" Jack Riley asked, following her gaze. "A foot fetish?"

She glared at him. Yes, he had big feet. But the man never wore anything but the disreputable high-tops that were probably Salvation Army rejects.

"All finished?" she asked, pointedly ignoring his comment.

A phone rang. Derek dived for it, clutching it like a lifeline. Brad seized the moment to slink out.

Without even glancing at the toxic-waste zone of his desk, Jack snatched up a pair of files. He shoved the first one at her. "Here's your goddamned sewage scandal. Art and all."

Derek hung up the phone and escaped.

"And this—" Jack slapped another file onto the first "—is the Santiago story. With art and a sidebar."

"But I didn't authorize—"

"Believe me, I know that, sweetheart." His voice was harsh with venom. "Listen to me, and listen good. The story runs, every word of it. Page one of the city section. Pictures and all."

"And if I kill the story?" she demanded.

He bent and grabbed a gym bag from under the desk. "Then I quit, Princess."

Whistling, he strode to the elevator bank.

Madeleine didn't know how long she stood there. She felt stung raw by his attack. He seemed to enjoy needling her. Today his scorn had a sharp edge. Keen as the bite of arctic air.

Shaken, she glanced over the sewage story. The man was good—she gave him that. He got people to say things they shouldn't. To reveal things better kept secret. And he managed to make sewage sound fascinating.

Then, reluctantly, she looked at the youth-center story. From the very first word, she was caught. For five years, the privately funded center had been a haven for troubled or runaway teens.

Now, suddenly, it had lost its funding. Well, why hadn't Riley explained all this? Of course, she would run the story. Who did he think she was, Ebenezer Scrooge? She started to scan for details.

"Miss?" A voice interrupted her before she had read three more words.

Now what? She looked up to see a compact, dapper man coming toward her.

"Yes?" she asked, smiling vaguely.

Lifting his hat, he gave the slightest of bows, evoking images of bygone courtliness. The tip of his cane lightly thumped the floor. "You're Madeleine Langston, aren't you?"

"Yes."

"Harry Fodgother." He set down his hat and a large parcel. He held out his hand. "Gentlemen's clothier."

Madeleine shook his hand. "How do you do? Have we met before?"

"Not in person." He flashed her a charming smile, looking like a cherub with a bald spot. "I've seen your picture, though. That was a nice one in Saturday's paper."

Lord. Had the whole world seen it?

"Did you like the tux?" he asked, sparing nothing for false modesty. "I did the tux."

"It was very ni—" Her grip tightened on the folders she held. "You did the tux."

"I did indeed. Quite a piece of work if I do say so myself."

"Who is he?" she demanded.

He cocked his head to one side. "Who's who?"

"John the Tux." She blushed. "I—I'm just so curious about him."

"Then you should ask him."

"He sort of…disappeared before I could ask him much about himself." Like his address, his line of work, she thought in self-disgust. Like his phone number.

"He was just passing through town," Harry said, not unsympathetically. "The tux was ready-to-wear. I made a few alterations."

Clearly he was not going to divulge anything more. Tailor-client privilege, she supposed.

"Say," Harry said, veering off the subject, showing no further sympathy for her lovesick yearning, "I'm delivering something for Jack Riley." He gestured at the big parcel. "He around?"

Her eyes widened. What business would Jack Riley have with a "gentlemen's clothier"? She smiled apologetically. "I'm afraid he just left."

Harry frowned. "Drat it! He needs these items right away."

She studied his parcel. "Could it be some sort of emergency?"

"That depends." Fodgother lifted the lid of the big oblong box. "He needs this for a Christmas party."

Madeleine found herself looking at the most beautiful, luxuriant Santa Claus suit she had ever seen. "Perhaps, I could help," she said without thinking.

Harry raised an eyebrow. "You're a lovely lady, miss, but I don't think you'd ever pass for the Fat Man."

"I meant, maybe I could take it to Ja—Mr. Riley."

"You're just the person to do it," Harry declared. He put the lid back on the box and scribbled a Brooklyn address on the parcel. "That's awfully nice of you, Miss Langston. You won't be sorry. Trust me."

Jack shared a table in the rec room with Sister Doyle. While kids played pool or chess or did homework, Jack and the director combed through the center's finances, looking for a ray of hope.

They found none. Santiago Youth Center was deep in debt and had zero cash reserves.

"So we've got three, maybe four days before we're flat broke," Jack explained to Sister Doyle. "Unless Miz Butter-Wouldn't-Melt-in-My-Mouth prints my story and we get a big surge in donations."

"What makes you think she wouldn't print the story, dear?" Sister Doyle asked.

"'We're a Manhattan newspaper.'" He mimicked Madeleine's snooty East Coast accent.

"Did you explain why it needed to run?"

"Oh, sure. Tell her she needs to run a story about the greed of her own board of trustees? Cute." Jack took a sip of the hot tea Sister Doyle was always making.

He couldn't believe how much it hurt to learn what Madeleine was really like. She drove him crazy. He wanted to think of her as a fragile woman with sad eyes and an amazingly bold touch. But common sense told him she was too rich and spoiled to be amused by any one man for long. "How's Maria, by the way?"

"Very well, under the circumstances." Sister Doyle glanced at the girl, who sat with an afghan in her lap and paged through an illustrated child-care manual. "I just don't understand José. I always considered him a responsible young man, one of our success stories. But he just up and left her."

"Where'll she and the kid go?" he asked in frustration.

"If the center closes and José never shows up, that's anyone's guess."

Jack slammed the ledger shut, removed his glasses and wearily rubbed his eyes. "Hang in there, Sister. We'll figure something out. It'll probably involve me groveling on my knees to Madeleine Langston, but I'll do what has to be done."

He ambled over to join a pair of boys whose geometry study had degenerated into dueling practice with pencils. With good-humored ease, Jack settled down with them and got them back on track. He had always loved the moment when a kid's interest was engaged. That "aha" look was beyond price.

And now his work here would soon be over.

Suddenly Marco, at the pool table, gave a low whistle.

"*¡Ay, mujer!*" Raul said. Both boys stared at the door.

Looking like one of the snowflakes in *The Nutcracker*, Madeleine Langston drifted in. She wore a white faux fur and soft boots and white gloves. The cold wind had nipped a coral hue into her cheeks and lips. Her blue eyes scanned the room. Jack had never seen anything more beautiful. Why did she have to have such a cold heart? Beauty was wasted on her.

She looked a bit uncomfortable and a *lot* out of place in the rec room of the center. Jack pushed up from the table and crossed the room to her.

"Hi," he said.

Silence. She stared at him. His nerves rattled like sleigh bells. Had she seen through him at last? Did she know the truth about Friday night?

"Hello." She seemed far less self-assured than she did at the paper. "Uh, I brought you something." She handed him a big box. "It's from a friend of yours. Harry Fodgother."

Jack sucked in his breath. Had Harry fessed up? No way. If he had, she wouldn't be speaking to him.

"The Santa suit." Jack took the box and set it down. "Thanks."

"He—Harry said you needed it tonight."

"He did?" Jack cracked a smile. The crafty little guy. Must be looking for a way to throw Madeleine at him. That damned photo. It was like magic. It convinced even the world's biggest skeptics that they were two people in love.

"I guess he got mixed up. I don't need it until Christmas Eve. But thanks for bringing it over."

"You're welcome. So you're going to play Santa?"

"I talked Derek into it. He'll be great."

"Uh-huh." Her gaze darted around the room. "So this is the Santiago Youth Center."

"Yep. Want to take a look around?"

She hesitated, and that moment of hesitation seared Jack with anger. "I realize it's a lot neater and cleaner to stay in your office and write the occasional check rather than actually work with these kids," he muttered in her ear. "But for their sakes, act as if you *care.*"

"You're a bastard, Jack Riley," she whispered through gritted teeth.

And then, miraculously, she was all smiles as she greeted Sister Doyle and the kids. At first she was a little stiff with them, but she insisted on having Marco teach her to shoot pool and before long was laughing and failing miserably to sink a single ball. Her skill at chess was undisputed, though, and she finished off André, their best player, in record time.

Amazing. The woman was amazing. The kids were

nuts for her. Jack watched her as she spoke in an animated way across the chessboard. The fuzzy white sweater she wore, decked with a single strand of pearls, made her look as soft and sweet as an angel. He couldn't figure her out. Her personae ranged from Marilyn Monroe to Joan Crawford to Doris Day. He expected her to start singing *"Que sera sera"* any minute now.

After a while, she excused herself and went to sit with Maria. Jack pretended not to listen in, but he craned his neck to hear their conversation. What could Madeleine find to talk about with a girl from the barrio?

"I guess *you're* getting ready for a big event," Madeleine said.

Maria gestured at the book in her lap. "Guess so. There's so much to do. I don't know how I'll ever do it all. You got kids?"

"No. But I want babies one day." Madeleine laughed at herself. "I need to work on getting a date first. I'm not too swift in that department."

Maria smoothed the afghan over her stomach. "I'm *way* too swift. At least, I was. *Madre de Dios.*" Her voice shook.

Madeleine took her hand. "Honey, there's not a mother in the world who doesn't have those thoughts, believe me. I won't kid you—this is going to be the hardest challenge of your life. But if you hang in there and work at it and love your child with all your heart, you'll make it."

"That's what Sister Doyle keeps telling me."

"Sister Doyle is right. Are you—" Madeleine broke off, clearly groping for words. "Are you by yourself?"

"Yeah." Maria sniffed. "I really love José, and I thought he loved me and the baby, but he's gone now. Jack said he'd look for him, but I'm not holding my breath.'' She flipped through the pages of her book. ''So it's just me and my giant stomach. I've been staying here, but that'll change day after Christmas.''

Madeleine nodded. ''I heard about that.''

Jack felt a bitter surge of satisfaction. So, she had read his piece, at least.

''After that, I don't know,'' Maria said glumly. ''Guess I need a miracle.''

Madeleine laughed softly. ''Miracles happen. Here.'' She handed the girl a business card. ''That's the number of my cellular phone. You can call me anytime, day or night. Okay?''

''Thanks,'' Maria said, tucking the card into her book.

Madeleine grew serious as Jack held her coat for her later and helped her put it on. ''I can't believe you'd let this place close,'' she said. They were out in the dim hallway.

His acid laugh echoed off the tile walls. ''Lady, it's not up to me. *You're* the one who cut off the funding.'' He stalked down the narrow stairs in front of her and yanked open the door to the street. A blast of winter air and snow flurries slapped him in the face.

Madeleine stood unmoving. She seemed heedless of the cold air and blowing snow. ''*What* did you say?'' she demanded.

''The funding,'' he repeated, speaking slowly. ''Hey, call me small-minded, but I just had a little-bitty problem with the decision of your board of trustees.''

Madeleine Langston did a most unexpected thing. She plopped down on the second-to-last step. ''Wait a minute, Riley,'' she said. ''You're losing me, here. What does *my* board of trustees have to do with *your* youth center?''

He thought for a long time. Was it possible she didn't

know? "They yanked the funding. I figured you were in on the decision. Didn't you read the article?"

"Harry interrupted me before I finished. I'd already decided to run it, though." She looked more confused—and more beautiful—than ever. "Riley, let's go," she said, rising and stepping outside.

He followed her to the most amazing car he had ever seen. Low-slung, bright red and aggressively Italian, it had already attracted a small flock of neighborhood kids.

"Where are we going?" he asked.

She hit a remote button on her key chain, unlocking the doors, and tossed him the set of keys. "Your place," she said. "You've got some explaining to do."

"Just my luck," he muttered, feeling the engine purr to life. His pleasure was almost sexual. "My one chance to drive a Maserati and we only get to go twelve blocks."

"Well, you'll cover it in record time," she said simply.

And he did, falling in love with the car like a teenager, worshiping the way the Maserati handled, reluctantly angling it into a parking space in front of his walk-up.

"It'll be safe here," he said. In just the few minutes it had taken them to drive here, the snow had come down thicker. "Mr. Costello doesn't miss a thing."

He waved at a portly older man who sat in the window of the ground-floor apartment. Mr. Costello pointed his TV remote control at the car and nodded approvingly.

"And now, Miz Langston," Jack said, holding open the door, "I guess we'll get down to business."

Chapter Eight

Madeleine had been trying all evening to cling to her anger at Jack Riley, but the more time she spent with him, the harder it was.

Oh, he was the same exasperating smart-aleck she had always known him to be. But tonight she'd learned something important about him.

Jack Riley had a heart as big as Manhattan.

She would never forget her first glimpse of him at the youth center. He'd been working with two boys on their math, gently encouraging, keeping them on task when too many adults would have given up in despair.

"Here we are," he said, pushing open the door to a second-story apartment. "Home, sweet home. Come see how the other half lives."

"What's that supposed to mean?" she asked, annoyed.

He flipped on a light. "Oh, I don't know. Something just tells me you live in nicer digs than I do."

She shrugged out of her coat and looked around. The place was small and old, cluttered and unaccountably homey feeling. One wall had floor-to-ceiling shelves crammed with books. A workspace, even more disgraceful than his desk at the paper, held a computer, a stereo and mountains of files. The screen saver floating across the computer monitor was X-rated.

"Charming," she remarked.

"I never said I wasn't a sexist pig." He walked over to the tiny kitchen, separated from the living area by a counter with two stools. "What can I get you? Tea? Coffee? I make great—" He broke off. "How about tea?"

"Fine," she said.

He banged around in the kitchen, hollering as he put on water. "Make yourself at home."

"Thanks." She wandered slowly around the room. The personal items intrigued her. There was a picture of Jack as a young boy sitting on the tailgate of a pickup truck. He had one arm around a laughing mongrel dog and his long, bare legs dangled almost to the ground.

Good Lord, she thought. Jack Riley had been a beautiful boy.

There was a picture of his parents, looking very loving and salt-of-the-earth against a backdrop of rolling hills. And a photo of a dark-haired girl; it was a cheap studio portrait, but she exuded a fresh-faced beauty that even the yellowing photo paper couldn't dim.

Feeling an unaccountable stab of discomfort, Madeleine moved on to the next framed item—a diploma from the University of Texas. He had graduated magna cum laude.

"You never said you were from Texas," she called out.

"Never said I wasn't," he called back.

"And who's the girl?"

There was a second of dead silence. Then he said, "Her name was Annie."

Madeleine felt a sudden chill. "'Was'?"

"Yeah. She, uh, died young. It's been six years."

Madeleine closed her eyes and inhaled slowly, shakily. "Tell me it gets easier."

He poked his head around the corner of the kitchenette. "It gets easier."

She smiled. "Thanks." She looked at a few badly hung certificates of appreciation. Apparently Jack Riley was a professional do-gooder. He had made a second career out of working with underprivileged youths.

He set a mug on the counter and filled it with tea. Without asking, he added a spoonful of sugar and handed her the mug.

"How did you know I take my tea with sugar?" she asked.

"Must be because you're so sweet," he said.

"Right. No, really—"

"'One sugar, no milk, Benny,'" he said, doing a wicked imitation of her order from the snack cart that came through the offices of the paper.

She laughed and sat down on a soft plaid sofa. "All right, Riley. You obviously think you have my number. How about starting at the beginning?"

He sat down next to her on the sofa. In the low light of a table lamp, he looked slightly less disreputable than usual. Discounting the slobbish attire and cocky attitude, he might almost be handsome.

"Either you're real good at pretending, lady, or you really are in the dark about all this."

"Have you ever known me to lie?"

"Only to spare my feelings." His admission was swift. "That's why I'm going to play along with you. It all started years ago when your father was still running the paper. I submitted a free-lance article. He liked it and he wanted to meet me. We hit it off, and I came to work for the paper."

Her father had always had a knack for finding talent. "I didn't even know my father knew you." She frowned. That was her one regret. She had never bothered with the paper until after her father was gone.

"We had an unusual arrangement, your old man and I."

"What sort of arrangement?"

"I was never too demanding in the salary department."

"I noticed. Is there a reason for that?"

"I took a small salary and the Santiago Youth Center got a huge grant."

She glanced at the faded beauty that had been Annie. "Does this have something to do with her, Jack?"

"In a way, yeah." He pushed his glasses up his nose. "You're a hell of a perceptive woman, Madeleine."

"What happened?"

He gazed at the photo, a faraway hurt in his eyes. "She couldn't stay off drugs, no matter how many times she said she'd quit. After a while, she stopped trying."

"But you never stop trying, do you?" Madeleine asked softly.

"I guess not. Anyway, your father pretty much funded the operation. He never made a big deal of it—just quietly contributed half the operating budget every year."

Warmth flared in her heart. "Ah, Daddy," she said with a sigh. She looked at Jack. "I might cry."

"*What?*"

She couldn't believe what she'd just said to him, but she said it again. "I might cry. It just sounds so much like something Daddy would have done—I—might—"

The tears came then, like a silent flood, and the next thing she knew, Jack Riley's arms were around her. She forgot that he was a slob who said hateful things about her and who held her entire life-style in disdain. He was simply a warm shoulder to cry on, and for a moment, that was all she needed. He smelled of clean laundry and something she could only call maleness. His arms were firm and solid, his hands soothing—and somehow, achingly familiar.

This was crazy. Was she really attracted to him or did she simply need comforting on the rebound? Yet it seemed to be more than that. Despite her hurt over John Patrick, Jack was filling her life up.

After a few moments, he riffled around under the end table and produced a box of Kleenex. She was surprised to see that he looked completely flustered. "You okay, Madeleine?"

She nodded and helped herself to a tissue.

"Just when I think I've got you figured out, you surprise me."

She smiled wanly. "I could say the same about you. Now. The funding."

"Your dad was a great guy," Jack said. "But it looks like the board of trustees of the paper was only too eager to put a lid on the charity."

She dabbed at her eyes. "I attended the last meeting, and nothing was said about—" She snapped her fingers. "Wait a minute. I had a memo just the other day. Something about a decision of the executive committee. I haven't had time to look it over."

"Somebody put it through without your signature, doll," Jack said. "Because starting the day after Christmas, the center's history."

"Sorry to douse your righteous rage, Jack," she countered, "but you're wrong. I'll make sure the center gets all the funding it needs to stay open. Same deal my father made you. In perpetuity."

He stared at her. Then, like the rising sun, a grin spread across his face. "Damn, Miz Langston," he said, the teasing note in his voice oddly welcome. "Financial prowess is so...so *sexy*. Especially to the financially challenged like myself."

She burst out laughing and flung a throw pillow at him. "You're shameless, Jack Riley. Shameless!"

"But I get what I want." He threw the pillow back at her.

Still laughing, she asked, "And what *do* you want, Riley?"

"Besides your money? Well—" He leaned forward and whispered something else, something that made her feel like he had lit a match to every nerve ending in her body.

She gasped. "I think you just singed my ear."

"I'll make it better." He kissed her ear, and before she knew it, his commanding mouth had captured hers in a long, deep kiss that was as demanding and earthy as Jack Riley himself.

She was shocked to find herself responding, arching toward him, opening her mouth. The taste of him, the searing intimacy, took command of all her faculties, and she stopped even trying to think or resist. He pressed her back on the sofa until they were half reclining, his hands moving over her soft angora sweater with a compelling mastery that left her breathless.

It took all her willpower to make a single sound of protest, to turn her head away. Her hands shook as she pressed against his chest, pushing at him.

Her cheeks flaming, she said, "Riley, don't."

He ran one finger down the side of her throat. "Aw, come on, Madeleine. We both want this. It's fun."

"I—I can't."

"Can't have fun?"

"Can't do this." She felt dizzy with confusion. Her heart was broken—wasn't it? Then how could she want *this* man? Was she turning into a slut in her old age? First the one-night stand, and now *Jack Riley?* Oh, that would make a cute picture for the society pages: Publishing Heiress Goes to Press with City Room Stud.

"What do you mean, you can't?" He kept doing this maddening thing with his finger, tracing her throat, her collarbones, through her sweater.

"I'm just not into casual affairs." She braced her hands on the sofa behind her and sat up. "I—they don't work for me."

"Whoever said anything about casual?" he asked. "Or affair, for that matter?"

"What else can it be?"

He chuckled and leaned forward. "It can be—" He whispered another suggestion in her ear.

She jumped up and stumbled back. "You are too much, Jack Riley. I need— Where's the bathroom?"

"Did I make you sick?"

"Just nervous."

With a lazy smile that caused an odd twist in her stomach, he pointed. She fled down a hall, closing the door behind her and leaning against it, her body shaking and her eyes squeezed shut.

Oh, God. What was she doing? Here she was, almost making it with Jack Riley, of all people. Was she crazy?

The worst of it was, she *wanted* him, in all his crudeness, his messiness, his insolence. There was something in him that she needed. It was purely ridiculous, she told herself, not to mention wanton and immoral, to crave intimacy with a man she barely knew. A man she was supposed to dislike.

A man diametrically opposed to her mystery date Friday night.

Her sanity was hanging by a thread. She had expected her first Christmas without her father to be rough, but she was going off the deep end. Jack Riley, of all people.

She turned on the water and let it run over her hands for a while, then washed her face. Jack Riley's bathroom was as cheerfully and unapologetically cluttered as the rest of the apartment. Turning to grab a clean towel from the rack behind her, she knocked over a plastic tumbler and bent to retrieve it from where it had fallen, right next to the cowboy boot.

Slowly drying her hands and face, Madeleine stared down at the boot. She shouldn't be surprised to see it, since she had just discovered Jack came from Texas, but she was amazed.

She bent and picked up the boot. Black leather. European goat. Made by Lucchese of San Antonio. Size twelve.

Her mind tried to grasp the significance of this, but for a few moments, she was numb, empty. She was like a trauma victim taking refuge in shock.

"Hey, Madeleine," Jack called. "You okay in there?"

"Uh, yes." Her voice sounded thin. Very carefully, she set down the boot.

You okay?

Sure, Jack, she thought. She forced herself to think things through. She wanted so desperately to be wrong.

"What can I expect from a woman who turns to mush over a guy in a tux and cowboy boots?"

She heard his taunting words echoing in her mind. The thing was, the photo had only showed the happy couple from the waist up. Jack couldn't have known about the boots.

Unless he'd been the one wearing them.

A sob built in Madeleine's throat, but she swallowed it. She wouldn't cry over this man. At least, not while he was watching. Crying meant she cared, and she refused to do that.

She stepped out of the bathroom, closing the door quietly behind her. Jack stood in the living room, regarding her quizzically.

She saw it all, then, the resemblance she should have noticed right from the first. The strong jaw, the beautiful hands. The drown-in-chocolate eyes. The long, lean-hipped body.

Her eyes had been as blind as her heart.

"I have to go," she said, enunciating each word. "I can't stay here."

"Madeleine, are you ill? Talk to me. What's wrong?"

Besides the hideous joke you played on me? her mind screamed. *Why, everything's just peachy.*

"It's late," she said, sounding the very soul of sane rationality. "I have to go."

"But—"

She snatched her coat. "Coming here with you was a mistake. It should never have happened. Goodbye, Jack."

Shoving her arms into her coat, she fled down the stairs and out the door. He came after her, calling her name, but she ignored him. She bolted into her car, stabbed the key into the ignition and roared off, the rear end fish-tailing on the snow-covered pavement.

Just once, she allowed herself to glance into the rear-view mirror. He was standing on the sidewalk, a tall, lanky silhouette backlit by the snow-hazed streetlight and a string of colored lights in Mr. Costello's window. For some reason, the image made the tears flow again. She promised herself it would be the last time she would ever weep for Jack Riley.

Chapter Nine

The next day, Jack took the subway in to the paper. The mindless clack and sway of the train, the blank looks on the commuters' faces and the bovine flow of foot traffic in the underground passageways suited his mood.

Now and then he encountered the annoyance of carolers and shoppers reminding him it was Christmas Eve, but he managed to ignore them.

On the way in to the city, he tried to prepare for his encounter with Madeleine. All his life he had worked with words, composing and shaping them into units of meaning. But today, the skill eluded him.

There were simply no words to explain to Madeleine why he'd done what he had. There was no way for him to explain to *himself* what had happened in that moment last night, when she had looked up at him and said, "I might cry."

That was the moment when he knew, finally and irrevocably, that he had fallen in love with her.

"Nice timing, Riley," he muttered under his breath as he scaled a small mountain of freshly plowed snow. "Just perfect."

He entered the building and jabbed his finger at the

elevator button. When he reached the city room, he didn't even pause at his desk, but went straight to Madeleine's office.

She looked up, serene as a Zen icon, when he stepped into the room. Damn, she was beautiful. Unruffled.

Jack felt encouraged. Perhaps she was, after all, unhurt. Maybe she viewed it as a game, a lark, a joke. Slumming with the hired help. Maybe she would see the humor in the situation.

Maybe the moon would fall out of the sky.

"Er, Madeleine..." His voice trailed off. His vocabulary had dwindled to a series of Cro-Magnon grunts. Until now, he hadn't realized that true love caused brain damage.

She indicated an open folder on her desk. "Your personnel file," she explained. "To your credit, you did stick as close as you could to the truth. Your real name is John—John Patrick Riley. You didn't lie about being from Texas...." She looked up at him, her blue eyes wide and devoid of accusation. "Tell me, did you plan it all out weeks in advance, or was it sort of a spur-of-the-moment practical joke?"

"Aw, come on, Madeleine, you're acting like I set out to hurt—"

"Or maybe there's another motive," she went on calmly, as if she hadn't heard him. "You know, maybe the guys in the city room had some sort of standing bet. Free Knicks tickets to the first one who can get the boss in the sack—"

"Jesus, Madeleine," he said sharply, closing the office door behind him with a *thwack*.

She blinked at the noise but didn't flinch. She was scary this way; cool and soulless and eerily calm. A stranger.

Then he noticed two things that betrayed her perfect facade. The fingernails on one hand had all been bitten off. And if he wasn't mistaken, her blouse was buttoned wrong.

Oh, God, Madeleine. I'm so sorry.

"Look," he said, "I never meant for it to go so far."

I never meant to fall in love with you.

She gave him a tight, controlled smile. "Who said I minded? Maybe it was what *I* wanted."

That stunned him. Had she known all along? Gone along with his deception simply because she wanted an excuse to have a man but not a commitment?

"If it's the funding you're worried about," she informed him, "you needn't. I've taken care of that. The Santiago Center will stay open. Just because *you're* a jerk doesn't mean those kids should suffer."

The acid in her voice stung him out of his state of shock and boosted him into a temper. "You are really something, Madeleine," he said. "You know that? Okay, so it's a deal. You write the checks but don't get your hands dirty. It works out just peachy, doesn't it?"

"Just peachy," she agreed coldly.

He could only stare. "Wow, lady. You are one cool customer."

"I suppose you're used to having the women you dump grovel at your size-twelve feet and scream 'You broke my heart!' Is that it?"

"No." Jack blew out a sigh of exasperation. "No, Maddy, I'm not."

"Fine. I'm not about to start sounding like some bad country-and-western ballad. Now, if you don't mind, I have work to do." The soul of efficiency, she found a large rubber stamp and *thunked* it down on his personnel sheet.

"Oh, and Jack," she said as he turned to go.

"What is it?"

"You're fired. Effective immediately."

Fax machines and E-mail worked overtime, and by ten in the morning, it seemed that all the world knew Jack Riley had been canned. Somehow, Madeleine managed to write an editorial for the next edition. The piece was a heartfelt commentary on the state of modern love, slamming home the truth that "happily ever after" was a myth. Reality was a girl like Maria—abandoned by her lover and homeless but for the kindness of strangers. Reality was the sterile emptiness of a one-night stand.

In order for her Christmas editorial not to sound too "bah, humbug," she added a plea for generosity to places like the Santiago Youth Center.

The piece was strong and tight. She knew instinctively that it was good.

By lunchtime, the phone started to ring. Several advertisers, angered by the firing of the paper's most popular writer, called to pull their ads in protest.

What had started out as a truly bad day quickly deteriorated into an unbearable one.

She muddled through the afternoon and let the entire staff leave early. It was Christmas Eve, after all. Just as the presses in the basement roared to life, Madeleine wandered out into the city room. Jack's abandoned desk drew her like a magnet.

Oh, God, I fired a man on Christmas Eve. What have I become?

The desk looked like a skeleton, devoid of the mess and personality and exuberance that had been the hallmarks of Jack Riley. She found herself remembering things that had meant nothing before she had gotten to know him. A lopsided coffee mug, which she now knew had been handcrafted by a child at the Santiago Center. An ink blotter with his name burned into the leather and the inscription To Mr. Riley, A Righteous Dude.

He had been a special man.

And she had run him out of her life—on Christmas Eve. She was beyond pathetic.

She released a shuddery sigh and told herself to forget him. As she turned to leave the room, she was surprised to discover she wasn't alone.

"What are you doing here?" she asked sharply.

Harry Fodgother gave her a sunny smile. "Looking for Jack. I guess I missed him, after all." Harry set a shopping bag on the empty desk. He took off his hat and subjected her to a long, nosy stare. "You look like your best friend up and died."

She sniffed, annoyed by his prying. "Aren't you working late on Christmas Eve?" she asked.

"It's just another day to me," he said. "I'm a Hanukkah type myself."

"Oh."

"But I was thinking I might make a donation to a Christian charity. That Santiago Center I read about in your paper."

"That would be wonderful, Mr. Fodgother. Jack will be pleased." She hated the way her voice caught when she said his name.

"Good. I owe him a lot. My life, if the truth be known."

She frowned. "I don't know what you mean."

Harry shrugged. "He's not the sort to boast. He saved my life. Last Friday night, it was. Two junkies were mugging me. Jack came on like a locomotive. Decked them both, and then they turned tail and ran. I'll never forget that.''

''Last Friday night?'' she repeated slowly.

''Precisely. He didn't want to accept a thing for his troubles, but I insisted. When he showed me your invitation, *I* became the locomotive. Gave him a whole new look.'' Harry winked. ''Poof! He certainly did turn out different, didn't he?''

''Like magic,'' she conceded, fascinated.

He twirled his cane. ''Miracles happen. I hope you had a good time that night. Jack had his doubts, but I swore he'd love every minute of it.''

We *both* loved every minute of it, she thought. Because it wasn't real. It was a fairy-tale illusion.

''Well,'' said Harry, cramming on his hat and moving toward the elevators. ''I'd best be going. Give that to Jack when you see him.'' He gestured at the shopping bag.

She picked it up. ''But I won't be seeing him.''

''You will. Trust me.''

Exasperated, she turned to give the parcel back to Harry. The little man was nowhere in sight. *He must be quicker than he looks,* she thought.

She was trying to decide what to do with the bag when her cellular phone rang. She dug it out of her handbag. ''Hello?''

''Miss Langston?''

''Maria! Are you all right?''

''I just called for a taxi. The baby's coming.''

Madeleine felt a thrill of pleasure and concern. ''How do you feel, sweetie?''

''Like—'' She gasped, breathing hard for a moment. ''Like the baby's coming. Miss Langston?''

''Yes?''

"Do you think you could…you know, come to the hospital? Just for a while…"

"Maria?"

"Yeah?"

"I wouldn't miss it for the world."

Chapter Ten

His parka flapping open and his hat long gone, Jack rushed down the green tile corridor of the hospital. Maria Garza was a lot more grown-up than he had suspected. Not wanting to disrupt the Christmas Eve festivities at the center, she had quietly called a cab and gone alone to the hospital.

The second Jack had found out, he'd raced over. Sister Doyle was managing the center. Families from the neighborhood had all come. Derek was playing a dapper Santa Claus and Brad was serving punch. The preppies had surprised Jack with their willingness to help out. Maybe they felt sorry for him for getting fired on Christmas.

Hell, he'd had it coming.

He skidded to a stop at the nurses' station of the maternity wing. "Maria Garza?" he asked.

The nurse peered at him over her reading glasses, then poked at her keyboard. "In labor. Looks like they're going to take her into Delivery pretty soon. You the father?"

"No, but—"

"*I'm* the father," said a worried voice.

Jack turned to see a young man in a construction-company parka, his hair mussed by the wind and his ears chapped, his feet dancing nervously on the tile floor. "What, you figure better late than never, José?"

José's eyes flashed, but only for an instant. "Yeah," he said. "That's what I figure. Look, Jack, I'm going to stay with her now. It'll be good. I got a steady job and a nice apartment in Queens. I just, I don't know. Quit calling her. It was stupid of me. I got scared."

"So how do you think Maria felt?"

He hung his head. "It won't happen again, man. I got a nice place, really. Just for the three of us." He lifted his chin. His face bore a maturity that had been lacking before. "If she'll have me."

Jack felt pride and cautious relief. "That's always the big question, isn't it, buddy? Whether or not she'll have you."

The nurse cleared her throat. "They're about to take her into Delivery. You'd better scrub up if you think you're going to be part of this."

The look of sheer wonder and excitement that lit José's face banished the last of Jack's doubts. "Go for it, man," he said. "Tell Maria I'm waiting out here."

To pass the time, he bought a pack of gum and wandered to the broad glass display window with a view of the nursery. There were just three babies there, sound asleep and incredibly tiny in their clear bassinets.

Like a kid looking in a candy-store window, Jack leaned against the glass and stared and stared. And stared. Man, he loved babies. Loved kids. He'd always wanted kids of his own, but in order to have that, he needed a certain component in his life. Namely, a wife.

And in all the years since Annie, he had found only one woman in the world he wanted to marry.

The problem was, she hated his guts.

"You know, it's funny how some things work out," said a soft, feminine voice from behind him.

Jack went rigid. He almost didn't dare turn around. He forced himself.

There stood Madeleine, her white coat draped over her arm and the faintest of smiles on her face.

"Maddy?" he asked, resisting the urge to grab her. "What are you doing here?"

"I've been here for a while. With Maria." She glanced down the corridor. "Not in my nice clean ivory tower writing checks."

His face flushed. "I shouldn't have said that."

"If not for you, Jack Riley, that's where I'd still be." He spread his arms. "Welcome to real life."

She looked down the hall again. "That boy—José— he seemed awfully young."

"They both are," said Jack. "But we have to believe they'll work hard to make it—"

"Hey, Riley!" A metal door swung open down the hall. Swathed in green surgical scrubs, José yelled, "It's a boy! A boy! Merry Christmas!" José disappeared back inside.

Jack felt the most ridiculous grin spread over his face. He saw the same look of pure happiness on Madeleine's face. Now she wasn't Grace Kelly or Doris Day or anyone but herself, with a special magic unique to her. The woman he loved.

"Wow," he said, holding out his pack of Juicy Fruit. "Let's celebrate."

She laughed and took a stick of gum.

"Almost midnight," he said. "Come here." He drew her out a rooftop door marked Patio. It was the outdoor smoking lounge for the maternity ward, but no smokers were out braving the cold night.

"I thought we'd see Santa Claus," he said, scanning the sky. "No such luck."

"It's beautiful." Her eyes shining with wonder, Madeleine looked down at the gleaming river, the profile of the Brooklyn Bridge, the winking Manhattan skyline looking its finest for Christmas Eve. She glanced back over her shoulder. "Isn't it beautiful?"

"Yeah," he said, his gaze never straying from her face.

Her smile fled. "Let's not talk about—"

"We have to talk about it." He took a step toward her. "I saw your editorial. Peeked at the mechanicals. Are things really that bleak? That hopeless?"

"Look at the facts, Jack," she said fiercely. "Look at what a game you made of fooling me."

"Look how easily you fell for a good suit and a smooth line," he countered.

"You set me up, Jack! Like I didn't have feelings, didn't mind being manipulated because you and some tailor were feeling playful one night." She stared off at the glittering skyline. "I admit, I was a sitting duck. Pathetic. Just ripe for Prince Charming."

He grasped her by the shoulders. As delicate as she looked, she felt surprisingly solid. "Look, this is real life now, not some goddamned fairy tale. It's messy and painful and *real*. If you can't deal with—"

"Jack?" she said, interrupting him.

"Yes?"

"Shut up."

He did, and gladly, for she stood on tiptoe and wound her arms around his neck. He kissed her with all the frenzied passion that had been clamoring in his heart. He was half afraid she would shrink from the intensity of it, but instead she welcomed him, opening her mouth to his, pressing her warmth against him, her passion matching his.

Distant church bells started to ring, heralding Christmas. Slowly, like a dreamer awakening, he lifted his mouth from hers and stared down into her face. "So now what?" he whispered.

"So we live happily ever after?"

"Sorry, Princess." He grinned apologetically. "No can do. I have too many character flaws. This frog won't change into a prince."

Her hand skimmed along his jawline, where the stubble grew. "I adore your flaws."

"Tell you what, Maddy. I'll give you something more interesting than 'happily ever after.'" Jack took a deep breath. It was the coldest night of the year, and he was sweating. This was it. The big plunge. And nothing had ever felt so right.

"What will you give me?" she asked softly.

"I'll give you the real thing. True love. Forever. All day. All night. For the rest of your life. How's that sound?"

"Like a dream come true. God. Listen to me." Tears glistened in her eyes. "I might cry."

"I can handle it."

"You make me crazy."

"You're pretty sexy for a crazy lady."

"Shut up and kiss me again. Merry Christmas, Jack Riley."

"Merry Christmas, my love."

* * * * *

Lady of the Night

Kate Hoffmann

1

"NEW YORK PLATES." From beneath the brim of his Panama hat, Hamilton Thompson watched a brown hatchback pull up to the general store. He hooked his thumbs under his suspenders and leaned back until his chair rested on the brick storefront, balanced on two spindly legs.

"Twenty bucks says she's jest a tourist passin' through," Claude Palmer said. The rangy black man scratched his bare chest beneath the bib of his overalls and yawned, then closed his eyes to resume his nap.

"I'd have to be dumber than a doodlebug to take them odds," Ham replied. "An' I ain't bettin' with you no more! People 'round town don't trust a bank president who's a gamblin' man." Besides, he knew better than to bet with his best friend, a man who had an uncanny knack for separating Ham from his hard-earned money. And it wasn't as if Claude needed the money. Now in retirement after a successful career as a commodities trader, Claude was walking in high cotton. He spent his mornings talking investments with Ham, his afternoons gardening, and the time on either side fishing.

"Shoot, I got to get back to the bank before they miss me," Ham said. "Some of us got to work for a livin'."

"Ten dollars says it ain't noon yet," Claude replied lazily.

Ham ignored the wager, his attention drawn to the young woman in the car. Through the windshield he tried to make out her features. Pale hair, high forehead, striking cheekbones and a wide, full mouth. Taken one by one, they were as ugly as homemade sin, but put together, he had to admit that the little lady had a powerful beauty that even he, a sixty-one-year-old married man, could appreciate. Her looks sparked a long-ago memory.

Ham slowly lowered his chair and concentrated on the stranger. Sure enough! If he didn't know better he'd swear he was looking upon the spitting image of the lovely Miss Lily Fontaine. He'd never forget that evening, nigh on forty-five years ago, when his daddy had took him down to the end of Edisto Street and paid one of Miss Lily's ladies twenty-five dollars to make his only son into a man.

He stared at the woman for a long moment before he turned to his best friend. "Claude, I b'lieve I'll take that bet," he said.

Claude's chair thumped down beside his. "Which bet would that be?"

"Both of 'um," Ham replied.

"Damn!" Annabeth Dupree shoved the gearshift into Park, slammed her fist on the dashboard of the ten-year-old car and bit back another curse, this one vivid enough to make a New York dockworker blush. The car's air conditioner belched out a blast of tepid air before it drew its last breath and expired with a groan.

"Don't you dare," she threatened, frantically pushing the dashboard buttons that controlled her last vestige of comfort in the stifling heat. But her pleas had no effect. Once again, the sorry excuse for transportation had gotten the better of her.

Her mind backtracked over her four-day odyssey from civilization in New York City to the main street of Magnolia Grove, South Carolina. Unfortunately she had chosen to travel south in the midst of a record-breaking heat wave. Though the scenery along the way had probably been lovely, she had spent most of her time staring at the odometer and counting down the mileage to the next service station. She'd seen the grimy interiors of seven stations along the way, and now, when faced with an idle bit of time, could recite verbatim the dire prognoses of all seven mechanics. Busted fan belt, leaky radiator, rusted muffler, bad fuel pump, corroded spark plugs, cracked distributor cap and blown fuse.

She shifted her murderous thoughts from the battered car to the slick salesman who'd sold her the lemon a week before. He had assured her that she was getting a dependable car for her money, then happily took her thousand dollars—the remains of her paltry life savings. Well, what did she know about buying a car? She'd lived in New York City for seventeen years without one. She knew even less about car repairs, only that her one remaining charge card had been maxed out with the last repair in Florence.

"Fine," she shouted to the car. "I give up. I'm here anyway, so what do I need you for?" She shut off the ignition, but the car continued to cough and sputter for half a minute before it gave one violent shudder and died. Annabeth looked up through the windshield to find two old men watching her from the wide front porch of Ben Early's General Store. They stared at her in open curiosity and she forced a friendly smile to her lips as she reached to open the car door.

If this town of fifteen hundred was going to be her new home, she would have to start by making a good impression, and shouting at her car wouldn't help. She had heard stories about the disdainful attitude Southerners held for Yankees. And though she had been born and raised in Atlanta, she'd left the deep South long ago, first for Boston boarding schools at age thirteen and then for New York and ballet school when she was sixteen. All traces of her accent had disappeared over her twenty years up north, leaving her with a definite East Coast edge to her voice that probably wouldn't endear her to the residents of the sleepy little town.

Satisfied that she was ready to face whatever the townspeople had to offer, she pulled on the door latch and pushed against the door. It wouldn't budge. She tried again after checking the lock and rattling the handle, but still the door wouldn't give way. A glance to the passenger side showed that door blocked by two overnight bags, a grocery bag full of books and Giselle's cat carrier. Somewhere, amidst the possessions she had stuffed into the tiny car, was her cat, probably prostrate from the heat by now.

Annabeth rolled down the window. Hot, humid air rushed in, nearly smothering her like a thick, wool blanket. She had once thought New York hot in June, but she had never realized what real heat and humidity were until this very moment. Her trendy black sleeveless turtleneck and black leggings suddenly clung damply to her body like a second skin, and the air was almost too heavy to breathe.

She tried the door once more for good measure, then decided that getting out of her sweltering automobile was more important than a good first impression. Grabbing the upper edge of the door, she shimmied out the window and dropped lightly to the ground beside the car. She smoothed a loose strand of her pale blond hair behind her ear and walked up the three steps to the porch.

"Good morning," she said, nodding at the two men.

They nodded back. The lanky black man pulled a watch from the front pocket of his overalls and glanced at it. Then he looked over at his round friend. "Told you, Ham. It's still mornin'."

The portly man called Ham squinted up into the sun. "Not by much I'd say, Clod." Annabeth stifled a smile. Clod and Ham. Southerners certainly had a way with nicknames.

"Twelve minutes left," Clod replied.

She watched Ham reach into his pants pocket and withdraw his wallet, then fish out a ten-dollar bill and hand it to Clod, before he returned his attention to her. "See y'all is from New York," Ham said. "I 'spect you're just passin' through."

"No," Annabeth answered. "Actually I'm here to stay." She frowned as Clod returned the ten-dollar bill to Ham, then withdrew another from his pocket and handed that over as well. "I was hoping you might be able to direct me to 453 Edisto Street."

Clod's eyes widened in surprise and a satisfied smile broke across Ham's face. "You'll be looking for Miss Lily's place then," Ham said.

"Yes. Do you know it?" Annabeth hoped there might be a few townspeople who remembered her grandmother. Though she had died fourteen years before, Miss Lily Fontaine had once run an exclusive finishing school for young ladies in Magnolia Grove: Miss Lily's School for Social Arts. The school, or what was left of it, was all that Annabeth owned, beyond the car from hell and her cat, Giselle. And whether she owned Giselle, or Giselle owned her, was still up for debate.

"Mos' folks 'round this part do," Clod drawled. "You kin of Miss Lily's?"

"Shoot, Clod, can't you see she's the spit of Miss Lily?" Ham asked.

Clod raised an eyebrow and glared at Ham. "I can see jest fine. I guess I didn't know Miss Lily as well as you did."

"You were a friend of my grandmother?" Annabeth asked.

Ham's face turned a deep shade of red. He reached into his pocket for a wrinkled handkerchief and wiped his brow. "I wouldn't say we were exactly friends," he answered. "More like acquaintances."

"Well, we'll have to get together after I've settled and you can tell me all about her. I'm afraid I never knew her."

Ham swallowed, then smiled nervously. Clod looked at his friend with what seemed like suppressed amusement. And Annabeth felt as if she were somehow missing out on the humor of the situation. Oh well, she couldn't hope to understand these people right off. Folks lived a different life in the rural South, laid-back and simple. Nothing like her hectic life-style in New York.

"What are you fixin' to do here on your visit?" Ham asked.

"Oh, I'm not here for a visit," Annabeth replied. "I plan to live here. I want to reopen Miss Lily's School for Social Arts. I want to make it just like it used to be."

The two men froze, their eyes wide. Slowly they turned to each other, disbelief coloring their expressions. Then they turned back to Annabeth. "Don't that beat a hen a-flyin'," they said softly, in perfect unison.

Annabeth frowned in confusion. "Yes...well...could you tell me how to find Miss Lily's?" she asked.

Clod grinned at her and stood up, then ambled to the edge of the porch. "You go down the road a piece until you see the Baptist Church. Take a right and then look for a big ol' brick house with a rose arbor over the front walk. That's Miss Bertie Jean Simpson's house. She's got the touch with roses. Take a left and you're on Edisto Street. Jest follow that to the edge of town. Can't miss the house. It's set back from the road a bit. There's a sign."

Annabeth held out her hand and the old man shook it. "Thank you...Clod."

The man smiled warmly. "The name's Claude, ma'am. Claude Palmer. It's a pleasure to make your acquaintance."

Annabeth felt the color rise in her cheeks. His name was Claude? How could she have missed that? She'd have to learn to decipher this South Carolina drawl if she ever hoped to get along. "The pleasure is mine...Claude." She turned to Ham and held out her hand, wondering if she had somehow misunderstood his name as well. "And it's been a pleasure meeting you...sir. I hope that we can get together soon and you can tell me all about my grandmother."

Ham snatched off his hat and shook her hand limply. "Surely, ma'am." He blushed again. "An' when you get around to choosin' a bank, y'all be sure to come down to my place. First Bank of Magnolia Grove. Money's all the same, no matter how it's earned."

Annabeth tried to interpret this last Southernism, but it made no more sense than the one about the hens aflying. "I'll do that," she said as she walked down the steps to her car. She pulled at the door handle, but the door refused to open, and she smiled sheepishly. Claude hurried down the steps, his movements sprightly for a man who seemed to operate at the speed of a dozing tortoise. Gallantly he yanked the door open and helped her inside. Then he gently closed the door. "Thank you, Claude," she said as she coaxed her car to life.

"No problem, ma'am," he replied in a kind voice.

She waved at both men as she pulled out of the parking lot and they waved back. Then Ham shouted something that sounded like "Y'all give the flowers our best, y'hear." Annabeth was tempted to ask him to repeat his farewell, but the sputtering of her car would have made it impossible to hear his words more clearly. He'd probably just tossed out another of those colorful Southern phrases that Annabeth would have to learn to understand. Give the flowers their best? What in the world could that mean?

As she drove down the tree-shaded streets of Magnolia Grove, the warm breeze buffeted through the interior of the car. Annabeth tentatively sniffed and was surprised at the sweet smell. Nothing like the noxious odor of bus exhaust and week-old New York garbage, the air was laden with the scent of flowers and green trees. A person could actually breathe through her nose here. She drew another breath, this time more deeply. Suddenly the air didn't seem as oppressively humid. And her surroundings didn't seem as backwardly rustic. This was home now and she'd made two new friends already.

Annabeth easily found Edisto Street and her breath caught in her throat at the sheer beauty before her. Immense tree boughs arched over the street, creating a lacy tunnel of greenery. She slowed the car and lingered over each magnificent house. Most were white clapboard with wide verandas across the first and second floors. Deep, multipaned windows flanked by tall shutters gave the homes a simple, symmetrical elegance, enhanced by graceful columns that supported the upper veranda and the overhanging roof.

As she took in the grandeur of the architecture, she watched for the plain brick building that she had visualized in her mind as Miss Lily's school. When the houses quickly gave way to undeveloped woods, she knew she had missed her destination. She turned the car around and backtracked. A weathered sign hung from a post in front of the next house she came to and she searched for a number. But the lettering on the sign was unreadable at a distance, so she turned to the brick pillars that marked the entrance to the front walk. There, partially hidden by a tangle of vines, were three tarnished brass numbers: 453.

Slowly Annabeth raised her gaze. Through the shade of three towering trees, past a sweeping lawn and overgrown gardens, she could make out her inheritance. Not a simple brick school, but an elegant, though slightly run-down, antebellum mansion. Italianate in style, it was the biggest house on Edisto Street and boasted a two-story veranda that surrounded the house on all four sides.

She grabbed for the door latch and gave the car door a hearty shove. This time it popped open and Annabeth stepped out. She walked numbly across the walk and took a closer look at the faded sign. Though most of the paint had peeled away, she could make out the words Lily's and Social. Slowly she released the breath she was holding. She was home!

"Well, Grandmother," Annabeth murmured. "If I'd known this was what you meant by a school, I'd have come sooner."

The lawyer from Charleston who handled the estate had claimed he had searched for Annabeth for over nine years before he tracked her down in New York five years ago. The news of her maternal grandmother's death, though long belated, had still come as a shock. Annabeth had been unaware of her grandmother's existence. And for some strange reason, Annabeth's mother, the socially prominent Camilla Fontaine Dupree Robbilard of the Atlanta Robbilards, had maintained a stony silence regarding Lily Fontaine. When she learned that her mother had refused to help the lawyer locate her, Annabeth's demands for an explanation had gone unanswered. Soon, the inheritance and her mother's strange behavior were put aside in lieu of a six-month guest engagement with the Paris Ballet and the company's tour of the Orient.

"How could you have known, Grandmother?" Annabeth whispered. "How could you have known that one day your gypsy granddaughter would need a home?"

Annabeth hurried back to the car and dug through her purse until she found the key that had been included with the papers for the house. The attorney had written that the house had been maintained with a small trust fund since her grandmother's death. Even from a distance, she could see that only the most essential work had been done. The house was badly in need of paint and the landscape needed tending before it swallowed up the house completely. But it was home and it was hers.

She found Giselle, asleep on the floor behind the driver's seat. She picked up the recalcitrant Himalayan and pushed her into the cat carrier. Then she grabbed her purse and the carrier and pushed open the rusty gate. A crumbling brick walk, covered in places by moss, paved the way to the front steps. As she stepped up onto the porch, key in hand, the sound of music drifted to her on the languid midday breeze, followed by soft voices and quiet laughter.

Curious, she walked along the front veranda and peeked around the corner of the house. The sound of voices increased in volume. There were people in the backyard. She walked toward the sound and froze as she came upon an open window. Music filtered through lace curtains and she recognized a Mozart string quartet. Someone was obviously in residence. In *her* house!

Tiptoeing to the back corner of the house, she listened carefully to the chattering and made out three distinct voices, all three female and elderly. Taking a deep breath, she stepped around the corner and onto the wide porch that spanned the back of the house.

Three gray-haired ladies sat gathered around a card table, each with a fistful of cards, their attention focused on their game. Though it was Monday, they looked as if they'd just come from church, garbed in light summer dresses complete with necklaces and earrings. Annabeth watched as they picked cards off a stack in the center of the table and discarded them on another. Finally the pudgy woman with her back to Annabeth shouted "Gin!" and spread her cards out on the table.

"You trashy poor and no 'count wench!" the imperious lady across from her scolded. "Why didn't you tell me you were collectin' diamonds?"

The winner laughed lightly. "Rose, darlin', I been collecting diamonds all my life. I'm not about to change my ways now." She scooped up the pile of coins at the center of the table and deposited them on the large cache beside her cards. "My, my, my. I guess I'm just livin' on the lucky side of the road today."

Rose gave the winner a withering look. "Daisy, dear, we've been livin' on the same side of the road for some time now," she said with thinly veiled sarcasm. "An' if you know what's good for you, you'll let me and Jasmine win back a piece of the change we've been losin' to you."

Daisy laughed again. "Rose, honey, I don't think I should have to—"

Jasmine, a lovely black woman with skin the color of café au lait, waved an elegant fan beside her face. "Dears, please stop your bickerin'," she said, her voice as sweet as the flower that bore her name. "I can't hear my Mozart through the din. Rose, I know you don't like losin', but if you'd pay closer attention to the cards that have been played, you'd stand a better chance. Daisy, if I see you dealin' off the bottom of the deck one more time, sugar, I swear by all that's right, I will never play gin rummy with you again. And, Rose, I'd appreciate it if you would watch your language, as well."

They both moved to protest, but Jasmine pointed at each of them in warning, then pressed her finger against her lips for a brief second before she smiled demurely. "I believe it's my deal, isn't it, ladies?"

Before they could begin another hand, Annabeth cleared her throat. Slowly all three ladies turned in her direction. She watched as they examined her with curious gazes. Then Rose pushed back her wicker chair and stood. "Can I help you?" she asked. She was a tall woman, with a thorny demeanor to match her name. Annabeth guessed she measured only a few inches shy of six feet. Rose began to walk around the table toward her, but Jasmine reached out and stopped her.

"She's come home," Jasmine whispered, her voice quivering with emotion.

Rose looked down at her in annoyance. "Who's come home?" she asked.

Daisy slowly stood and gazed at Annabeth, then spoke. "Don't you see? It's her."

Rose squinted at Annabeth, then snatched a pair of bifocals from the card table and peered through them. The cool expression on her face softened slightly and Annabeth almost sensed a smile behind her stern facade.

Jasmine pushed out of her chair and slowly approached Annabeth. She reached out and laid her palm on Annabeth's cheek and smiled. "You're Annabeth, aren't you?" A tear glimmered in the corner of her eye. "My, don't you look like your grandmother." Jasmine reached up and tucked a strand of hair behind Annabeth's ear. "Miss Lily told us all about you, 'bout your dancin' and all your early successes. After Miss Lily passed, we followed your career with great interest. And when that nosy lawyer from

Charleston came 'round years back askin' about you, we thought for sure you'd come." She smiled winsomely. "But when you didn't, we just decided we'd have to wait a bit longer. Then when we stopped findin' your name in the ballet magazines, I told the ladies you'd be stoppin' by soon."

Jasmine wrapped her arms around Annabeth and gave her a hug. Daisy followed suit and when Rose reluctantly approached and did the same, Daisy poked her in the arm. "I'm surprised at you, not recognizin' our Annabeth. If you'd wear your glasses, Rose darlin', the world wouldn't pass you by like a Fourth of July parade. And you'd probably have better luck at cards."

Rose glared at Daisy, then turned back to Annabeth and kissed her on both cheeks. "Welcome home, Annabeth. We are all so very glad to finally meet you."

Annabeth forced a bright smile. Beyond the names she had picked up from their card table conversation, she had no earthly idea who these three ladies were. "Daisy... Rose...Jasmine, I'm afraid you have me at a loss. You were friends of my grandmother?"

Rose answered first. "Not friends, exact—"

"Yes, dear," Jasmine interrupted, giving Rose a strained smile. "We were friends of Miss Lily."

"And you live here? All three of you?"

Rose again was the first to jump in. "Lived and work—"

This time Daisy interrupted. "Yes, dear. Miss Lily made arrangements that we be allowed to live here, in her house, until we either meet our maker...or meet some man willing to take us in holy matrimony. I'm afraid the first is more likely." She sighed dramatically. "But now that you're here, you'll probably want us to find another place to reside."

"Well, yes...I mean, no," Annabeth stammered. "I mean, I guess so."

She looked at the trio of hopeful faces. They were all over seventy if they were a day and they were obviously dear friends of Miss Lily, or her grandmother wouldn't have made arrangements for their comfort and security. And she hadn't bothered to read the small print in her grandmother's will. For all she knew, they had every legal right to be there.

"I didn't really expect roommates," she explained.

"We know, dear," Daisy sympathized. "It's a tangle, isn't it?" Her expression brightened. "Of course, if you'd be willin' to accept rent from us..." Daisy looked to her friends for agreement and they nodded. "It wouldn't be much, but it would help to get you settled here."

Annabeth considered her offer. The house was huge and she was without friends or relatives in the area. Maybe it would be best to allow the ladies to stay. At least for a little while. And she could certainly use the rent money until her school got started.

Annabeth smiled and nodded. "I'd like you to stay. I never knew my grandmother. In fact, I wasn't even aware that I had a grandmother until I received word of her death. All I know is that she and my mother had a falling out years ago." She reached out to clasp Jasmine's hand. "We'll worry about the rent later. This is your home," Annabeth said firmly. "And you all belong here." She held up the cat carrier and poked her finger through the wire mesh door to stroke Giselle's nose. "And now it's our home, too."

"TAKE A LOOK AT THIS."

Zach Tanner walked past the conference table and took a yellowed envelope from his corporate attorney's grasp.

Stopping at the window, he stared out at the skyline of Atlanta from his vantage point twenty-seven stories above the street. The sun was fading in the west, bringing much-needed relief from the heat that had plagued the city and the entire Southeast for over a week. Inside the conference room at Tanner Enterprises, on the top floor of Tanner Towers, the state-of-the-art ventilation system kept the room at a constant sixty-eight degrees. Ah, the beauty of technology. No expense had been spared in the design and construction of his most stunning development project. Zach smiled in satisfaction as he pulled a sheaf of papers from the envelope and examined them.

"What's this?" he asked.

"I believe that's the title to a piece of property located at 453 Edisto Street," John Crawford replied.

He perused the papers more carefully. "A house?"

"From what I can tell," John answered.

Zach frowned. "As far as I know, my grandfather never lived in Magnolia Grove. Why would he buy a house there? Is it rental property?"

"If it is, we haven't received any rents from it since the senator died three years ago. The property is just one of many that he owned in Magnolia Grove."

Zach thought he knew everything there was to know about his grandfather. As Senator DeWitt Tanner's only grandson, they had been close from the time Zach was born, and had grown even closer after the death of Zach's father in a hunting accident when Zach was sixteen. The old man took his only son's death hard. The senator's wife had died in childbirth many years before when Zach's father had been born, so there had been no more children or grandchildren. Only Zach to carry on the great family tradition of public service.

"This is the only one that appears to be vacant and residential," Crawford continued. "The rest are commercial buildings leased to various tenants and located in downtown Magnolia Grove. Your grandfather traveled all over the state during his term in the senate. Maybe he saw some kind of business potential in the town."

He'd come from a long line of South Carolina politicians, dating back to his great-great-grandfather. Zach's grandfather, a U.S. senator, had possessed even grander aspirations for his son, who had gotten as far as a state senator before he died. After the hunting accident, those aspirations had simply been transferred to the next available heir. Zach had been thirty-four when Senator DeWitt died and that he had not made his first steps into the political arena had been a great disappointment to the old man.

Zach took a deep breath and clenched his jaw, trying to ignore a niggling feeling of guilt. Sometimes he felt as if he had left a debt unpaid, a family legacy abandoned. Why the hell should he feel this way? He now enjoyed more financial success than all his ancestors combined. Tanner Enterprises was a huge real estate development company, the largest in the state of Georgia.

He turned his attention back to the task at hand. "Downtown Magnolia Grove. You make it sound like a booming metropolis."

"Not exactly." John shuffled through a stack of file folders and finally found a road map and unfolded it. He pointed to a small dot on the Edisto River. "Magnolia Grove, population 1,572."

"What's the outlook on economic growth in the town?" Zach asked absently as he paced the length of the room.

"Our people report that the town has enjoyed a booming seven percent growth in population."

"Not bad." Maybe his grandfather had been right about the town.

"They enjoyed that in 1961," John joked. "It seems that Magnolia Grove is the only town in South Carolina to experience a negative population growth in every year since 1964."

Zach stopped his pacing and turned to his attorney. Once again, he felt a brief stab of guilt before he spoke. "Sell it all. I'm willing to settle for ten percent below market just to clear this out of my portfolio before year end. I should have taken care of this right after I inherited, but I've been putting it off. How much do you think it's all worth?"

"Combined, I'd say around a million, give or take."

"Good. We could use the extra cash to cover the cost overruns on the Mitchell Street project. Maybe then our investors would be more comfortable with the changes I've proposed." And maybe, once he was rid of the last of his grandfather's legacy, he could also rid himself of the guilt that he had not fulfilled his family duty.

John gathered the documentation and returned them to the appropriate files. "Would you like me to arrange for one of our people to go over there and interview brokers?"

Zach was about to agree, then stopped to consider his options. He shook his head. "No, I think I'll go myself. Magnolia Grove was obviously important to my grandfather. I'd like to find out why he invested his money there. Besides, I'm due for a vacation and they say the fishing in South Carolina is great."

"Don't you and Missy have tickets to see that Pavarotti concert tomorrow night?"

"Melissa and I have come to a mutual parting of the ways," Zach said dryly.

"Her daddy's going to be disappointed. I think he fancied you as his son-in-law," John said. "And heir apparent to his construction company."

"And his daughter didn't say much to discourage the old man," Zach replied. "Don't get me wrong, Melissa is a beautiful, sweet-tempered woman that any man would be lucky to marry. But I don't want to get married."

"I've heard this song before," John said. "More than once."

"This was different. There was something missing. I don't know what it was." He paused and reflected for a long moment. "We never argued. She agreed with everything I said or did. Don't you find that strange?"

"Most men would find that enviable," John replied. "After all, hell hath no fury like a woman."

"Like a woman *scorned*," Zach corrected.

"Tell my wife that the next time I come home late for dinner."

"I guess I'm just not looking for a wife. Unfortunately Missy was looking for a husband." Zach picked up a manila folder and shuffled through it distractedly. "By the way, my secretary has the tickets. Box seats. Why don't you take your wife? I'm sure she'd enjoy the concert."

"Thanks," John replied. "She'd like that. Now what about your meeting with Senator Gaines and his cronies? That's scheduled for the day after tomorrow."

"Tell the honorable senator that I've changed my mind. I'm not interested in taking up a political career after all."

"Zach, you don't just blow off a U.S. senator without any explanation. He'll want to know *why* you've changed your mind."

Zach paused and smiled. "Just tell him that my business dealings couldn't stand the scrutiny. Tell him I've got one too many skeletons in my closet."

John shook his head. "Why are you doing this? With the support they've thrown behind you and your financial re-sources, you've got a virtual lock as the party's next candidate for state senator. People know and respect the Tanner name in Georgia. These boys have big plans for you, Zach. And you and I know there isn't a single skeleton in your closet. You're the most scrupulously honest man I know. You take after your granddaddy."

"Real estate development is riddled with payoffs and kickbacks. Don't worry, when you tell them, they won't be calling back. Besides, if I get out of town for a while, maybe Senator Gaines will cast his eyes in someone else's direction."

John sighed. "Okay. I'll have the keys to all the properties for you tomorrow morning along with the appropriate paperwork," John said. "And the contracts on the Donnelly joint venture will be ready to sign tomorrow at noon."

"Good," Zach said. "I'll plan to leave right after that. How long's the drive?"

"It's about two hundred miles," John said, handing him the road map. "The way you drive, I'd say two hours, max. But the highway patrol in the Palmetto State just loves to stop expensive sports cars with Georgia plates. Better make it four hours with a stop for dinner."

"I've got the phone and the fax in the car. If there are any problems, you can contact me. As soon as I've got a room, I'll let my secretary know where I can be reached. If all goes well, we should have this tidied up in short order. I'll plan to be back sometime next week."

THE HOUSE ON Edisto Street was silent. The "Flowers," as the townspeople called Daisy, Rose and Jasmine collectively, had gone out for an evening of bingo at the Fireman's Hall. Anxious for some solitude after two days of constant company and mother-hen fussing, Annabeth slowly wandered from room to room, admiring the decor

in the soft evening light. Each room was a picture of subdued elegance and she had the strange sense that she had
inherited her love of fine antiques from her grandmother.
It was hard to believe that the house and all its lovely fur-
nishings were now hers.

She wandered back to the grand entryway and remembered her first impression of the sweeping staircase. Tara,
she had thought. I'm living at Tara.

The lower floor held her favorite room, the ballroom. In
between sets of French doors that led out to the veranda,
ornately framed floor-to-ceiling mirrors reflected the light
from a crystal chandelier. A cherrywood grand piano sat
in the corner, its highly polished surface glowing in the
soft light. She looked longingly at the glowing, hardwood
floor, a surface perfect for dancing. How she wished she
could slip into her toe shoes and turn a combination of pir-
ouettes and jetés the length of the room, to dance again for
the sheer joy of it.

Annabeth examined herself critically in the mirror. She
still had a dancer's body, reed-thin and lithe, even though
she hadn't danced in nearly two years. Strange, that her
life could change so drastically in such a short time. She
had been at the top of her form, dancing lead roles with
City Ballet and featured roles with prestigious European
companies. And then suddenly, one stupid combination
had ended it all. She could still recall the pop of her knee as
it buckled under her, could still remember the gasp from
the audience. She had known her body well enough to
know it was all over in that split second. Recovery would
be long and painful, and a return to her position as prima
ballerina impossible.

Over the next two years, her life had slowly unraveled.
The company kept her on during her rehabilitation, but
even management realized it was only a matter of time be-

fore they would have to cut her loose. After sixteen months of halfhearted progress, she had been called into the director's office. At the time, she thought it ironic that the company had kept her on just until she could walk again, then handed her her walking papers.

Numb, she'd gone home that day to the penthouse apartment she shared with David and decided that she would finally accept the marriage proposal that he had offered once a year since they had been together. David was thirteen years older and so wealthy that her friends jokingly referred to him as "Daddy Bigbucks." But, fearful for her future, she was willing to overlook his faults and the lack of true passion between them for the financial stability he offered. From the age of eighteen through the prime of her career, he had supported her while she spent her sizable salary on living, and dressing, in a manner befitting a prima ballerina. She had nothing left besides a small savings account with a seven-thousand-dollar balance. David could at least give her a life and a future.

But she soon learned that David didn't want a future with a washed-up ballerina and her bum knee. Good old dependable David was nothing more than a ballet "groupie" and she was his trophy—a trophy that was now tarnished in his eyes. He thrived on the glitter and glamour that surrounded Annabeth, and when she couldn't provide it, he moved on to someone younger and healthier, a dancer with a perfect body and a talent to match.

Reeling from her realization, Annabeth had spent the next eight months moving between the living room couches and guest rooms of old friends, pawning anything of value she owned and blowing the money on maintaining her image as a star. She tried to convince the company to hire her as an instructor, but there had been no funding. She even made a brief attempt to break into Broadway, but her tap and modern abilities were rusty and required two healthy legs. Her career was over and she was ill trained for anything but dancing.

Everything had always been handed to her, every decision made for her. From her mother's ultimatum that Annabeth would become a ballerina to David's decree that they live together. From the roles she would dance to the verdict that she would never perform again. Then, suddenly, the life that had been so safe and predictable was gone. She felt like a child, cast adrift and alone, without any of the skills needed to survive. How ironic! Annabeth had always thought she had absolute control over her own life and everyone in it. Then, in a blink of an eye, her life had careened out of control. And she had no idea where to find the brakes.

"So many changes in such a short time," she murmured to herself.

Annabeth leaned forward and placed her palms on the mirror, then slowly stretched her calf muscles, her gaze fixed on her reflection. She lifted her bad knee and pointed her toe, then grasped her thigh and began to rotate her lower leg. Her gauzy skirt slithered up her thigh. The telltale *click* that she used to feel in the joint was gone. Slowly she turned to the side and extended her leg in front of her, still watching her form in the mirror. The shooting pain that she usually experienced on extension never came. Carefully she drew her leg up higher, grasping the back of her thigh with her fingers and hyperextending the knee until her leg was nearly beside her ear. A sharp pain shot from her kneecap to her hip and she winced.

She repeated the exercise on the other side and was surprised when her knee supported her weight with only a dull ache. Annabeth stared long and hard at her reflection. She was a dancer; she had been a dancer since she had put on her first pair of toe shoes when she was nine. And if she couldn't dance for an audience, then she would dance for herself.

Annabeth spun away from the mirror and raced through the ballroom and up the stairs to her bedroom. Tearing through the bags and boxes that were still left unpacked, she finally found her toe shoes. With an excited laugh, she slapped them together and ran back to the ballroom.

She stripped off her skirt and tossed it over a Chippendale settee, then sat down on the floor in just her underwear and a body-hugging midriff top. With movements borne of long practice, she wrapped the ribbons of the toe shoes in her own intricately personal way around her ankles. As she worked, her gaze was caught by the ugly red scar that bisected her right knee, a vivid reminder of her limitations.

She stood and walked over to Jasmine's stereo system, testing the feel of the shoes. The Mozart disc was still inside the player and she flipped on the power and pressed the Play button. As the first strains of a string quartet echoed through the ballroom, she walked to the door and turned off the lights.

The last rays of the sun filtered through the open windows and French doors, and the room was bathed in a soft, golden light. A gentle breeze rustled the leaves of the live oak trees on the front lawn and a blue jay's raucous call echoed on the sultry air.

In the magic of a peaceful summer evening, Annabeth felt as if a great weight had been lifted from her shoulders. For the first time in years, she could dance for the simple pleasure of it. It didn't make any difference whether she could still perform for a cheering audience, whether she could still outdance the rest of the world. The audience was gone and she was alone now, free of the pressures and the fears. She had a home now, and a future, and no one could take that away from her.

Annabeth slowly limbered up, diligently tending to each muscle and joint until she felt a long-lost feeling of fluidity inhabit her body. As she began to dance, she closed her eyes and lost herself in the ebb and flow of her movement, the crescendos of the music and the steady beat of her pulse. Darkness fell and still she danced, blind to all but the feel of her body drifting through the warm, night air. The moon rose and cast the ballroom in its pale rays and she danced on.

Finally the music stopped and Annabeth stilled, her muscles quivering and her breath coming in short gasps. Perspiration soaked her top and dampened her forehead. With a deep sigh, she lifted her hair off her neck and turned to restart the music.

That's when she saw him. A tall form haloed by the light from the moon, standing in the opening of the French doors. She froze, rooted in one spot, her heart pounding in her chest, her blood racing through her veins. They stared at each other for a long time, unmoving and silent.

Then he stepped toward her and she screamed.

2

HER EARSPLITTING SCREAM echoed through the empty house and died on the sultry night breeze. Annabeth crouched in a self-defensive pose, one of many moves she had learned in classes she'd taken during her time in New York City. The intruder froze in his tracks. Though she couldn't see his face in the dark, she could sense that he was reconsidering his choice of a victim. If he got within striking distance, she would be ready with a sharp knee to the groin. And after that, she'd pop him in the nose with the heel of her hand. Burglars in the backwater South had no idea what they faced in a well-prepared New Yorker.

She waited and watched warily, but the man made no further attempt to approach. He also made no move to retreat.

"If you don't leave now, I swear, I'll scream again," she warned, trying to keep the fear from entering her voice.

"Give me a minute," he replied dryly. "I'll warn the crystal."

Surprised by his sarcastic comeback, she took a tentative step to the side, hoping to make out his expression from a new angle. He didn't sound like an ordinary criminal. His rich voice held just a hint of a southern drawl, and was not threatening, but almost mocking. She had learned to stop a physical attack, but she had no defense for a sharp-tongued mugger.

In the dark, his tall, broad-shouldered form seemed deceptively menacing and her mind formed an image of arctic eyes and a scarred visage. Another rush of adrenaline pumped through her veins. Annabeth knew that she was no match for a man of his physical size. He was at least eight or nine inches taller than her five-foot-five height and he outweighed her measly postdancing weight of one hundred and twelve by a good seventy, well-muscled pounds. She would have to rely on her wits to maintain control of the situation.

"My husband's in the other room," she lied. "He's got a gun and he's an excellent shot."

"I'm looking forward to meeting him," the man said.

He turned toward the door as he waited for her nonexistent husband to appear. His profile materialized from the shadow that had hidden his face and she caught the outline of a straight nose and firm chin in the silvery moonlight. Strong, determined features, almost classic in their masculine balance. Not at all what she had expected. She squinted her eyes and saw a flicker of movement near his lips. She could swear the corners of his mouth were turned up in a smile. After a long minute, he turned back to her. His smooth voice broke the strained silence.

"I don't think he heard you. I'd ask you to scream again, but I've grown rather attached to my eardrums. Maybe you could just call his name. Or maybe, I should call him. What's his name?"

He'd called her bluff. She remained silent, trying to decide her next move. If the man was bent on burglary, he was taking his sweet time about it. She shivered as she considered the other possibilities for his break-in. Could he intend to attack her?

"You don't remember his name?" he asked. "Let me guess. Could it be...Bubba? Or how about Moose? I know. Your husband's name is Killer, right?"

She had only one choice left. She'd make a run for it, through the house and out the front door. Once outside, she could race next door for help. Her plans for escape ground to a halt. She was dressed in a top that stopped at her midriff, bikini underwear and pink satin toe shoes, not the ensemble she would have chosen for her first call at the neighbors.

Her gaze returned to the intruder. He had an athletic build with a narrow waist and long legs. If he chose to follow her, he'd probably catch her. And if he didn't follow, there was no telling what he might steal from the house, before she could return with the police. No, she wouldn't run. Until he made another threatening move, she would stay and protect her property.

"You don't have a husband, do you?" he asked.

She tipped her chin up defiantly.

"Hmm. No Bubba, no gun and definitely not dressed for a social call. I guess the only choice left is to call the authorities."

He couldn't possibly be serious! Annabeth squinted and tried again to read his expression in the dark. Yeah, right. The last thing he wanted was for her to call the police. She was certain he was teasing her, toying with her like a cat would a mouse. If only he would turn a bit toward the stream of moonlight that lit the room, she might be able to read his expression. Maybe it was time to call *his* bluff.

"All right," she said firmly. "I'll do just that." She turned and, with outward calm, walked to the doorway that led to the rear of the house and the kitchen phone. Her pulse pounded in her head and she waited for the sound of footsteps behind her. When she got to the door, she reached out with a shaking hand and opened it. As soon as she passed out of his line of sight, she felt her knees turn to rubber.

A wave of relief washed over her as she pulled the door closed and locked it with the skeleton key. She was safe! Gathering her wits, she stumbled through the dark kitchen to the phone and dialed 911. After thirty seconds without a connection she realized that a community the size of Magnolia Grove probably didn't have the emergency service. With a nervous moan and trembling fingers, she dialed the operator.

"This is Sue Ellen. Is that you, Miss Daisy?"

A local operator? Leave it to Magnolia Grove to scorn the technological superiority of Ma Bell.

"This is Annabeth Dupree," she whispered. "Get me the police."

"Annabeth? Miss Lily's Annabeth? Miss Jasmine told me you were home."

"Yes, I'm home," Annabeth replied impatiently. "Now, please, connect me with the police station, or the sheriff's office, or wherever it is you keep your law enforcement officials. It's an emergency."

"Well, darlin', I could connect you, but no one would be there. Sheriff Yancey went home before suppertime. He don't allow emergencies after five."

"He what?" she shrieked. "Then call his home! There's an intruder in my house!"

"An intruder? Darlin', you must be mistaken. We don't have any crime in Magnolia Grove. Maybe it's just old Mr. Peabody. He likes to wander in and out of folks' houses. Some say he's crazy as a betsybug, but I say he's harmless. Just give him a little snack and send him on his way."

"Call the sheriff, Sue Ellen."

"I told you, Sheriff Yancey don't like bein' disturbed unless it's a real emergency. Why don't you go look and see if the intruder is still there. Maybe he decided to leave."

"Listen, Sue Ellen. I want you to get Sheriff Yancey on

the phone and tell him to get over to 453 Edisto Street. There is an intruder in my house and my safety is in danger." Her frustration had reached its breaking point. "He has a gun!" she shouted. "A big gun! And a knife. And I'm sure I saw him on 'Criminal Close-Up' last week."

"Oh my," Sue Ellen replied. "You mean the episode where that—"

"Call him!" Annabeth screamed into the phone. "Now!"

The line went mercifully dead. Annabeth closed her eyes and sighed. She put the phone back softly into the cradle, then turned. She'd have to find a place to hide until the sheriff arrived. Someplace he'd never find her.

"'Criminal Close-Up?'"

Annabeth yelped at the sound of his voice behind her, then scurried to the other side of the kitchen. Damn! She'd never thought to lock the other door to the kitchen. Backing up against the counter, she kept her eyes on the shadowy form. Slowly she reached behind her and searched the tiled surface for a weapon she could use. Her fingertips found the handle of what felt like a kitchen knife and she inched it toward her.

Then, in one lithe movement, she grabbed the knife and darted for the light switch. White light flooded the room. She cried out as the glare stuck her eyes and she blinked hard. Holding the knife out in front of her, she backed toward the counter and squinted to see. "I want you out of my house, now!" she shouted.

A deep laugh resounded through the kitchen. When her vision finally adjusted to the light, she found herself staring into a pair of intensely blue eyes. Blue eyes that were filled with humor, not malice. He looked nothing like she expected of a criminal—no shifty eyes, no scarred features. Only an openly handsome face. He was dressed in an expensive golf shirt and a pair of finely pressed khaki pants.

His dark brown hair brushed the collar of his shirt and was perfectly windblown. He looked suspiciously like he had just stepped off the pages of an exclusive men's magazine. Either the burglary business had been extremely good to him or he wasn't a burglar. She was beginning to suspect that the latter was the case.

"What are you laughing at?" she demanded.

His eyes drifted down to the weapon she held. Her gaze followed his until it came to rest on the potato masher she held gripped in her right hand.

"Do you have a permit for that?" he asked.

She slammed the utensil onto the counter. "I've called the sheriff. He'll be here any minute."

"And will your husband be with him?"

She shot him a withering glare. "All right. I'm not married. But the sheriff *is* on his way. And then you'll be charged with breaking and entering. You're going to go to jail," she added smugly, though she wondered if a town that claimed to have no crime actually had a jail.

He smiled. "I don't think so. If anyone's going to jail, it'll be you."

Annabeth laughed harshly. "Me? This is my house and you're the intruder here."

"We'll see about that." He crossed his arms and leaned casually against the edge of the counter. His gaze slowly drifted down to her toes and back up to her face, and she grew uncomfortable under his close scrutiny. Yes, she was dressed in nothing more than her underwear, but she'd made quick costume changes backstage in front of ogling stagehands more times than she could count. So why did her unclothed state suddenly cause acute discomfort? She couldn't let him sense a weakness in her, so she returned his sardonic stare with a malevolent one of her own.

They stood in the kitchen, sizing each other up, bent on

intimidation. Then suddenly, a grin split his cool expression and he laughed. Shocked at another mercurial shift in his mood, she watched as he turned his attention from her and surveyed the kitchen. His gaze stopped on the pot of coffee left over from the Flowers' dinner. He looked at her and arched his brow questioningly.

"Oh, no," she protested. "I'm not offering you coffee. You broke into my house and now you expect me to treat you like a guest?"

He shot her a sexy grin. A very disarming, disturbing grin that sent a shiver skittering along her spine. "Where's your Southern hospitality? Besides, I didn't have to break in. The French doors were open. I knocked, but you didn't hear me. You were...occupied."

Annabeth winced inwardly. He'd watched her dance. Though she had danced in front of audiences all over the world, she somehow felt uncomfortable with the knowledge that this stranger had enjoyed his own private performance. A performance in which she had discarded her control and reserve and danced for the sensual pleasure her movements gave her. A performance flawed by her injury and lack of practice.

They waited in a tense silence for another few minutes before she decided that his staring into a coffee cup would be infinitely better than his staring at her bare legs. With an irritated sigh, she retrieved a mug from the cabinet, poured him a cup of coffee and placed it on the counter beside him, then scrambled back to her spot across the kitchen.

He took the mug and raised his brow again.

"Drink it black," she said. "There's a limit to my hospitality."

He smiled. "Thanks," he said wryly.

Once again, his gaze wandered around the room. "This

is a nice house," he commented benignly. "Have you lived here long?"

"No," she shot back. "Have you been a criminal for long?" She ground her teeth. Who was this guy? He acted as if he had every right in the world to be standing in *her* kitchen enjoying a cup of *her* coffee. And there was something about his manner that told her he wouldn't leave until he was good and ready. He exuded an inbred confidence that made her feel the fool for even suspecting he had criminal intent.

He took a sip of his coffee, then glanced at his watch. "You weren't bluffing about the sheriff, too, were you? I'd really like to get this little problem cleared up."

"Who are you?" she demanded. "And what right do you have—"

As if the sheriff was also at his personal command, the front doorbell rang. Annabeth glanced in the direction of the entry hall, then quickly slipped past the stranger and hurried to the door. "We'll get this *problem* cleared up, all right," she muttered as she flipped on the entry hall lights.

As she walked across the marble floor, she heard his footsteps right behind her. She turned around and gave him an annoyed glare and he stopped in the middle of the hall and crossed his arms over his chest. She felt his eyes bore into her back as she turned to approach the door.

Just as she reached for the knob, he spoke. "Although I find your Yankee fashion sense incredibly stimulating, we Southerners do tend to dress for important occasions such as a police interrogation," he said.

She spun around and looked down at her bare legs and midriff. He grinned and raised his brow in a familiar way that was really beginning to irritate her. "Wait right there," she commanded, pointing to the floor at his feet.

She ran into the ballroom and tugged on her skirt, then

rushed back to the entry hall. She was surprised to find him still standing in the same spot, certain that he would have deliberately answered the door just to goad her. Giving him a haughty look, she strode to the door and pulled it open.

The sheriff's form filled the doorway. He was huge, immense, as tall as he was wide. His cherubic face and white hair seemed out of place on a body that rivaled that of a New York Giants middle linebacker. Even though he looked close to retirement age, she was sure he could easily take out three or four New York muggers without breaking a sweat. Sheriff Yancey could certainly handle one amateur intruder with a talent for sarcasm.

He looked her over thoroughly. "You must be Annabeth Dupree."

Annabeth nodded and grabbed his hand to draw him inside. "I'm so glad you're here, Sheriff. And I'm sorry to disturb your evening, but there's been a break-in."

"A break-in," the sheriff repeated gruffly.

"Yes," Annabeth replied. "This man broke—"

The sheriff held up his hand to stop her explanation, then slowly pulled a pad and pencil out of his back pocket. He touched the pencil to his tongue before scribbling something down. "When did this break-in occur?"

"When did it occur?" Annabeth asked. "What kind of question is that? Can't you see that he's—"

"Miss Dupree," the sheriff interrupted. "I'm the sheriff here and I'll be askin' the questions. You're the witness, so you'd be the one doin' the answerin'. Just answer my questions straight away and we'll get to the bottom of this."

"That's what I'm trying to do. If you'd just allow me to explain..."

The sheriff glanced up at the stranger. "Did Mr. Tanner here see anything?" he inquired.

Annabeth spun around. "Mr. Tanner?" she asked.

The stranger nodded and smiled. "Miss Dupree."

Annabeth turned back to the sheriff. "You know this man?"

"Mr. Tanner stopped at the station on his way into town," the sheriff replied. "He's here to take care of some family business. I knew his granddaddy, the senator."

Annabeth glanced back and forth between the pair. "Well, arrest this man!" she demanded. "I don't care if his granddaddy is the mayor of Magnolia Grove. He's the one who broke into my house."

The sheriff looked at her as if she'd just lost her mind. "Everybody knows Hoot Wilkins is the mayor of Magnolia Grove. Mr. Tanner's granddaddy jest owned a considerable piece of this here town."

"And I suppose that includes the jail and the man who runs it?" Annabeth inquired sarcastically.

A thunderous expression crossed Sheriff Yancey's face before he calmed himself, touched the pencil to his tongue and scribbled something else on his notepad. "You say Mr. Zach Tanner's the one who broke in here?"

"Miss Dupree has it turned around," Tanner replied smoothly. "She's the trespasser here. I think it would be best if you arrested her now, Sheriff."

"Sheriff, how could I possibly trespass in my own house?"

"*My* house," Tanner said.

Annabeth slowly turned to face the stranger. "No, *my* house," she countered stubbornly. "Your house is the one with the bars on the windows and the guard towers in the front yard."

He shook his head.

Annabeth clenched her fists until her nails bit into her palms. "I would truly love to continue this battle of wits with you, Mr. Tanner," she said in an icy tone, "but you're obviously unarmed. You're also having a serious real estate delusion. My grandmother left me this house in her will. I have the papers to prove it."

He seemed taken aback by her blunt statement and for a brief moment, a frown creased his brow. "You say you have papers that prove you own this house?"

Annabeth nodded curtly.

"That's strange. I also hold papers that prove I own this house. The house was left to me in my grandfather's will."

"That's impossible!" Annabeth gasped. She looked to the sheriff for agreement. "He's lying."

The sheriff's amused gaze moved back and forth between the two of them. Slowly he put his pencil and notepad away, then rubbed his hands together and chuckled. "Now don't this take the whole biscuit. Maybe I oughta take a look at those papers."

ZACH LAY ON THE BED and stared at the ceiling, his hands folded over his bare chest. He had stripped down to his silk boxer shorts and still he found no relief from the heat. The Breeze Inn, Magnolia Grove's only motel, promised air-conditioning and a color television in every room. The marginally cool air the ancient air conditioner provided wasn't worth the noise. And the color television brought in only one channel, which had gone off the air at midnight.

With a disgusted sigh, Zach pushed himself up and walked to the door. He yanked it open and braced his hands on the frame to stare through the screen door. The breeze that had rustled the sprawling live oak on the motel lawn had died shortly after he had checked in and the heat now hung oppressively in the air. A huge thermometer, illuminated by the yellow porch light, hung from a nail on the outside wall of the motel office. It read eighty-four degrees.

In the distance, flashes of heat lightning brightened the horizon, but the Charleston newspaper that he had picked up at the gas station predicted no rain for at least another week. Another week. He might be stuck in this stuffy motel room for at least that long. His plans for a quick stop in Magnolia Grove and a leisurely fishing trip afterward had evaporated like a puddle on hot pavement. It had happened the minute he had stepped through the French doors at 453 Edisto Street. The minute he had laid eyes on Annabeth Dupree.

The Edisto Street property had been the last on his tour of Tanner holdings in the town. He had planned to just drive by before finding a room for the night. But as he passed, he noticed light spilling from the windows of the upper floor and decided to investigate. The house was listed as unoccupied in John Crawford's report and he paid his attorney well to never be wrong.

The vision that greeted him as he stepped onto the gallery and through the open French doors was burned indelibly into his brain. Like precious few experiences in his thirty-seven years, it was an image he would not soon forget.

She moved like a wisp of fog in the sea wind, swaying and drifting in a sensuous counterpoint to the Mozart and the soft evening breeze. At first, he thought he had stumbled upon some spirit, a phantasm who haunted the mansion by night and would disappear in the light of day. But then, as his eyes adjusted to the dark, he saw she was no illusion. A specter wouldn't wear sexy black lace panties and pink satin toe shoes. A ghost wouldn't perspire until damp tendrils of hair clung to her long, graceful neck. And a spirit wouldn't favor her right knee.

He'd watched her dance for a long time, unable to move, unwilling to break the spell that she wove with her movements. He felt like a helpless insect trapped in a spider's web, mesmerized by the woman who held him prisoner, loath to cut the invisible silken threads that bound him. He had decided to reach out and touch her, just to be sure she was no mirage. He had stepped toward her, his fingers tingling with the need.

And then she'd screamed.

In that single instant, his blithe spirit had turned into a shrieking banshee. Geez, the woman had a scream that could split atoms. And an attitude that could make a guy think long and hard about getting within firing range. He'd never encountered a woman quite like her. Zach usually preferred ladies to be ladies, quiet and demure, born and bred Southern belles. This woman probably preferred threepenny nails over chicken salad for lunch.

But still, he had to admit, there was something about Miss Annabeth Dupree that made him want to stop and take a second look. Even through her stubborn facade, he could sense an underlying vulnerability. He had been tempted to find the chinks in her fiery facade, to expose her weak points. The only problem was, looking at her was like looking straight into the sun. Interesting for curiosity's sake but definitely dangerous as a practice.

Maybe that was for the best. At least he wouldn't feel bad about putting her out on the street. Annabeth Dupree could take care of herself, of that he was sure. She was a survivor.

Zach shoved away from the door and walked over to the small desk. Pushing thoughts of Annabeth Dupree from his mind, he plugged the phone line into his laptop computer and accessed the mainframe at Tanner Enterprises.

First, he sent a memo to his secretary, giving her the

name of his motel and the room number. Then he sent a note to John Crawford outlining the dispute over the title to the Edisto Street property. Sheriff Yancey had advised him to visit city hall and Judge Otis Clemmons for an eviction notice for Annabeth Dupree.

If she left quietly, all the better. And if she decided to fight him in court, Zach was sure his claim to the house would be reaffirmed. He knew real estate law better than he knew his own name, and though he hadn't actually practiced since the early days of Tanner Enterprises, a law degree from Harvard had to carry a least a little weight with Judge Clemmons. Maybe his grandfather's insistence on an Ivy League education would finally be of more use than just making him an attractive candidate for office.

Then, after he took care of business, maybe he'd scout a few good fishing spots in the area.

Zach flipped off his computer, then stood up and stretched. The walls of the stuffy room were beginning to close in on him. He found a pair of baggy khaki shorts and a T-shirt in his suitcase and pulled them on. After a brief search for his keys, he walked out the door to his car. The dead silence of the night was almost deafening and he wondered whether he was the only one in the entire town who was awake.

Minutes later, he turned off the main street of Magnolia Grove onto Palmetto and then took a left on Edisto Street. He pulled up at the front gate and stared at the house across the wide, sweeping lawn and through the majestic oaks. A pair of coach lights on either side of the front door illuminated the lower gallery.

Zach's gaze was drawn to the French doors that opened into the ballroom. In his mind's eye, he could see her as he had earlier that evening. He had to admit that she was beautiful in an unconventional way. Cheekbones that were almost too high, hair that was almost too pale and eyes that were too green to resist. And he was sure, if given the opportunity, he could span her tiny waist with his hands.

He shook his head. Annabeth Dupree was also too much trouble. And her occupancy of 453 Edisto Street was standing between him and a future free of the Tanner family tradition.

Zach put the car back in gear and took a last look at the house. He understood Annabeth's attachment to the house; it was an extraordinary piece of property. What he couldn't understand was why his grandfather owned a house that he never intended to live in, especially one so grand? And what about the handwritten deed that Annabeth Dupree held, giving her grandmother the house? He had only examined it for a brief moment, but he recognized his grandfather's writing. Why would his grandfather have handed the property over to a woman Zach had never even heard of?

"HEAR YE, hear ye, hear ye. The municipal court of the city of Magnolia Grove in the great state of South Carolina is now called to order. The honorable Judge Otis R. Clemmons residing. All rise."

Annabeth stood and watched as the man who would decide her fate stepped onto his bench and sat down. Though she desperately wanted to imbue him with kind, compassionate qualities, she was forced to admit that he looked more like a crotchety old sourpuss than a beneficent savior. His black robes and a slightly hooked nose gave him an uncanny resemblance to a huge buzzard. Annabeth suddenly regretted that she hadn't spent the last of her money on a lawyer, someone who could plead her case to the forboding judge.

Annabeth opened the manila envelope on her lap and withdrew the deed that proved the house hers. Though a lawyer might make a more eloquent argument, the plain fact was she had only one piece of evidence to present. She picked up a second piece of paper and stared at it. Bold letters across the front made her squirm in her seat. Notice of Eviction.

The order to vacate had come yesterday along with a summons to appear in court. The Flowers had been beside themselves with worry, hovering over her with more questions and concerns than she could answer. She suspected Zach Tanner was just trying to rattle her cage with complicated legalities and empty threats. Annabeth had assured the ladies that once the judge saw her deed, she would be proved the house's true owner. Despite Zach Tanner's well-aimed salvos, they would not be put out on the street.

Annabeth risked a glance over at her adversary. He was dressed in a finely tailored suit and tie, the picture of professional competence. He looked at home in these surroundings, among these people. She wondered if her Yankee ties would have any effect on the case. While it was clear by Zach's gentle drawl that he was a Southerner, Annabeth's voice betrayed her as an outsider as soon as she spoke.

"Tanner versus Dupree in the matter of eviction," the court commissioner called. "Case number seventy-six. Would the parties step forward, please?"

Annabeth rose and walked to the front of the courtroom. Zach did the same. The judge slipped a pair of reading glasses on and perused the papers laid before him. After a long moment, he looked up.

"Zachary Tanner," the judge said in a stern voice. "You any relation to DeWitt Tanner?"

Zach nodded. "He was my grandfather, sir. Did you know him?"

"Your granddaddy was quite the politician," the judge replied, examining Annabeth's opponent with a critical eye.

"Yes, sir, he was." Zach glanced over at Annabeth with a self-satisfied smile. Annabeth's temper rose. The nerve of him, using his family ties to sway the judge to his side.

"Young man, do you think my relationship with your granddaddy might help your case?"

"Of course not, sir."

The judge narrowed his eyes and pinched his mouth in what Annabeth assumed was a smile. "Good. Because your granddaddy and I stood on opposite sides of the cow pasture when it came to our politics." He turned to Annabeth. "And who might you be?"

"My name is Annabeth Dupree and I own the house at 453 Edisto Street." She handed him the deed.

"Humph." He turned back to Zach and shook a finger at him. "See there. That's what I like. Get right down to business. None of this talk of relatives and such."

Annabeth felt a warm rush of satisfaction. Maybe she had been wrong about the judge. He definitely was showing his partiality to her side. She directed a smug smile back to her opponent.

"I also hold a deed to the house," Zach said, ignoring her look and handing the judge another document.

He examined both papers then frowned. "Miss Dupree, how have you come to possess this deed?"

"I inherited the deed and the house from my grandmother, sir. Miss Lily Fontaine."

Judge Clemmons's bushy gray eyebrows shot up. "Your grandmother was Lily Fontaine?"

"Yes, sir. Did you know her?"

"Only in a purely professional way. Your grandmother and I had occasion to meet once or twice. But like Mr. Tanner's grandfather, we also found ourselves with a cow pasture or two between us."

He handed them their documents, cleared his throat and turned to Annabeth. "As the claim to ownership of the property at 453 Edisto Street is in dispute, I hereby order a court date set for August third at which time I will rule on the eviction notice. Miss Dupree, it appears you have at least a moral argument for your claim to ownership. A handwritten deed is a powerful piece of evidence. But that deed does not appear to be perfected. You will either have to prove it was duly registered or you'll have to prove that DeWitt Tanner's indisputable intent was to deed Miss Fontaine the property."

He turned to Zach. "Mr. Tanner, you have the legal argument. Your deed has been registered, but according to the race notice laws, it may be invalid if Miss Dupree can prove that her deed supercedes it in any way. A title search and a clear chain of title would help your case. Though it is not necessary for you to retain counsel, real estate law can be quite confusing. I suggest you both avail yourselves of the services of a competent attorney."

"I'll be serving as my own counsel, your honor," Zach said. "I hold a law degree from Harvard and am quite familiar with real estate law."

Annabeth's irritation rose. He had a law degree? Next, he'd be claiming he was personal friends with the governor.

The judge stared at him, unimpressed. "Yes, I do suppose you are." He struck his gavel. "I'll see you both back here in five weeks."

"Wait!" Annabeth cried.

The judge gave her an annoyed look. "What is it, Miss Dupree?"

She quickly handed him the eviction notice. "What about this? It says we have to vacate the property within thirty days."

The judge looked at the paper. "The notice to evict will be stayed until after this case is resolved."

Zach stepped forward. "Sir, until title to the property is decided, I don't think either of us should occupy the house."

"You want to put Miss Dupree out on the street?" the judge asked.

"Your Honor," Annabeth pleaded. "I have three seventy-year-old tenants living in the house with me. These ladies are like family to me. Putting us out would cause undue stress and may prove harmful to their health."

"Your Honor," Zach continued. "If you grant Miss Dupree and her 'family' the right to stay in the house, then I believe I should be allowed residency also."

"What?" Annabeth gasped. "You can't be serious."

The judge frowned. "You want me to allow you to move in with Miss Dupree?"

Zach nodded. "She already has tenants, sir. And there is a detached servants' cottage that is unoccupied. It's not as if we'd be alone in the house. It would simply be another landlord-tenant relationship."

Annabeth instantly regretted bringing the Flowers into her fight. Zach had easily turned their presence against her. "Why are you doing this?" she whispered.

"Miss Dupree," he replied in a soft, even voice. "Everyone knows that possession is nine-tenths of the law. I'm merely taking what's rightfully mine."

"It is not yours." She ground out the words. "That house is mine."

The judge cleared his throat again. "Mr. Tanner, you've put me in an awkward position and one I don't relish. Miss Dupree, you have a choice. Either you and your tenants can vacate the house until this dispute is resolved, or you can allow Mr. Tanner residency. The decision is yours."

Shocked at the strange turn of events, Annabeth looked back and forth between the two men. Choice? How could they call either option a choice? Zach Tanner had backed her into a corner. Without the Flowers as chaperones, the judge would never have allowed Zach to move in. But she couldn't throw the Flowers out just to maintain her hold on the property. They *were* her family now.

Annabeth drew a deep breath and gathered her resolve. There was no way she would surrender to this man! Not without a fight. If possession was nine-tenths of the law then she'd keep possession of her house, even if it meant facing that despicable Zachary Tanner across the breakfast table for the next fifty years.

"Miss Dupree, have you made a decision?" the judge asked.

Annabeth looked up at the judge and forced a smile. "Yes, Your Honor, I have."

3

ANNABETH AWOKE to the sounds of morning drifting through the open windows of her bedroom. The mockingbirds and blue jays in the oaks had set up a strident chorus, punctuated by the exotic cries of Miss Daisy's pet peacock, a bird Annabeth had yet to glimpse though it wandered the grounds at will. Strains of Mozart drifted up the grand staircase, and somewhere outside, the sound of a spade meeting dirt signaled that Miss Jasmine was hard at work in her garden. Rose was probably in her usual place, preparing breakfast in the kitchen, and Daisy never rose before ten.

Annabeth glanced at the clock beside her bed and groaned. Seven-thirty. Breakfast was served at eight and those who didn't make Rose's punctual start were left with only an icy frown and a bowl of lukewarm grits that could have doubled as industrial adhesive. After a long stretch and a leisurely yawn, Annabeth pulled herself from the comfort of the ornately turned tester bed. She had slept in a canopy bed as a child, but according to Daisy, this rosewood bed was not just any bed, but a valuable work of antique art that had arrived by boxcar one Christmas Day as a gift to Miss Lily from the school's "benefactor."

Annabeth had mentally added it to the long list of beautiful items that Miss Daisy had attributed to this mysterious "benefactor." But now, as she stared at the bed, she wondered why the benefactor of an exclusive girl's finishing school would give the headmistress a gift so personal. Usually benefactors gave money for more practical and useful items, items that were necessary for the proper running of a school. An elegant dining room table was certainly needed to teach the proper placement of sterling silver, bone china and leaded crystal. The lovely works of art were probably used to teach appreciation of the finer things in life to aspiring socialites. And the grand piano in the ballroom would have been needed for dancing and music lessons. But what lessons could possibly have required an exquisitely carved tester bed with silk sheets?

Annabeth sighed. Who was she to quibble about propriety? She loved the bed and the bedroom set and every other stick of furniture in the house. Thank goodness this generous benefactor had the good taste to choose timeless pieces.

She brushed her damp, tousled hair from her forehead and walked over to the window. The humidity and heat still hung in the air with only a breath of a breeze stirring the yards and yards of mosquito netting draped over the open windows. The weather forecast promised no relief from the punishing heat wave that smothered the southeast. She grabbed an oversize T-shirt from the armoire and pulled it over her naked body, then attempted to coax Giselle from beneath the massive piece of furniture. Her cat still hadn't adjusted to the new surroundings and refused to be drawn out of her hiding place.

Giving up on the cat, she walked to the window, pushed aside the netting and stepped out onto the veranda. Unlike the French doors on the lower veranda, the second story had huge windows that nearly reached the floor and sashes that were high enough to stroll beneath.

Her bedroom overlooked the backyard and as she stepped to the railing, she caught sight of Miss Jasmine, kneeling amid a tangle of rosebushes. She stretched sinuously and was about to call a greeting when a deep voice sounded from behind her.

"Morning."

With a gasp, Annabeth spun around to meet the penetrating blue gaze of Zach Tanner. He was sprawled in a wicker rocker, dressed in a pair of baggy cotton trousers and a loose-fitting shirt that had yet to be buttoned. His feet were bare and he balanced a mug of coffee on his flat stomach. As her eyes traveled the length of his bare torso, from his wide chest to his muscled abdomen, she felt a shiver course through her. Rubbing her arms, she wondered if the heat wave had finally broken, then knew that the weather had nothing to do with her reaction.

By the time her eyes moved back to his face, he was smiling. "Is it just you," he drawled, "or do all Yankees run around in little more than their underwear?" He challenged her narrow-eyed glare with a raised brow. "If that's the case, maybe I ought to spend more time up north. We Southerners tend to be a bit more decorous in our mode of public dress."

"What are you doing here?" she demanded.

"Don't you remember? You invited me to stay until our dispute over this lovely property is resolved."

"I didn't invite you. The judge ordered me. And you're supposed to be staying in the servants' quarters, not in the main house. Certainly not skulking about on the veranda outside my bedroom window."

He frowned, then took a deliberately lazy sip of his coffee. "Hmm. I don't remember the judge saying anything about restricting my access to the house."

"Well, I'm saying it now," Annabeth replied. "Stay away from the main house." She affected a drawl that surpassed his. "Any proper Southern gentlemen would know that your presence might do irreparable harm to the reputations of the ladies living in this household. So, I'd appreciate it if you would kindly drag your sorry self out of that chair and retire to a more 'decorous' location. A location well out of my delicate eyesight."

He threw back his head and laughed. "My, my, someone woke up this mornin' in a powerful ashy mood, didn't she?"

Annabeth crossed her arms beneath her breasts, trying to control her temper and the blush that threatened her imperturbable expression. Under different circumstances she might just find him incredibly attractive, that sexy grin and rumpled hair, those bottomless blue eyes and a body that begged to be admired. But the man had an uncanny knack for unnerving her.

"Don't you have somewhere you need to be?" she asked. "Like a job?"

"I'm on vacation. A long, well-deserved vacation. And I'm going fishing."

"I hear the Amazon's lovely this time of year. The mosquitos and the malaria and all those alligators and poisonous snakes. Maybe you ought to reconsider your vacation destination."

He set his coffee cup on the table beside his chair, then stood up and held out his hands in surrender. "Call me a fool," he said, "but I'll take my chances here."

Annabeth bit back a stinging reply, knowing that he would only counter with a clever one of his own. This verbal one-upmanship they were playing was guaranteed to drive her mad in short order. She would just have to ignore him, pretend he was invisible. And before she knew it, he would be gone, booted back out on the street where he belonged.

Still, a man like Zach Tanner had a strange talent for

making his presence known. Like a powerful magnet, he'd only need to enter a room and every eye would instantly be drawn to him—to that unshakable confidence and subdued sexuality. Yes, Zach Tanner was absolute ruler of his domain, and right now, his domain happened to be *her* domain—the property at 453 Edisto Street.

"I have an idea," he said, moving to stand before her, so close she could smell his after-shave and the fresh scent of his shampoo. Annabeth was tempted to close her eyes and draw a deep breath, but instead she took a safe step back until she felt the railing against her thighs.

"Maybe you and I should call a cease-fire," he continued. "After all, we're going to be living in the same house for the next month. We could try to be civil to each other."

Annabeth swallowed hard. "Such a gentleman," she replied softly, her eyes fixed on his smooth chest. "Maybe I've misjudged you. But seeing as how you're determined to put us all out, you'll forgive me if I don't trust your intentions."

Zach held his hand out to her. "Come on, Annabeth. Like you, I'm just interested in the truth. Why don't we put our personal differences behind us and let Judge Clemmons settle our legal differences."

She risked a look up at him. His smile was open and genuine and somehow, she was tempted to trust him. Some instinct told her that Zach Tanner was an honorable man, probably the first truly honorable man she had ever met. Hesitantly she reached out. Their palms met and he wrapped her fingers in the warm strength of his, holding on to her hand for much longer than a businesslike handshake required.

"All right," Annabeth said, shaking his hand firmly. "A truce. As for the war, may the best woman win."

Zach squeezed her hand. "Strange. The saying's a bit different here in the South."

"I'm not from the South," Annabeth countered.

Slowly he drew her hand to his lips and placed a gentle kiss below her wrist. The breath that Annabeth held slowly escaped her lips and she felt paralyzed, her mind focused on the firm pressure of his mouth on her skin. He lowered her hand and looked deeply into her eyes. "Geography's only a small part of it, Annabeth. Whether you want to admit it or not, you've got Rebel blood running through your veins." With that he turned and sauntered toward the stairs.

Annabeth stood frozen in place, long after the sound of his footsteps disappeared on the veranda below her. Then, with a frustrated groan, she turned and stalked back into her bedroom.

Sure, a truce with Zach seemed like a sensible plan. And Annabeth was certain she had the fortitude to face him day after day, without letting her temper take over. She only hoped her hormones would be so cooperative. Yanking clothes from the armoire, she hurriedly dressed.

When she arrived in the kitchen, she was irritated to see Zach seated at the table, stuffing a biscuit dripping with honey into his mouth. His shirt was properly buttoned and he had found his shoes. Annabeth gave him a benign smile, poured herself a cup of coffee, grabbed the front page of the Charleston paper and sat down at the opposite end of the huge table. She hid behind the paper and listened as Zach lavished compliments on Miss Rose's cooking. She waited for Rose's acidic retort, knowing how prickly the woman was in the morning. But to her utter surprise, Rose fussed and cooed over the man as if he were the king of the Confederacy come to Sunday dinner.

Annabeth forced a pleasant good morning when Rose

placed a plate before her. Though she tried to ignore their conversation, it wasn't long before the talk turned from polite chitchat to something of greater interest.

"I've lived here for nearly fifty years," Rose said. "Jasmine and Daisy, too."

"Did you know my grandfather, DeWitt Tanner?"

Rose laughed and Annabeth slowly lowered her paper, startled by the strange sound coming from a woman who until now she had regarded as humorless.

"Of course," Rose replied. "We all knew Senator De-Witt. He was Miss Lily's—"

"Benefactor," Jasmine interrupted from the doorway. With a sweet smile, she pulled off her gardening gloves and floated into the room, kissing Annabeth softly on the cheek on her way to the table. "Good morning, dear." She took her usual spot and Rose placed a plate before her. "Your grandfather was a kind and generous man," she told Zach. "All of us were quite fond of him and saddened to hear of his passing. Weren't we, Rose?"

Rose gave Jasmine an odd look, then pursed her lips in a tight line and nodded.

"I don't understand," Annabeth interrupted. "Tanner's grandfather was a benefactor of Miss Lily's school?"

"The only benefactor," Rose muttered.

"The benefactor who bought the Hepplewhite dining room set and the first-edition Byron in the library?" Annabeth probed.

"Yes, dear," Jasmine replied as she spread her linen napkin on her lap.

"And the Baccarat crystal and the Limoges china?"

Jasmine took a tiny sip of her coffee. "Of course, dear. The senator was a man of fine taste. Didn't Daisy go over all this with you?"

"Well, yes," Annabeth replied, "but she didn't tell me

the benefactor was a Tanner. And she didn't tell me that you all have lived here for almost fifty years."

"Then Miss Lily and my grandfather were friends?" Zach interrupted, his brow furrowed.

Annabeth saw Rose and Jasmine exchange an uncomfortable glance across the table, a look she'd seen more than once since her arrival.

"Very good friends," Jasmine said.

"Very good," Rose echoed.

Zach took a last gulp of coffee, then wiped his mouth with his napkin. "It's odd that my grandfather never mentioned Miss Lily. Or the school."

"Rose, darlin', wherever did you get these peach preserves?" Jasmine asked, blithely changing the subject in another behavior that was becoming quite familiar to Annabeth. Whenever talk turned to the past, the Flowers would only provide the most basic information. Annabeth knew little more about her grandmother than she did when she arrived in Magnolia Grove. As for her grandfather, all the Flowers would say was that he was killed in World War II. Which was more than she had ever managed to get from her own mother.

Zach shrugged and pushed away from the table. "Ladies, the breakfast and the company were superb." He nodded at Rose and Jasmine, then turned to Annabeth. "I'm off to the Amazon," he teased. "Let's hope the fish are biting and the gators are napping."

Annabeth watched Zach leave, then turned to Jasmine. "Why didn't you tell me about this sooner? If you've lived here for fifty years, you must know something about the title to this house. Didn't my grandmother ever talk about who legally owned it? Or how much she paid for it?"

Jasmine studied her plate, picking at her breakfast with a sterling silver fork. "Your grandmother preferred to keep her business affairs to herself. She took very good care of her employees and we didn't need to know more."

"You *worked* for my grandmother?" Annabeth asked.

"Yes, dear, I thought we explained that all."

"But, I—I just assumed you were old friends. So what did you do at Miss Lily's? Were you teachers?"

Miss Jasmine smiled demurely. "Teachers?"

"You heard the girl," Rose said. "Tell Annabeth what we did at Miss Lily's."

Jasmine reached over the peach preserves and patted Annabeth's hand. "That's exactly what we were, dear. We were teachers. Rose, did I hear you say that the Senior Center is planning a trip to Atlantic City? Annabeth, darlin', you wouldn't mind if we took a little vacation, would you?"

With the skill of a battlefield general and the manners of a socialite, Jasmine had once again delivered a conversational about-face. Well, Annabeth was tired of vague answers and conspiratorial looks. There had to be some way to learn more about her grandmother and her relationship with her benefactor. She had to prove her ownership of this house, and if the Flowers wouldn't help her, then she would have to help herself.

THE MUDDY RIVER RAN as slow as molasses in January. Zach cast his line out from the rickety pier and watched as the lure floated along with the sluggish current. His shirt lay crumpled in a ball beside him and his pants were rolled up to his knees. The sun beat down on his back and his body was covered with a fine sheen of perspiration. The heat wave had tightened its grip on the day and the temperature was nearing one hundred degrees.

A sudden sense of déjà vu washed over him and he glanced up and looked from side to side. He had come to a place much like this when he was a child, on a blazing summer day, in a long, blue convertible, with his grandfather at the wheel. His surroundings suddenly seemed familiar. He could nearly feel the rough bark of the willows that hung over the water. And the smell of the river drifting in the air was as near to him as the scent of his mother's perfume.

Zach's gaze came back to his line. It was almost noon and he hadn't had a single nibble. Without a fish to fight, his mind seemed determined to drift in Annabeth's direction. She appeared in a lazy series of images: her delicately shaped legs, the gentle curve of neck, her pale hair damp with perspiration.

Groaning in disgust, Zach yanked sharply on his fishing rod and reached for the reel. Life at Miss Lily's promised to be sheer torture if he couldn't put this bothersome attraction for Annabeth Dupree aside. He had never met a woman quite like her, and there lay the source of his fascination. Zach usually found himself drawn to demure blue-blooded belles, women who were safe and undemanding and looked good beside him at obligatory social events.

But Annabeth was no weak-willed, what-ever-you-say-dear, country club princess. She wasn't a woman to be molded and shaped to fit a man's requirements for a proper mate. Every inch of her slender frame shouted "Take me as I am or don't take me at all." Like a northern wildflower, she stood out among the delicate, brightly colored hothouse blooms of the South. And he found himself strangely fascinated by her strength and tenacity, her subtle beauty and hidden vulnerability.

Maybe he ought to just give her the house. It was clear that she would do anything in her power to keep it, just short of murdering him. And though Zach considered himself a charitable person, giving away this part of his grandfather's estate could do more than just ease his conscience. The young ladies of Magnolia Grove would benefit from Annabeth's new school. And in the process, he might be able to rid himself of another link in the Tanner family legacy.

Zach cast his line back into the river. Giving her the house would make her happy. Maybe she would even grace him with that incredibly beautiful smile of hers, a smile that seemed to fade whenever he entered a room. And maybe they would be able to get past the mistrust that seemed to charge the air whenever they were close. They might even become friends.

Zach distractedly began to reel his line in. What would it feel like for the two of them to be on the same side? How would it feel to have Annabeth's unwavering loyalty and stubborn strength in his corner? A man could do important things with a woman like Annabeth beside him.

With a sharp movement, Zach drew back on the rod and let the line fly into the middle of the river. "Hell and sulfur," he muttered in an oath his grandfather was particularly fond of.

What was he doing—thinking of Annabeth as simply a means to succeed? When would he stop fighting this battle? No matter how hard he tried, he still thought about his future in his grandfather's terms, subconsciously fitting every decision he made into some strange master plan. But then his conscious mind would rebel.

He had turned down numerous civic appointments, including a spot on the symphony board, for fear it would send the message that he was ready to enter the political arena. He avoided charitable events, knowing that the question of his political future would inevitably come up. A large check always compensated for his conspicuous absence. And he had deliberately steered clear of any hint of a serious relationship with a woman because he knew that voters didn't elect single men to office.

A gentle tug on Zach's line startled him into awareness and he pulled sharply back to set the hook. But he hadn't been quick enough and the fish let go, sending the lure flying through the air.

"You fish like a city boy. Didn't your granddaddy teach you anything?"

Zach turned to see a tall black man ambling down the pier, a bamboo fishing pole in one had and a tin can in the other.

"Fishin's supposed to be relaxin'. The senator, he knew that. We used to get a real chuckle from some of the folks who come down here from the city. Senator says they fished like they played golf. Turned it into some personal mission, as if they could will a fish onto their line as easy as they could place a chip shot on the green."

The gray-haired man dropped the tin can on the pier and held out his hand. "Name's Claude Parker."

Zach took his hand. "Nice to meet you, Claude. I'm—"

"Tanner," Claude interrupted. "Zach Tanner. Tanner Enterprises in Atlanta. You're living over at Miss Lily's."

Zach shook his head. "Why am I not surprised?" he asked dryly.

"This is a small town, son. Person can't sneeze without half the town saying 'God bless.' 'Sides, most folks knew your granddaddy. You favor him. Anybody ever tell you that?"

"Yeah, all the time," Zach replied.

They stood in silence as the old man watched Zach cast his line into the river.

"Aren't you going to fish?" Zach asked.

Claude shook his head. "Naw. My spot's down the river a piece."

Once again, they stood in companionable silence, the old man observing and Zach's impatience with his futile activity growing. "All right, tell me, what am I doing wrong?"

"You city boys don't know beeswax from a bull's foot. It's not the *catchin'*, boy, its the *fishin'*," the old man replied. "That's why they call it *fishin'*. Relax, and enjoy yourself."

"I'd enjoy it a lot more if I caught a fish."

"Well, there ain't no fish roundabout here."

Zach slowly turned to face him. "I'm beginning to realize that," he said irritably.

Claude shook his head resignedly. "All right, get your gear and follow me. Your granddaddy knew when to cut his losses and move on. I guess you do, too."

Zach reeled in his line and grabbed his tackle box, then followed Claude as he walked along a narrow footpath parallel to the river.

"Did you know my grandfather well?" Zach asked.

"Most folks did," Claude replied, over his shoulder. "He owned half the town."

"Did you know Lily Fontaine?"

"Yep. Most folks did."

"I guess you also know that Annabeth Dupree claims that my grandfather deeded the house on Edisto Street to her grandmother, Miss Lily."

"Yep."

"You wouldn't care to shed any light on that particular transaction, would you?"

"Nope."

"I didn't think so," Zach said sardonically. "It's strange. I've been asking around town about my grandfather and that house, and everybody remembers DeWitt Tanner like he was a favorite uncle, but nobody wants to talk about him. I asked Sheriff Yancey, Judge Clemmons, the Flowers, even Ben Early down at the General Store. And now you. I have a feeling I'm not getting the whole story."

Claude stopped and turned to face Zach. "Your granddaddy was a fine man," he said. "He did good for a lot of folks 'round here. He paid LeRoy Burnett's mortgage off after LeRoy got hurt and couldn't work no more. He lent Miss Emmaline the money to start her beauty parlor after her husband run off and left her with five little ones. He paid to rebuild the Baptist Church after the Christmas tree started on fire and the church burnt to the ground on Christmas Eve."

"What about Miss Lily? Why did he give her the house on Edisto Street?" Zach asked.

"Miss Lily was a true lady—kind and generous and sympathetic. She never said a bad word about nobody. She could always see both sides of a story. She was strong and determined and folks knew they could always count on her not to judge."

"But that's not the whole story, is it," Zach said, looking the man directly in the eyes.

"Sometimes the truth don't matter. And it's not my place to be telling tales. If you want more, you're goin' to have to get it someplace else."

"Dammit, how am I going to do that if no one will talk to me?"

"Don't get all cross-legged now. You'll find a way. You're a Tanner, after all."

"So, you're not going to tell me any more?"

Claude drew a deep breath and sighed. "Listen, I'm not so sure you shouldn't have known the whole story from the jump, no matter what most folks think. Though, I can't guarantee you're gonna like what you find. But, I 'spose there's nothin' to stop you from going down to the library. Miss Blanche, the librarian, knows everything about this town and she's near eighty years old. She and the amen corner biddies in her sewing circle practically stitched this town's moral fiber. And she don't have no problem with tellin' tales."

"She'll talk?"

Claude laughed and shook his head. "Between her and Miss Sue Ellen at the phone company, this town don't need CNN."

A half hour later, Zach pushed open the front door to the Magnolia Grove Lending Library. As he stepped into the lobby, he was stopped dead in his tracks by a familiar face. There, on the wall before him, hung a portrait of DeWitt Tanner. Zach slowly walked over to the painting and looked at the brass plate on the wall beside it. He recognized the name of the artist; it was the same man who had painted the portrait of his grandfather that hung in the State Capitol in Columbia. But here the artist had captured him in earlier times. Zach quickly did the arithmetic. DeWitt had been the same age as Zach when he sat for this portrait.

He stared at the painting, examining each feature of his grandfather's young face until a strange realization overcame him. The piercing blue eyes, the strong jawline, the straight nose and nearly black hair, were identical to those he saw in the mirror every day as he shaved.

His first real memories of his grandfather were of a white-haired man who steadfastly refused to exercise or give up his meat-and-potatoes diet. A man with sad eyes, but a quick smile. A man troubled by the aches and pains of the old and overworked, but blessed with extraordinary energy and a zest for life. An honorable man who valued the truth and tradition.

Zach stood in the lobby for a long time, trying to reconcile the man he saw with the man he had always known. Did the young man in the portrait ever chafe under the Tanner family legacy as Zach did? Had he ever considered defying his family and giving up public service for a private life?

Had he been as captivated by Lily Fontaine as Zach was by Annabeth Dupree, so much that he had given her the house on Edisto Street?

Zach tore himself away from the portrait and strode to the main desk. He wouldn't leave this library until he had all the facts. He'd find out who really owned the house. Miss Blanche would know. But as he approached the librarian's desk, his determination ebbed. The woman behind the desk was not Miss Blanche, but a woman quite a bit younger than eighty years.

"May I help you?" she asked in a proper librarian's tone and without the slightest drawl.

"I was hoping to speak with Miss Blanche," Zach replied.

A slight hint of irritation crossed the young woman's plain features. "Miss Blanche only works in the mornings. She left at noon. I'm Catherine Jacobs. *Ms.* Catherine Jacobs. I'm sure I can help you with whatever it is you're looking for."

"No, thanks. I'll come back tomorrow morning," Zach said. He turned to walk away.

"I *can* help you." The desperation in the librarian's voice stopped him. "I know how much everyone in this town trusts Miss Blanche, but I do have a masters degree in Library Science. They didn't hire me to shelve books all day long. Now, why don't you tell me what you want and I'll find it for you!" The last was a hysterical command.

"All right," Zach said as he reluctantly turned back to her. "I'm looking for information about Senator DeWitt Tanner. He was a prominent figure in this town during the forties and fifties. I was wondering if you might have some newspaper clippings."

"One moment, please," the librarian said, smoothing her hair and regaining control of her emotions. She returned almost immediately with three manila file folders, stuffed with yellowed clippings. "We also have a lovely portrait of the senator in our lobby."

Once she settled Zach at a table, she opened each and explained that the clippings were arranged by date. "Please try to keep them in the proper order," she warned. "Miss Blanche would have my head if she knew I allowed you to go through these. The clipping files are her pride and joy. She doesn't let anyone touch them. Not even me." Catherine Jacobs smiled smugly. "But Miss Blanche isn't here now, is she? And I'm in charge."

"Thank you," Zach said. "I'm sure these will be very helpful."

"You're very welcome. If there is anything else I can do for you, please don't hesitate to ask."

As Zach looked through the clippings, he felt the librarian's eyes on him and wondered if she had made the connection between him and the portrait. He skimmed each clipping from the *Magnolia Grove Monitor*, increasingly surprised at his grandfather's involvement in the community. The clippings began in 1946 and ended in 1981, and covered the spectrum of his grandfather's civic philanthropy in Magnolia Grove. But by the time he reached the end of the last file, he still hadn't found any reference to the house on Edisto Street. He could only speculate that his grandfather had purchased the house as a place to stay on his frequent trips to Magnolia Grove. But how did Miss Lily end up with a deed to the property?

"Is there anything else I can find for you?"

Zach looked up into Ms. Jacobs's hopeful expression. "No, there isn't." He closed the folders and handed them to her, avoiding her crestfallen expression. "I'm sorry," he muttered.

"Are you sure?"

Zach stood up. "Yes. Thank you, Ms. Jacobs."

"We have many other reference sources," she added, tagging after him as he walked toward the door. "We haven't even tried the periodical file. And there's the old city records. In fact, why don't you sit down and I'll bring you the city directories. You'd be surprised at the information one can find in those old directories."

"Would you be able to tell me if DeWitt Tanner ever lived in Magnolia Grove?"

She smiled and nodded. "Of course. I'll be right back."

Minutes later, she returned with four musty volumes. "You know, I've always considered myself a bit of an amateur sleuth. We librarians love a good mystery."

"Did you find anything?" Zach asked.

"I looked for DeWitt Tanner's name in the directories from 1930 through 1960 and he isn't listed anywhere. I'm afraid he didn't reside in Magnolia Grove. But I don't think we should give up yet. What else would you like me to try?"

"Nothing. I think I might have more luck at the courthouse."

"Are you sure?"

Zach started toward the door again, then stopped. "On second thought, see if you have a file on Lily Fontaine."

Ms. Jacobs gave him a grateful smile and hurried off.

When she returned, she looked disappointed. "We have a file on Lily Fontaine, but there's only one clipping." She handed Zach the folder, then excitedly hurried off to help another patron who was just walking through the door.

Zach opened the folder, bracing himself for another item of little revelation. A single clipping slipped from the folder and fluttered to the floor. He picked it up and read the date penciled into the corner of the clipping. Monday, July 18, 1949. His eyes moved to the headline.

New Sheriff Resigns

Zach stared at the headline, trying to decipher the meaning. What did a sheriff's resignation have to do with Miss Lily's School for Social Arts?

After only three weeks in office, Sheriff Hiram B. Hawkins has handed in his resignation. The resignation came about after an ill-conceived raid on Miss Lily's School for Social Arts last Friday evening. Miss Lily and three of her ladies were arrested and taken to the city jail. Bail was posted within a half hour. After an emergency late-night meeting with members of the town council, called by Senator DeWitt Tanner, Hawkins handed in his resignation and the charges were dropped. Before leaving town for a new position with the Columbia Police Department, Hawkins issued a formal apology to Miss Lily Fontaine and her employees. In related news, Silas P. Yancey, a hometown war hero, is under consideration as Hawkins's replacement.

Zach strode over to the circulation counter where Miss Catherine was helping her other patron. "I need something else, Miss Jacobs," he interrupted. "I need to look at old city records, the sheriff's arrest reports from July of 1949. Do you know where I might find those?"

"Why, yes," she replied. "We have a city archive in the basement. I'm sure those records would be there. Just let me finish up with Mr. Dooley and I'll go down and get the records you're looking for."

Zach returned to the table and leaned against it, tapping his foot impatiently as he watched Ms. Jacobs complete her task. As she worked, the librarian became engaged in a rather heated series of whispers with the elderly Mr. Dooley. Finally, after what seemed like hours, she approached Zach but avoided his gaze.

"I'm afraid I was wrong, Mr. Tanner. Those records aren't here. They were destroyed...I mean, burned...in a fire...a big fire. It burned everything," she added softly.

Zach raised a brow and fixed her with a discerning stare. "You're lying," he accused. "I want to see those records. Now."

"I don't think that would be pos—"

"Ms. Jacobs, I have always considered librarians the guardians of the First Amendment," Zach said solemnly, in a voice that would have put most politicians to shame. "We have entrusted our most valuable freedom to you. Within these walls are the books and newspapers that stand for free speech and open expression of ideas. And you, Ms. Jacobs, are the caretaker of that freedom, a patriot as important as Betsy Ross or Paul Revere." Maybe he ought to reconsider a career in politics, Zach thought wryly. He could almost hear the "Battle Hymn of the Republic" playing in the background.

"I am?" she breathed.

Zach gave her his most sincere, press-the-flesh smile.

"Ms. Jacobs, I need to see those records. Will you show them to me?"

The woman blinked only once, so mesmerized was she by his stirring speech. "I would consider it my patriotic duty, Mr. Tanner. Follow me."

It took Zach nearly a half hour to find the reports from 1949. Ms. Jacobs had left him alone to tend to her other duties, but pointed him in the right direction. The sheriff's logs had mildewed with age but were still legible. He flipped through the log dated July through September 1949, then skimmed down the page headed July 18. There was a record of four arrests and he recognized all four names: Lily, Rose, Jasmine and Daisy. He ran a finger along the page until he found the charge. Though the single word proved his growing suspicion, it still shocked him.

Suddenly everything became crystal clear. The house. Miss Lily. His grandfather's ties to Magnolia Grove.

Rage at his grandfather's betrayal welled up from deep inside him. How could he have been so blind? He had worked all his life to emulate DeWitt Tanner—a man he'd considered honorable and invincible. And now, to find that it was all a lie. His grandfather, who had maintained a pristine ethical code in his professional life, had been taken in by the charms of a woman like Lily Fontaine.

He felt as if he had been manipulated—by his grandfather, by Miss Lily. And by Annabeth Dupree. He had almost fallen for her sweet, innocent act, had actually considered giving her the house! But she was no different than her grandmother, and he wasn't about to allow himself to repeat his grandfather's mistake.

An overwhelming urge to place blame burned through him. He would make Annabeth Dupree pay for the shame Miss Lily had brought upon his grandfather's memory.

And he'd make her pay for her attempt to manipulate him. But most of all, he'd make her pay for his ludicrous attraction to her.

Zach looked down at the word once again, secretly hoping that he had misread it. No, there was no use denying the truth. All the pieces fit.

Miss Lily's School for Social Arts was a bordello. Annabeth Dupree's grandmother was the town madam. And DeWitt Tanner had been a loyal, and very generous, customer.

THE NEWSPAPER OFFICE was empty as Annabeth opened the door. The interior was cool and dim, an oasis from the stifling humidity outside. A small bell on the door announced her arrival and an elderly gentleman in a printer's apron appeared from the back room. His cheek was smudged with ink and the sparse hair on the top of his head stood on end, as if he'd recently grabbed hold of a high-voltage wire.

"Afternoon. What can I do for you?"

"I'm Annabeth Dupree, the new owner of Miss Lily's School for the Social Arts. I'd like to place an ad in your paper."

The man's initial look of surprise was immediately cloaked by a bright smile. He held out his hand, then thought better of it after seeing that it was covered with ink. Instead he nodded and self-consciously scratched his chin, leaving a black smudge behind. "Eugene Stillweather. Editor, publisher and head pressman of the *Magnolia Grove Monitor*. You got somethin' you want to sell?"

"I guess you could say that," Annabeth replied. "I'm going to be reopening Miss Lily's and I'd like to run an ad for our open house."

Eugene frowned, then fumbled for a pencil and paper. "You say you're going to reopen Miss Lily's?"

"Yes," Annabeth replied excitedly. "I'm going to make it just like it used to be, only better."

He cleared his throat. "Hmm. And how might that be?"

"We're going to teach the social graces—I'll offer the usual classes in etiquette, comportment, and good manners. But there will be much more emphasis on dancing— ballet, modern, tap and ballroom. Mothers can sign their daughters up for just one class, or the whole series of classes. I want you to list those things in the advertisement. All ages are welcome. The open house is from 7:00 p.m. to 9:00 p.m. next Tuesday evening. And refreshments will be served. You don't think it's too late to run an ad, do you? I want people to notice it."

"Oh, people will notice it all right," Eugene mumbled. He rubbed his forehead and left behind an ink mark the size of a golf ball.

"And I thought I might have you print some invitations. About one hundred. I'll deliver those myself to some of the homes in the neighborhood. I want to make a good impression on our neighbors. Here's what I'd like printed." Annabeth handed him a crumpled piece of paper. She'd worked all morning on the wording, trying to get it just right.

He leaned over the counter and scrutinized her copy, cupping his chin in his hand and nodding distractedly. "I'm sure the neighbors will get all excited when they hear Miss Lily's is reopening. Especially Miss Blanche and her sewing circle," he said under his breath. "Yeah, excited might not even cover it."

"Good. I think there's a real need for a place like Miss Lily's, especially in this day and age."

He straightened and examined her with a somber eye.

An impression of four fingers blackened his cheek and Annabeth bit back the urge to giggle. If she didn't finish her business soon, his face would be unrecognizable beneath the layer of ink.

"You really think you can make a go of Miss Lily's?" he asked. "Like you said, times have changed. Folks 'round here might get the wrong idea if you place an ad like that."

"The wrong idea? What do you mean?" she demanded. "I'm perfectly capable of running the school. I was a professional dancer in New York from the time I was sixteen. And my mother practically raised me on Emily Post and Letitia Baldrige."

The man's complexion turned a bright shade of red under the black. "Oh...well, that's not exactly what I meant. Hmm... Sixteen? Say, did you ever hear of a dancer named Letty LaRue. She does this thing with fans and feathers. As graceful as a bird, she was. I saw her once in New Orleans at a place called The Gilded Cage. She was a professional, too."

Annabeth smiled tightly. Why did everyone assume professional dancer meant show girl? She couldn't count the number of times she'd been asked whether she had been a Rockette or whether she'd ever danced in Vegas. "I'm sure she was," Annabeth replied. "But I plan to teach ballet and ballroom dancing. You know, the waltz and the cha-cha."

Eugene swallowed convulsively, his eyes wide. "The cha-cha?" he said, his voice cracking.

"Yes. And I want you to make sure you put that in the ad. The waltz and the cha-cha. Now, how much will the ad and the invitations cost?"

"Have you discussed this with the Flowers?"

Annabeth resisted the urge to vent her temper on the man. What did she need? Sanction from the Flowers and approval from the town board? She was throwing a party, not painting her house purple. She couldn't say boo in this town without letting everyone know ahead of time. "Daisy, Rose and Jasmine have nothing to do with this. This is my business and I'm going to make a success of it. How much?"

"All right," Eugene acquiesced. "That will be $67.00 for the ad and $23.50 for the invitations. You can pay me when you pick up the invitations tomorrow."

"Thank you, Mr. Stillweather."

He called out to her just as she opened the door. "Miss Dupree, when you see Miss Daisy, would you have her give me a call? Tell her it's urgent."

"Is there a message you'd like me to give her?" Annabeth asked.

"No. Just ask her to call me."

Annabeth nodded and stepped back outside into the smothering heat. What an odd little man. If she didn't know better, she'd think he didn't want to sell her an ad in his paper. But that made no sense at all.

She started down the sidewalk, her mood bright. Her business plan had been set in motion. And even if Judge Clemmons ruled in favor of Zach, she might be able to persuade him to sell the house to her. Her business would be up and running. And she could prove to the bank that she had a source of income. There were so many possibilities. Maybe a bed and breakfast or a tearoom for the Flowers to run. They could even open a gift shop in the old servants' cottage. Her excitement began to grow with every step she took.

As she crossed Main Street she caught sight of a familiar figure leaving the library. She called to Zach and he looked in her direction. Then, as if he didn't recognize her, he quickly turned away and continued down the street. Annabeth hurried to catch up with him, calling as she approached. When he didn't respond, she tapped him on the shoulder. He stopped cold. The muscles across his back tensed and slowly, he faced her, his eyes as cold and blue and distant as the Arctic Ocean.

"Hi," she said shyly. "I thought you were going fishing. What were you doing at the library?"

"Research," he said.

He turned away and she quickly fell into step beside him. "On the house?" she asked.

He nodded, keeping his eyes fixed on the sidewalk in front of him.

"Did you learn anything?" Annabeth asked, not sure if she really wanted to hear the answer. What if he had found the proof of ownership he needed? She needed more time!

He stopped suddenly then opened his mouth as if he were about to speak. But then he changed his mind and continued down the sidewalk at a faster pace. A small measure of relief shot through Annabeth as she hurried after him. "I placed an ad for my open house," Annabeth offered.

"Don't you think that was a little premature?" His expression was strained and a muscle twitched in his jaw. He looked as if he were about ready to explode with anger.

"I wanted to talk to you about that," Annabeth said. "If the judge rules in your favor, I'd like to make an offer to buy the house from you."

"It's not for sale," Zach said, stepping off the sidewalk and crossing the street.

"What?" Annabeth cried, grabbing his elbow and yanking him to a stop in the middle of the street.

Zach looked down at her hand disdainfully and pulled

out of her grip. "If the judge rules in my favor, I'm not interested in selling."

"But your business is in Atlanta. You can't live here. What would you do with the house?"

"Oh, I don't know," he said sarcastically. "Maybe I'll just set fire to it and watch it burn to the ground."

Annabeth gaped at him, shocked speechless. He was serious! "Zach, what's wrong? Why are you so angry? I thought we had decided to be friends."

"What's wrong?" Zach mocked with a bitter laugh. "You want to know what's wrong?" He reached out and grabbed a lock of her hair, rubbing it between his fingers. "This is what's wrong," he said. He brushed his knuckles against her cheek and along her lower lip. "And this." Suddenly, he grabbed her upper arms and pulled her against his body. She turned her face up to his and looked into his blazing eyes. They stared at each other for a long, electric moment, her heart fluttering in her chest and her breathing erratic. He lowered his head until his lips hovered above hers. She could feel his warm breath on her mouth and she closed her eyes.

"So much like your grandmother," he said. "Just how far will *you* go to get what you want, Annabeth?" Then, just as suddenly as he had pulled her to him, he released her. She stumbled backward. "Stay away from me," he warned. Then he turned and strode across the street.

This time Annabeth didn't follow. She stood rooted to the spot in the middle of Main Street, bewildered by Zach Tanner's bizarre change of mood. "Fine!" she shouted after him. "I'd be happy to stay out of your way. Thrilled! Ecstatic! And you can just stay out of *my* way as well."

A horn blared and Annabeth jumped as a car screeched to a stop a few feet away from where she stood. Calming herself, she spun on her heel and walked in the opposite direction, only to find Miss Sue Ellen standing on the sidewalk in front of the phone company. Annabeth nodded curtly as she passed. After a few more steps she risked a glance back over her shoulder. Miss Sue Ellen had already rushed inside.

Annabeth groaned and cursed silently. Within minutes, the gossips would know all the down-and-dirty details. Annabeth's argument with Zach Tanner in the middle of Main Street would give them all plenty of fat to chew for the next few days.

4

THE MANTEL CLOCK in the ladies' drawing room chimed eight times. Though Annabeth tried to ignore the sound, she couldn't help but count along. Had she put the wrong date or time in her ad? She grabbed the newspaper tucked beside her on the settee and reread the ad. Everything appeared to be correct. Had her invitations been ignored? She had carefully placed the hand-addressed envelopes in the mailboxes of all the houses in the neighborhood. How could anyone mistake her invitations for junk mail?

Annabeth carelessly shoved the newspaper aside, then braced her elbows on her knees and buried her face in her hands. Was there anything more embarrassing than throwing a party and having no one attend? The humiliation was almost outstripped by the overwhelming anxiety she felt. After all, this was her life, her future, and she had counted on at least a handful of students to get her school started. Certainly there was at least one little girl in Magnolia Grove who dreamed of becoming a prima ballerina, one mother who believed in the value of good manners.

Maybe she should have listened to the Flowers. They had gently tried to tell her that the attendance at her open house might not meet her high expectations. The town was small, they explained. Young ladies were busy with other activities and maybe the need for a finishing school was a thing of the past. Annabeth had brushed off their gloomy forecast and remained stubbornly optimistic.

At least Zach Tanner wasn't around to relish in her failure. True to his promise he had stayed out of her way and she had gladly reciprocated. He'd left for Atlanta on Friday, but had promised Jasmine he would return by the next weekend to help her plant a new dogwood tree in her garden.

Annabeth looked toward the door to the ladies' parlor. The Flowers were involved in a heated game of gin rummy, but she had caught them peeking at her from behind the partially closed door at regular intervals. Somehow, their concern and compassion made the disappointment a little easier to take. They cared about her feelings and Annabeth loved them for it.

She glanced dejectedly at her watch. How much longer should she wait before she gave up all hope? The sound of footsteps on the front porch brought her upright, and she slowly stood and waited for the bell to ring. But, instead, the door swung open.

He stopped short when he saw her and they stared at each other for a long moment, the tension between them humming like a live wire. Strangely she wasn't as unhappy to see him as she expected. He'd been gone for only four days, but she had... She had what? Missed him? Annabeth felt the color rise in her cheeks.

"Hi," she said softly.

His gaze wandered from her face to the simple black cotton sundress she wore. For an instant, his cold expression seemed to thaw a bit, and she smiled hesitantly in response. But then his jaw tightened and he hoisted the strap of his garment bag onto his shoulder. He was still intensely angry with her, though she hadn't a clue as to why. "I thought you'd be busy with your *guests*," he said, closing the door behind him.

She shook her head, trying to decipher his mood. "Nobody came." She bit her lower lip and watched for his response.

He shrugged. "It's probably for the best. After all, this house will be mine in a few weeks. And you'll have to leave anyway."

Annabeth bristled at his arrogance. So maybe she hadn't missed him after all! She rose and walked toward him. "Why did you come back?" she demanded. "Why didn't you just stay in Atlanta where you belong?"

"I came back to get what's rightfully mine. This is my house and I intend to live here until the judge confirms that fact."

She tipped her chin up defiantly. "What makes you so sure Judge Clemmons will rule in your favor?"

"Because, I'm willing to do whatever it takes to prove that this house is mine."

She stood in front of him, her fists clenched in anger, her spine stiff with indignation. "But you don't even want the house. A week ago you threatened to burn it to the ground. *You* just want it because *I* want it."

He closed the narrow distance between them, until they stood toe-to-toe, like two prize fighters ready to square off. He was bent on intimidation but she wasn't about to back down. Her anger got the better of her and she threw the first verbal punch. "You're a spoiled, petulant child," she said.

"And you're an acid-tongued shrew," he countered.

"Overbearing lout."

"Conniving hussy."

"Stubborn jackass."

"Pushy little wench."

She drew her hand back to slap his face but he caught her wrist an instant before she made contact. He held her hand so near to his face that she could feel the heat of his anger radiating off his strong jaw. Suddenly she was tempted to smooth away the tension with her fingertips, to caress his beard-roughened cheek. Why couldn't they stop this animosity between them? Why couldn't they just be nice to each other? He was the one who'd broken their truce, not her.

She tried to pull away, but he tightened his grip. She watched in astonishment as he slowly turned and placed an insolent kiss on her open palm. Closing his eyes, his mouth still pressed against her skin, she felt him draw a shaky breath, as if he were fighting the urge to go one step further. Then, he opened his eyes and looked directly at her. Where she expected warmth and passion, she saw only an icy distance.

"Be careful, Annie," he said, squeezing her hand until her fingers crumpled in his. "A smart lady knows where her favors are best spent. Your grandmother knew that and my grandfather paid the price. But I'm not about to let history repeat itself." He dropped her hand as if it were on fire, then strode past her. The sound of his footsteps disappeared into the back of the house.

Annabeth rubbed her palms together, trying to remove the brand that his lips had left behind. She wanted desperately to rekindle her anger, but was left only with a nagging sense of loss.

She should hate Zach Tanner, but instead she found herself fascinated by him. He was a mass of contradictions, one day gently teasing her into a truce and the next, hurling insults at her like hand grenades. And all the time, there was an inexplicable magnetism between them, drawing them together against their will. Their cease-fire had lasted little more than a day and now that he had returned, the fighting had resumed at a more feverish pitch than before.

But she didn't want to fight with him. She was tired of the tension and the bitter accusations. She longed to share a few sentences of polite conversation. She wanted to see his sexy mouth curled up in a smile, to see his eyes turn to azure rather than ice when he looked at her.

She didn't even know why he was so angry. Had she said or done something to invite his wrath? If she knew what it was, maybe she could apologize and they could at least live in peace for the next few weeks. But considering Zach's black mood, Annabeth wasn't about to initiate peace talks tonight. Tomorrow, she would ask Daisy to find out what his problem was. Zach had a soft spot for the Flowers and could refuse them nothing. And Daisy could wheedle an enlightening conversation out of a marble statue. Zach would be no match for her.

With a sigh, Annabeth walked toward the staircase, the echo of Zach's words still ringing in her ears. All right, so the finishing school might not work, but there was still the bed and breakfast or the tearoom or the gift shop. She hadn't expended all her options yet. If the house really was hers, she had plenty of time to regroup and try another plan. And if it wasn't, she still had a few weeks to make peace with Zach and convince him to sell her the house.

"Going to bed, dear?"

Annabeth turned and smiled warmly at the three ladies who crowded the parlor doorway. "I think so."

"Are you all right, Annabeth?" Jasmine asked. "We heard you arguing with Zachary."

How sweet they were to show their concern. She felt as if she were part of a real family again, living with people who cared about her, who wanted her to be happy. She'd lost that security at a young age, when she was sent to boarding school, and she hadn't felt it again until this very moment. "I don't want to think about it now...I'll think about this all tomorrow," she added in her best imitation of Scarlett O'Hara. "After all, tomorrow is another day." With that, she slowly mounted the stairs backward, her wrist pressed to her forehead in a dramatic fashion. The Flowers giggled, more in relief at her acceptance of the situation than at her joke.

She was halfway up the stairs when the doorbell rang. Annabeth froze in mid-exit and stared at the door. The bell rang again and the Flowers looked at her anxiously. Her hand dropped to grip the banister.

"Are you expecting anyone?" Annabeth asked.

Daisy shook her head. "Would you like me to get that, Annabeth?"

"No!" Annabeth shouted. "I mean, no, thank you, Daisy," she amended in a more refined voice. "I'll get it."

She raced down the stairs, slowing within a few feet of the door. Pausing briefly, she smoothed her loose cotton dress before opening the door.

Five elderly gentlemen stood on the doorstep and Annabeth's heart fell. She recognized Claude Parker's face among the group and forced a smile. "Good evening."

"Good evening," they all said in unison. The scent of bay rum drifted in on the humid breeze. They watched her expectantly, nervous grins twitching across each freshly shaved face.

"Is there something I can help you with?" Annabeth asked.

The dapper gentleman in the front removed his straw hat and spoke for the group. "We've come for the lessons," he said. "We're here to...cha-cha."

"You're here for dance lessons?" Annabeth inquired. The four strangers nodded enthusiastically, but Claude just continued grinning, clearly uncomfortable with the prospect. "Well, of course, come in." The five men filed in and Annabeth turned to the Flowers and gave them an incredulous shrug. "I guess it's never too late to learn to cha-cha," Annabeth said.

"See, Claude," the heavyset man with the white shoes said. "I told you." He turned to Annabeth. "I'm George Culpepper. Claude said that Miss Lily's wasn't givin' cha-cha lessons anymore. But I saw your ad and there it was, plain as day. Cha-cha. That's what it said."

"Yes, that's what it said. Well, why don't we go into the ballroom and get acquainted," Annabeth said, leading the group through the foyer. As she passed the Flowers, she frantically signaled for them to follow. They looked back and forth at each other with wide-eyed expressions, then fell into step behind the gentlemen.

"Have any of you gentlemen ever taken dancing lessons before?" Annabeth inquired.

"Walter used to come here all the time," Mr. Culpepper volunteered, indicating the dapper man in the seersucker suit. George and Walter. It would be important to remember every student's name.

"You used to come here, to Miss Lily's, for dancing lessons?"

Walter nodded and a spot of red appeared on each cheek. The room was warm even though the French doors had been thrown open to catch what breeze there was. She wondered how much exertion this group could take. They all looked between sixty and seventy-five years of age, but with the exception of George, they were reasonably fit.

"His wife, God rest her soul, was a regular harpy, wasn't she, Walter?" the man in the plaid golf pants added. "I don't mean to be speakin' ill of the dead, after all she was my sister, but that woman had a tongue on her that made a man feel like a kerosene cat in hell with gasoline drawers on."

"And what is your name?" Annabeth asked.

"Edward Durrant. And this here's Lewis Atwater and I guess you know Claude."

Annabeth nodded at each of the men, committing their names to memory. "Would you gentlemen care for some refreshments?"

"If you don't mind, ma'am, we'd like to get right to it. After all, we aren't gettin' any younger," George joked. The others were clearly embarrassed by George's clumsy reply.

"All right. Since there are five of you, Miss Daisy, Miss Jasmine and Miss Rose will serve as dancing partners. I'm afraid one of you will have to sit out each dance, but that shouldn't cause a problem." She looked over to the Flowers and saw them huddled in a corner, involved in a rather animated but whispered exchange. "Ladies," she called. "Please, don't be shy. I'm an excellent teacher and I'm sure we'll all be cha-cha experts in no time. Daisy, why don't you dance with George. Rose and Edward can be partners and Jasmine and Claude can pair up. I'll dance with Walter, since he's had some experience. And Lewis can sit the first dance out."

Annabeth rushed over to the stereo and found the ballroom dancing compact discs that she had purchased in New York. She slid a disc into the player and adjusted the volume. The rhythm of a cha-cha echoed through the room.

"Now, I want you to watch my movements. Step, step, cha, cha, cha," she chanted. "Everybody now, step, step, cha, cha, cha. Step, step, cha, cha, cha."

The gentlemen stood like pillars of stone and watched her in consternation. Every now and then, they glanced at each other, frowned, then turned back to her with confused expressions.

"Come on, it's not so difficult," Annabeth urged. "Walter, why don't you demonstrate with me?"

Walter looked to his companions for encouragement and Claude gave him a gentle push out onto the dance floor. Annabeth placed his right hand on her waist and crooked his left arm up. Giving directions along with the music, Annabeth worked through the steps until Walter fell into the rhythm of the dance.

"See," she said, "that wasn't so hard. Now, why don't we all try this together. Just follow along and have fun."

It didn't take long before the gentlemen overcame their insecurities and stepped onto the floor. At first, their movements were clumsy and the dance was peppered with apologies for squashed toes and missed steps. But after thirty minutes and a litany of encouraging comments from Annabeth, everyone seemed to be well on his way to mastering the cha-cha.

Without giving her students time to take a breath, she moved right into the waltz and from there, to a basic lesson on the fox-trot. Annabeth took her turn with each of the men, laughing and teasing them as they moved around the room. She hadn't had as much fun or felt as pleased with herself in a long time. Ballroom dancing was terrific exercise and she had to admit, her five students looked like they were enjoying themselves.

As she moved around the room with Lewis, leading him through the waltz, she glanced up from the elderly man's feet to find Zach watching her through the open French doors. Though his features were partially hidden in shadow, she could feel his eyes on her as he followed her movements around the room.

Had he come back to gloat? Or was he looking for another argument? A bolt of anger shot through her and she turned her attention back to Lewis, deliberately ignoring

Zach's presence. She was certain he enjoyed some measure of satisfaction at the sight before him. So what if the evening hadn't turned out quite as she had imagined? Her students were a bit older than she had anticipated, but they were students nonetheless.

She risked a glance up as she and Lewis passed the door, prepared to offer him a cool glare. But when their eyes met, she found no hostility in his expression. He watched her with a disturbing intensity, as if all his anger had transformed—into desire. Their eyes met again and again as Lewis spun her around the dance floor, but Zach's expression remained unchanged.

For a fleeting moment, she wondered what it would be like to be wrapped in *his* arms, to lose herself in the gentle sway of *his* movements and to brush against his body then teasingly turn away. She could tell by the way he moved that he would be a wonderful dancer. He had a confident, athletic grace, as if each muscle in his body was attuned to the world around him.

They danced out of Zach's field of vision and Annabeth closed her eyes, immersing herself in the fantasy. The waltz was such a sensual dance. She remembered reading that it had once been considered quite scandalous, a man and a woman locked in a virtual embrace, their bodies pressed together as they whirled around the dance floor and whispered suggestive endearments to each other. And then, when the music stopped, a walk in the garden and a stolen kiss.

"Miss Annabeth?"

Lewis's voice intruded into her thoughts and she opened her eyes with a start. The music had shifted to another cha-cha and she stumbled once as she tried to adjust to the rhythm. Her foot came down hard on Lewis's instep and he winced in pain.

"Oh, Lewis, I'm so sorry! Why don't we sit this one out. Would you like some refreshments?"

Annabeth looped her arm in his and pulled him toward a table set with delicate finger sandwiches and watery punch. The ice had melted long before in the heat of the room and the lettuce on the sandwiches looked a bit wilted, but she grabbed a plate and stacked it high, then poured him a cup of pale green punch. As she showed him to a settee, she glanced over to the open French doors.

Zach was gone, disappearing back into the shadows of the night like a phantom lover. Annabeth walked over to the stereo then pressed her palms to her warm cheeks. Why did his nearness cause such an intense reaction in her? He merely had to look at her and a flush of anticipation would set her nerves on fire. She snatched up a CD case and fanned herself.

It had to be the heat. The temperature hadn't dropped below eighty degrees since she'd arrived. She felt restless and frustrated and on edge, as if she were ready to snap like a piece of dry tinder or burst into flames until she was nothing but ash.

She tossed the CD case onto the table. Zach Tanner was out to destroy her happiness, to steal everything she had ever wanted. Yet in her muddled mind he had somehow become intertwined with that want, and she felt herself longing to draw him closer, to make him part of her dreams.

Annabeth turned and observed her students. Rose and Daisy were still on the dance floor, partnered with Walter and Edward in a lively foxtrot. Jasmine was enjoying a cup of punch and an animated conversation with Claude as they sat this dance out. Lewis was still nursing his sore foot by stuffing himself with finger sandwiches and George stood at the open French doors, puffing on a huge cigar.

Suddenly Annabeth felt incredibly tired. She glanced at her watch and was shocked to see that it was nearly ten-thirty. "Gentlemen," she called, "and ladies. I'm afraid we're going to have to call it an evening." She gradually herded them toward the front door as the Flowers, all glowing under the abundance of male attention, said their goodbyes.

"Why don't we plan to meet again next Tuesday evening?" Annabeth said. "That will be our regular class day, if that's all right with everyone. We'll review what we learned tonight, then start on the tango and the rumba."

They all nodded in agreement, but when she opened the door and led them out onto the porch, the group refused to leave. "Is there something else?" Annabeth asked.

Walter stepped forward. "We were wondering how much we owe you."

"Owe me?"

"For the lessons," George said.

Annabeth smiled and shook her head. "Oh, the lessons." How could she have been so dense? This was, after all, her means of support. She had almost let them get away without paying. "Well, I guess ten dollars each would be fine."

They pulled out their wallets and handed her the money, then bid her good-night before they walked down the steps to their cars. She strolled back into the house and closed the door behind her, then turned and leaned back against it.

With a triumphant smile, she waved the money at the Flowers. "We did it!" she cried. "Miss Lily's is back in business!" She rushed over and gave each one of them a hug and a kiss. They chattered on about the evening's success, reviewing the progress of each of her gentlemen students, until the doorbell rang.

"It's probably one of my *students*," Annabeth said playfully. "Did Walter forget his hat?"

Annabeth swung the door open and to her surprise, came face-to-face with the towering bulk of Sheriff Yancey. He stepped inside then pulled a small card from his shirt pocket.

"Annabeth Dupree," he said, in a terribly serious tone of voice. "You are under arrest."

THE CELL DOOR SLAMMED behind Annabeth and Sheriff Yancey turned the key in the lock.

"I know my rights!" Annabeth shouted. "You have to tell me why you've arrested me. What are the charges? I get one phone call. Have you ever heard of probable cause?"

"We got 'Perry Mason' here, too," Sheriff Yancey replied as he lumbered to his desk and sat down. "And 'L.A. Law.' Why don't you just simmer down and you and I will have a little heart-to-heart chat."

"I'm not telling you anything until you tell me why I've been arrested."

"We had an anonymous phone call about the possibility of illegal activities at Miss Lily's."

Annabeth gasped. "Illegal activities? I was teaching a group of elderly men the cha-cha. Since when has dancing been illegal?"

Sheriff Yancey leaned back in his chair and put his feet up on his desk. "Long time back, folks turned a blind eye to all those cha-cha lessons goin' on at Miss Lily's. But times have changed and you're livin' in the heart of the Bible Belt now. Money changed hands and that kind of dancin' can land a person in jail."

"What are you talking about? The cha-cha's not illegal,

nor is taking money for dancing lessons. Why have you arrested me? What are the charges?''

"Suspicion of panderin'.''

"Pandering? You mean like begging for money on the street corner?''

The front door of the sheriff's office opened and Annabeth watched as the Flowers walked in. Jasmine stepped up to the sheriff's desk and withdrew her wallet from her purse. "We've come to post bail, Sheriff Yancey.''

"Don't you dare give him a single cent,'' Annabeth cried. "He's charging me with panhandling and I'm innocent.''

"Not panhandlin'. Pandering,'' Sheriff Yancey explained. "That's a whole different sort of thing.''

"Well, maybe you could explain it to me,'' Annabeth said sharply. "I think I have a right to know why I was arrested.''

Sheriff Yancey picked up a clipboard from his desk and stared at it, flipping back and forth between several pages. "Well, to cut the tail off the dog, there seems to be some argument around town about your intentions at Miss Lily's. We'd like to clear this up before it gets out of hand. Certain folks, Miss Blanche and her sewin' circle for one, claim you intend to reopen Miss Lily's as an—er, house of ill repute. And when Miss Blanche gets hold of a notion, she don't let up. She starts rattlin' on in my wife's ear and my wife, she starts soundin' like the devil's own grandmother, and 'fore you know it, I'm ready to do jest about anythin' for a minute of peace and quiet. The Flowers, on the other hand, claim that you're runnin' a regular dancin' school.''

"You thought I was running a house of ill repute?'' Annabeth asked. "Where would you get an idea like that?''

"Well, that ad you ran in the paper, for one. It did say cha-cha lessons, didn't it?''

Jasmine stood up and approached the cell. "Sheriff, I think it's time we explained everything to Annabeth. Would you excuse us, please?"

Sheriff Yancey nodded, pulled his considerable bulk from his chair and unlocked the cell door. The three ladies filed in and sat primly on the edge of the bed, their hands folded in their laps.

Daisy leaned toward Jasmine and whispered, "Hasn't changed much in forty years, has it, dear?"

Jasmine looked around. "Weren't the walls green the last time we were here?"

Rose nodded. "Yes, dear, I believe they were," she replied.

Annabeth cleared her throat and the three pulled themselves away from their observation of the cell and directed their attention toward her.

"What does he mean?" Annabeth asked. "A house of ill repute? Is he talking about a bordello?"

"Yes, dear, I'm afraid he is," Jasmine replied. "We're sorry you had to learn about it this way, but we had hoped that with everyone's help, we might spare you the details of the past."

Apprehension twisted at Annabeth's heart. "What are you saying?"

"Annabeth, Miss Lily's was never a finishing school for young ladies," Daisy explained. "I think the popular term in our times was cathouse. Some refer to it as a disorderly house, the more vulgar call it a chicken ranch. I personally prefer bordello, though. It has such an...Italian flavor to it."

"And—and my grandmother?"

"She was what we called the madam. She ran the house."

"I don't believe it," Annabeth gasped.

"It's true," they replied.

"Why didn't you tell me?" Annabeth demanded. "How could you expect to keep something like this a secret?"

"We wanted to tell—at least Rose did," Jasmine replied. "But we were afraid we'd lose you and we've come to love you like our own granddaughter. Most of the folks in this town are willing to forgive and forget what Miss Lily's once was. They prefer to remember Miss Lily for the person she became after she got out of the business, not for the occupation she chose early in her life. And they didn't want to throw the past up at you."

"You all worked for her," Annabeth said. "But you weren't teachers, you were...I can't even say it, much less believe it."

"None of us makes any excuses for what we did," Rose continued. "At the time, it seemed like the only option available. You forget, Annabeth, society is much more accepting of a woman's mistakes these days. And all of us made mistakes that society couldn't forgive. We did what we had to do to survive. And Miss Lily made sure that we did it with as much dignity and security as we could."

"But I can't believe that my grandmother would... could... Why?" Annabeth cried angrily.

"Your grandmother had a child to care for," Daisy continued. "She wanted your mother to be safe from all the vicious tongues and wagging fingers. When Lily was twenty-two, she fell deeply in love with a young man, a soldier, and they planned to be married. He left for the army and he never came back. He was killed in the war when your mother was just a little girl. Lily made the mistake of loving him and trusting him, but she was determined to keep your mother's birth from being a mistake, too. She sent your mother to live with relatives, and later to private boarding schools. She gave her the best place in society that she could—the place that Miss Lily had been denied because of one tragic mistake. And when your mother was old enough, Lily told her the truth."

"That's why my mother never spoke of her. If her friends at the country club only knew they'd... Oh, God, did my father know?"

"Yes, dear," Daisy said. "He always tried to talk Camilla into burying the hatchet. But she wouldn't listen."

"I'm not surprised. My mother is rather fond of her hatchet," Annabeth said sarcastically. "And she never listened to Daddy, anyway. What about my stepfather?"

"I'm not sure," Jasmine replied. "Probably not. After your father passed away and Lily tried to make contact, Camilla refused to have anything to do with her. But Lily figured there wasn't much Camilla could say about it after Lily was dead. So she left you this house. I think she somehow sensed that you'd understand and you'd forgive her." Tears formed in the corners of Jasmine's eyes. She brushed them away and smiled apologetically. "Are you sorry you came?"

Annabeth's gaze moved from Jasmine to Daisy to Rose. She opened her mouth, ready to tell the Flowers what she thought of their subterfuge and secrets. But they looked so devastated, so remorseful. She took a shaky breath. "No," she said softly. "I'm not sorry I came. And I'm not ashamed of my grandmother. I guess she did what she had to do. I've done some things in my life that I'm not very proud of. But I don't dwell on the past and neither should you."

"You're so much like Lily," Rose said gruffly. "She would have loved knowing you. She would have been so proud of you."

Annabeth laughed. "Proud of me? I'm flat broke, I've got no career prospects, I'm about to be evicted. And now

I've been arrested. I'll be the talk of the town. Miss Sue Ellen's phone lines will be on fire within the hour."

"Don't worry, dear," Daisy assured her. "We were all arrested once, and it didn't harm our reputations in the least."

"We didn't have any reputations left to harm," Rose countered.

"Speak for yourself, Rose," Daisy replied. "*I* definitely had a reputation. And remember, Jasmine and I weren't charged with assaultin' an officer of the law. All of our charges were dropped. But *you* had to spend the night in jail."

"Rose spent a night in the slammer?" Annabeth asked. "Our Rose is an ex-jailbird?"

Daisy giggled and nodded. "She hauled off and punched Sheriff Hiram Hawkins, right over there by his desk. She decked him all right. Cleaned his plow. He was seein' stars the next day at breakfast."

"There's one thing I don't understand," Annabeth said. "What about all this cha-cha business? Is it really illegal to cha-cha in Magnolia Grove?"

"Oh, dear," Daisy replied, blushing. "Well, you see, cha-cha is merely a polite way of referring to...well, you know."

Annabeth groaned. "Oh, my God. Cha-cha! That ad. And the editor at the paper. And those five men that came for lessons. They all thought I meant—"

The Flowers nodded in unison.

"Ladies, I think it's time to get our Annabeth out of here," Jasmine said. "Rose, why don't you explain this misunderstanding to Sheriff Yancey. I'll call Sue Ellen and give her the whole story. She's always been able to pacify Miss Blanche and her biddies. By morning, this whole embarrassing episode will be behind us and our lives will be back to normal.''

Annabeth forced a smile. Normal? Just how was life supposed to be normal? She was living in a former brothel, with three seventy-year-old former ladies of the evening, in a town filled with crazy people who thought she was prepared to set up shop as a madam.

Suddenly New York City seemed like the sanest place on earth.

THE AIR WAS STILL with the sleepy silence of a hot summer night. Zach stared at the ceiling, his hands behind his head, and watched the fan whirl the stifling air in his room into a feeble imitation of a breeze. The dance music that had drifted through the screen door from the house had gone silent hours before, leaving him with just his thoughts for company.

Closing his eyes, he tried to clear his mind of all that had happened in the past week. But it was no use. Unbidden, his mind returned to the instant this mess had all started. He remembered the shock and disbelief he had felt as he read the police report, and his immediate suspicion that Annabeth truly intended to reopen the "school." How he wanted to throw all his accusations at her that day on the street, but something inside stopped him. Maybe it was that silly newspaper ad she had placed for her school or her bubbling excitement over the grand opening. Though he had wanted to believe she had immoral intent, he was certain she knew nothing of her grandmother's past.

Still, over the past week, he'd maintained a constant state of anger, bitter over his grandfather's duplicity and enraged at Lily Fontaine's part in all of it. He'd looked for someone to blame, anyone, for the betrayal and hurt he felt. To that end, he had tried to recall Annabeth's every

word, her every glance, hoping to find manipulation and
scheming agendas, until she could be the one punished for
her grandmother's crimes.

But when he walked in the front door that evening to see
her, sitting forlornly in the foyer, waiting for the "students" that would never arrive, the ice that encased his
heart cracked. And though he wanted to deny it, he
couldn't ignore the rush of affection he felt for her. It was
as if she held some kind of spell over him, weaving her
magic through his heart and mind until he was powerless
to resist.

Zach sighed and raked his fingers through his hair. So
what had he done? He'd lashed out at her, venting his confusion and frustration, wanting her to share in some of the
hurt he felt, wanting her to pay for his attraction to her.
And in the midst of all the name-calling, he'd almost told
her the whole sordid truth. But then he had touched her,
kissed her palm and looked into her wide, green eyes, and
he knew he couldn't hurt her.

She knew nothing of Lily Fontaine's occupation. And
she deserved none of the blame for her grandmother's per-
fidy. The Flowers, and the rest of the town for that matter,
were keeping silent on the subject, though he couldn't
fathom why. It was if they had made a pact to protect Annabeth from the past. And he realized that he, too, wanted
to protect her. So he had walked away from her and joined
in their conspiracy of silence.

He wasn't angry at Annabeth, he admitted to himself.
He was angry at his grandfather. His grandfather had
preached to him about honesty and ethics, the responsibility a politician had to his constituents and to his country,
and the price he'd paid to maintain his ethical standards.
Zach had always considered DeWitt Tanner above the
sneaky maneuvering and white lies and little cover-ups

that came with a political career—he had been the perfect politician.

But his grandfather had led a double life, like a two-sided coin, shiny and pure on one side, and tarnished and dirty on the other. And all along, Zach had been the naive fool, worshiping his grandfather, trying so hard to emulate him. It was as if his grandfather had died again, as if the memory of the man had suddenly been snatched from him, leaving a gaping void.

And Lily Fontaine had taken that memory away. She was the one to blame. She'd preyed on his grandfather's weaknesses and led him into all of this, seduced him into forgetting who and what he was. His grandfather never would have risked his career unless she'd held some sort of magnetic power over him.

Zach pushed himself up and swung his legs off the bed. Well, he and his grandfather were alike in yet another way. Neither one of them could stay away from the women who lived at 453 Edisto Street. Neither one could rid himself of a dangerous fascination.

He rubbed his eyes, then stood up. It was nearly 3:00 a.m. Maybe a drive would clear his head. Or a drink, he decided. Miss Rose kept a supply of fine brandy in the kitchen.

The walk to the main house was filled with the quiet sounds of the night, crickets chirping and the whir of June bugs in the bushes, the soft flutter of moths as they threw themselves against the porch light. He wore only his wrinkled cotton trousers, yet by the time he reached the door, a light sheen of perspiration covered his body. The heat refused to break, even in the darkest hour of night.

The glow from the porch light made it easy to find his way around the kitchen and locate Rose's stash of liquor. He pulled out a bottle of brandy, grabbed a tall iced tea glass from the dish drainer and sloshed a good measure into the glass. As he drank, the brandy worked its way through his bloodstream, relaxing him. He hadn't eaten since he gulped down a take-out sandwich at his desk in the office. And after the drive back and his confrontation with Annabeth, he had been too tired.

He wasn't sure how long he sat at the kitchen table, nursing the brandy, but suddenly she was there with him, standing in the doorway, a slender shadow with hair limned golden by the porch light. She wore a thin cotton nightgown, pale and flowing, and made nearly translucent from the light behind her. His eyes had adjusted to the lack of light and he could make out every perfect feature of her face as she stepped into the kitchen.

"You're up late," he murmured, turning away from her and quelling an uncomfortable tightening in his groin.

"I took a walk," she said in a voice as soft as the night breeze. "I couldn't sleep."

"Bad dreams or a guilty conscience?" he teased.

She flipped the light on above the sink and ran herself a glass of water, then turned and leaned against the counter. "Don't start," Annabeth warned. "I've had a miserable night and I'm not about to end it in another argument with you."

He didn't want to argue with her, either. "What's wrong?" he asked. "Everyone looked like they were having a fine time. Though I was a bit surprised by your student body. I expected them to be younger. And I didn't see a party dress or a single pair of patent leather shoes in the bunch."

"The dance class was fine. That's not what I'm talking about."

He raised a brow and waited for her to continue.

She sighed and shook her head, then took a place opposite him at the table. "I might as well tell you. The whole town will be buzzing about it tomorrow. I was arrested. It seems the townfolk were worried I was running a brothel."

Zach stifled a smile. What he wouldn't have given to see Sheriff Yancey haul Annabeth Dupree away to jail, kicking and screaming and threatening bodily harm. He felt a small measure of relief along with his amusement. Maybe she knew the whole truth about her grandmother now.

"What, no snide comments?" she taunted.

Zach shook his head. "Sounds like a miserable night to me."

Annabeth studied his face in the meager light, before realization gradually dawned. Her expression grew cold. "You knew about this the whole time, didn't you? You knew all about Miss Lily's."

"Not the whole time," Zach said, fighting the urge to reach out and take her hand. "I found out last week."

"I suppose you were planning to use this to embarrass me in court. Or were you hoping to blackmail me into leaving town?"

"No, that's not what I was thinking."

She placed her palms on the table and stood up. "You said you'd do anything to get me out of this house. Embarrassing me and the Flowers in front of the whole town might just do it. Well, it's not going to work."

He slammed his palms on the table and shot to his feet, leaning over to meet her threatening posture. "Dammit, Annabeth, I'd never do that."

"Ha! You expect me to believe that? I didn't just fall off the turnip truck, Zach Tanner. I've known men like you. You admitted it yourself. You'll stop at nothing to get what you want."

"I'd never do anything to hurt the Flowers," he admitted. "Or you."

She stared at him, astonished and clearly uncomfortable with his confession. Then she slowly lowered herself back into her chair and took a long drink of water.

Zach sat down. "I was angry and I needed to blame someone, so I blamed you. And your grandmother. Annabeth, my grandfather represented everything that was noble in a man. He is so much a part of who I am, of the man I've become, that sometimes I'm not sure where he ends and I begin. And yet he had this secret life he lived here in Magnolia Grove, a life that was...unacceptable by society's standards."

"Maybe you shouldn't be so worried about what's acceptable. They were adults, Zach, and they made their own choices. Why don't you just accept them for who they are...or were. Maybe they cared about each other. Or maybe they were simply friends."

"My grandfather was a very lonely man, Annabeth. He was strong, but I think he was vulnerable, too. He knew the risks of getting involved with a woman like Miss Lily, but that didn't stop him. It could have ruined him politically."

"You talk about her like she had some disease," she said defensively. "He gave her this house. He certainly wasn't in any hurry for her to get out of the business."

"What she did was against the law, Annabeth."

"You apply a double standard when it's convenient for your argument. Some people might argue that *she* was the victim. Besides, who are you to judge? Can you tell me you've never broken the speed limit? Or postdated a check? Or bet on a football game?"

"That's different."

"It's still breaking the law. And since I've done all three,

I won't presume to sit in judgment on my grandmother's sins. I'm here because of her. She had no husband. She could have decided not to have my mother, but she didn't. She went against everything society dictated and did what she felt was right."

"A true Pollyanna," Zach said with a bitter laugh. "You've been in the South too long, Annie B. Your edge is starting to dull."

"Don't you think your grandfather would have had a good reason risking his political career? Maybe he was just doing what felt right."

"Is that why he kept this dirty little secret for his entire life? Because it felt right?"

She was silent for a long time. He knew his words had hurt her, but the resentment at his grandfather boiled out of control at times.

"Is that why you want to burn the house down?" she asked softly. "Because of what it represents?"

Zach tipped his head back and rubbed his eyes with the heels of his hands. "Right now, as far as I'm concerned you can have it, lock, stock and termites. I'll give it to you. I just want to forget this town and this house and everyone in it."

He glanced over at her. She stared at him long and hard. He expected at least a smile, but her expression was unreadable.

"A few years ago, I might have accepted," she said. "Even a few weeks ago, I'd have jumped at the chance. But I don't need a man to hand me my life. My grandmother made her choices and it's about time I started making mine."

"You don't want the house?" Zach asked in disbelief.

"Of course I want the house. I just don't want you to *give* me the house. For the first time in my life, I'm learning to stand on my own, and I like it. All my life, other people have decided what was best for me, told me what to do and when to do it. I never had to make any decisions for myself. But I'm running my own life now and I'm making my own decisions. I want to be worth something, I want to feel like I've accomplished something. I want to be a responsible adult and make my own place in the world." She smiled slyly. "Besides, your grandfather already gave my grandmother the house. You can't give me something you don't possess."

"Then we're going to let this go to court?" Zach asked.

She drew a deep breath and nodded. "Yes. I think that would be best."

"You might lose."

"I might win. But either way, I won't have to compromise myself. I won't owe anything to anyone."

Zach smiled. "You know, Annie B., I think my grandfather would have liked you."

"What about you?" Annabeth said softly.

"I like you, too," Zach replied.

"Me, too," she said in a shy voice. "I mean, I like you, too." She dipped her head in embarrassment and fidgeted with her water glass. "Will you promise me something?" she asked hesitantly. "Will you promise me there'll be no more secrets between us? I think the more we know about the past, the easier it will be for both of us."

"Deal," he replied, holding out his hand. She placed her slender fingers in his and he grasped them lightly. She felt so small and delicate, as if her bones might break if he squeezed too hard. But Zach knew she wasn't weak and defenseless. She was strong and determined. And beautiful.

He wanted her to stay for just a minute longer, to be sure this tentative friendship they had started was real.

"I—I should get to bed," Annabeth said. "I've had a long day." She stood up, but he kept her hand wrapped in his.

She moved toward him, trying gently to free her fingers from his. "I really should go," she said.

Slowly Zach rose and stood before her, drawing her hands to his chest. Her fingers felt cool on his hot skin. He bent his head and brushed his lips against hers. Her mouth was as soft and sweet as he had imagined. When she didn't pull away, he kissed her again, this time lingering slightly to taste her more fully. Then he drew back and looked into her wide eyes.

"You shouldn't have done that," Annabeth said, breathless. "It wouldn't be good for us to get..." She sighed. "Well, you know what I mean. We can be friends, but with the court case and all, it might—"

He placed his finger over her lips. "I don't care," he said. "Maybe I did it because it felt right." He let go of her other hand and walked to the door. "Good night, Annie B. Sleep tight." With that, he pushed the screen door open and walked out.

He wasn't sure how long she stood in the kitchen staring after him. But as he walked back to his room, he imagined it was a good, long time.

5

"I WANT YOU TO TELL ME everything you know about DeWitt Tanner and my grandmother." Annabeth looked at each of the Flowers, her expression direct and uncompromising. "This is important. It may be the key to keeping this house."

The three ladies sat at a small table in the ladies' drawing room, teacups and plates of delicate sugar cookies surrounding the remains of a serious game of poker. The steamy midday heat had driven them into the cool, dim confines of the house, but it wouldn't be long before the interior and exterior temperatures were in balance and they'd all be sipping cold drinks and fanning themselves with magazines. Lord, this heat was really starting to get on her nerves.

"What would you like to know?" Jasmine offered. "We don't know much, but we'll tell you all we can."

"All right, let's start at the beginning. When did they meet?" Annabeth asked.

Jasmine and Rose turned to Daisy. "I was the first to come to work for Miss Lily and that was in 1946," Daisy explained. "I think they met right after the war. Miss Lily didn't talk much about their relationship. She kept that part of her life very private. Senator DeWitt was a state senator at that time and I suppose it would have caused quite a scandal if the public knew they even associated."

"Why? Was he married?"

"Oh, no," Daisy replied. "His wife had died some years before. I believe she died givin' birth to Zach's father."

"What else do you know?"

"Well, he used to come 'round on a regular basis," Jasmine said. "Once a month, sometimes twice. Whenever he came, he and Miss Lily would shut themselves in the gentlemen's parlor and wouldn't come out for the entire day."

Annabeth toyed with a stack of poker chips, her eyes downcast. "So they were...conducting business in there?"

"No, no," Rose said. "Not in the way you think. Your grandmother was the madam. She didn't do *that* kind of business."

"So, what *were* they doing?"

Rose continued. "I'd sometimes bring them lunch and they'd be deep in the midst of a discussion. Sometimes it was politics, sometimes investments. Once they had a huge argument about the War Between the States. You could hear the shoutin' all over the house. And other times, I'd walk in and they'd just be laughin' over some private joke. I'm not sure if they were ever...intimate."

The revelation startled Annabeth. "They never...?"

"Not that we know of, dear," Jasmine answered. "We never asked."

"What do you know about his involvement in Miss Lily's school?"

"He was a very generous man," Jasmine explained. "He loved to surprise Miss Lily with gifts. But he never bought her anything personal, like jewelry or dresses. It was always somethin' for the house. Art, antiques, books, even the bed was bought for its aesthetic rather than practical value."

"So, he gave her nearly everything in this house," Annabeth contemplated out loud. "And he gave her the house itself. But they weren't intimate."

The Flowers nodded.

"And this house was a...what did you call it, Daisy? A chicken ranch?"

"A bordello, dear," Daisy insisted.

A satisfied smile slowly curved Annabeth's lips. "Sounds suspiciously like a business partnership to me. My grandmother may have run Miss Lily's, but the *dishonorable* DeWitt Tanner was up to his neck in it as well. Now, what about the profits?" Annabeth asked. "How much went to Tanner?"

The Flowers looked deeply shocked at her blunt question.

"I'm sorry if this offends your sensibilities," she said. "But this could be very important."

"Nothing," Rose replied.

"Nothing?"

"Not a cent," Daisy confirmed. "Miss Lily gave us half the money we earned right away and the other half she invested for us. When we all decided it was time to get out of the business in 1955, she handed each of us an investment portfolio she had put together. Let me tell you, none of us have had to worry about our future. How much are we worth now, Rose?"

"At least a million, last I looked," Rose said.

It was Annabeth's turn to look shocked. "You own over a million dollars in stocks and bonds and you're each paying me fifty dollars a month in rent?"

"We were prepared to pay more," Daisy explained, "but you didn't ask for more."

"With *that* kind of money, *you* can buy this house," Annabeth said.

Daisy shook her head. "Oh, no. That wouldn't be right. This house belongs to you. Besides, rentin' is a much more economically sound option for ladies of our age. We wouldn't want to tie our cash up in a house.''

Annabeth sighed inwardly. Beneath those genteel Southern exteriors beat the hearts of shrewd business-women. She had to give them credit; they knew how to look out for themselves. Yet, this discovery did nothing to help her cause. Unless she could prove a business partner-ship between her grandmother and Zach's grandfather, she might have a hard time explaining the deed to the house. But what businessman in his right mind would in-vest in a business that returned no profits?

Unless, of course, he got his profits in trade. In a strange way, that might prove that Miss Lily bought the house from Tanner, that it wasn't a gift. But, according to the Flowers, Miss Lily and DeWitt Tanner didn't share an in-timate relationship.

So just what kind of relationship did they share? Tanner gave Miss Lily gifts and Miss Lily accepted them. The whole setup sounded suspiciously like Annabeth's rela-tionship with "Daddy Bigbucks." David had lavished gifts on her and she had accepted them all with delight. Yet, she knew she should have refused them. He had been trying to buy her love and deep inside, she knew it wasn't for sale.

Was that what it was like between Miss Lily and DeWitt Tanner? Had he offered gifts in the hopes of gaining Miss Lily's affection? Had she strung him along, knowing she'd never return his feelings? Annabeth looked around the ladies' drawing room. If this was so, DeWitt Tanner cer-tainly was too persistent, and possibly too bewitched, for his own good.

So, which was it? Were they business partners or was it a case of unrequited lust? Annabeth struggled to put the clues together, but the puzzle pieces didn't quite fit.

Maybe she was approaching this the wrong way. Maybe the house wasn't a gift.

"Is there any chance that my grandmother may have paid for the house? Either in actual money or…trade?"

"Well," Rose replied. "There is a possibility, but I really couldn't say for certain."

"Is there anything else you can tell me?" Annabeth pleaded. "The deed I have for the house is dated 1955. You say that's when you all decided to get out of the business. Do you remember Miss Lily mentioning anything about buying the house from the senator at that time?"

"As we told you," Jasmine said, "Miss Lily kept all her business affairs to herself. She was always scribbling in her journals, but the only one she ever showed the journals to was Senator DeWitt. She was meticulous about her books. Each penny she spent was recorded."

Annabeth tried to contain her excitement. This could be the break she was looking for. Miss Lily's journals could hold the truth about the house and its rightful owner. "Do you know where these journals might be?" she asked calmly.

A frown furrowed Daisy's brow. She looked to Jasmine. "Do you remember where we put all of Miss Lily's papers? I seem to recall moving them from the gentlemen's drawing room, but where did we put them?"

"I think we moved them to the loft in the servants' quarters," Jasmine replied.

"No, I'm certain they're in an old trunk out in the carriage house," Rose insisted. "Or maybe we put them in the box of things we sent back to the senator."

"That was so long ago, nearly fourteen years," Jasmine said dismally. "And we were all so distraught over your grandmother's death."

Annabeth reached out and squeezed Miss Jasmine's

hand. "Don't worry. If the journals are still around, I'll find them."

"Do you think you'll be able to prove the house is yours?" she asked.

"I'm going to try."

"It's not like we couldn't be happy in another house, but we've grown rather attached to livin' here," Daisy said. "It's our home and it would be devastatin' to leave."

"I can't believe Zachary would just throw us out on the street," Rose said. "He's such a nice young man. Maybe if you were a bit nicer to him he'd—"

"Zachary Tanner is not going to put you ladies out on the street," Annabeth said. "Or me for that matter. Not if I have anything to say about it."

"Did I just hear my name?" Zach stood in the doorway of the drawing room, dressed in shorts and a T-shirt, a teasing grin on his face.

Rose turned to him and smiled. "Annabeth was just sayin' that she'll never—"

Annabeth jumped up from her place at the table. "I was just sayin' that you ladies look like you could use some iced tea," she interrupted. "Why don't I get you some, then we'll leave you to your card game?"

Annabeth grabbed the empty teacups and hurried out of the room. Zach followed her to the kitchen. He leaned against the counter and watched as she took three iced tea glasses from the cupboard.

"I'm glad I found you," he said. "I wanted to talk to you."

She opened the refrigerator and let the cool air rush out against her warm cheeks. Just the sight of Zach brought back memories of the kiss they had shared in the kitchen the night before. The sensation of his lips, gentle yet powerful, still lingered in her mind. She wanted to experience it all over again and she felt tempted to throw her arms around his neck and try. But she wasn't one to act on impulse, especially when it came to Zach Tanner.

"What would you like to discuss?" she said, grabbing a pitcher of tea and placing it on the counter. She slammed the refrigerator door and opened the freezer. If she could have crawled inside, she would have, just to spare herself this overpowering heat that crept slowly up her body, stealing her breath and making her heart race.

Did he want to bring up their encounter? Or did he want to kiss her again? Maybe he wanted something more... intimate. And then what?

She grabbed the ancient metal ice cube tray and placed it on the counter, then struggled to pull the lever up and free the ice cubes. It was stuck firmly. She impatiently slammed the tray on the counter and tried again.

Zach wrapped his arms around her and took the tray from her hands, then deftly pulled the lever up. His body pressed against the length of hers until every nerve in her body pulsed with longing. She felt faint, weak-kneed, flustered by his nearness.

"Thank you," she murmured. Preoccupied with her raging reactions, Annabeth flipped the ice tray over. The ice cubes tumbled out, scattering across the counter and skidding across the tile floor. She tried to bend down and pick them up, but Zach's arms still encircled her body, pinning her to the counter. She slowly slid down and under his arms, then grabbed an ice cube from the floor.

"What did you want to discuss?" she repeated as she crawled along the kitchen floor and gathered the fallen cubes.

She stood and he took an ice cube from her hands. A grin quirked the corners of his mouth as he ran the ice slowly from her shoulder to her wrist. "I wanted to ask if you'd like to spend the afternoon with me," he said seductively. She felt the cold slither slowly back up her arm, then trace her collarbone.

"What would we do?" she asked, stifling a shiver.

He touched the ice cube to her lips and gave her a slow smile. "We could pack up cold drinks, suntan lotion, a picnic lunch...and go fishing."

Annabeth licked the cold water from her bottom lip and laughed nervously. "Fishing? As in sitting in a boat all afternoon, under the hot sun, putting worms on a hook and waiting for a fish to bite? That kind of fishing?"

Zach traced her lower lip with his thumb, following the path of the ice cube, his hot touch a startling contrast to the freezing ice cube. "That's about it. Except we'll fish from a pier. You might like it. After all, I'll be there and I promise you won't have to touch a worm or a fish. If you like, you can just sit on the pier and look beautiful. That way, if I don't catch anything, the afternoon won't be a total loss."

Annabeth relished his compliment. She was tempted to say yes; she'd like nothing more than to spend an afternoon alone with Zach. But her grandmother's journals were her first priority and she was anxious to begin searching for them. "Can—can I take a rain check?" Annabeth asked. "I've got some work to do here at the house and I promised Miss Rose I'd take her grocery shopping." The last was an outright lie, but Annabeth knew he wouldn't pressure her with the Flowers as an excuse.

"All right," he said. "We'll go another time." Before she had a chance to move, he bent over her and brushed a kiss across her lips. Then he placed the melting ice cube into her hands. "I guess I'll see you later, Annie B."

Annabeth watched him walk out the back door. With frozen fingers, she dropped the pile of ice into the sink and slowly released her long-held breath. His kiss had seemed so natural, so right, as if he'd been kissing her for years. A sweet, undemanding, affectionate kiss.

She wished he would have stayed just a little longer so they could try it again and again.

IT WAS LATE AFTERNOON by the time Annabeth found the journals in the attic, stored inside an old wardrobe. She pulled out all ten of the thick leather-bound books and stacked them on the dusty floor. The temperature in the attic was unbearable, but Annabeth was determined to examine every entry in the books. After three trips up and down the attic ladder clutching an armful of books, she was dripping with perspiration and coated with dust. She locked her bedroom door, threw herself on her bed and opened the first journal.

Her grandmother's handwriting crossed the page in tidy, precise script. Jasmine had been right. Miss Lily had been meticulous about her accounting. Every penny, down to the nine pennies spent for soap in December of 1948, was accounted for. She scanned the book for 1955, looking for a payout for the house. When she found nothing, Annabeth flipped back through the book until she found a page detailing business revenues. Once again, the accounting balanced to the penny. Annabeth's grandmother had invested the Flowers money in the stock market, taking a small share for the household expenses, but leaving the rest to appreciate in value and collect dividends.

She continued through the book, looking for the accounting of her grandmother's partnership with DeWitt Tanner. As she paged through the final section of the journal, she found what she was looking for. In one neat, long column, she totaled twelve deposits to Miss Lily's accounts. But unlike the other detailed entries, these deposits had no explanations alongside, just the initials *DT*.

There was only one explanation. The money had to have come from DeWitt Tanner! They *had* been business partners. Over the years, Tanner had invested his money in Miss Lily's and this proved it. She turned the page, expecting to find a listing of the dividends paid to Miss Lily's major investor, but the next page only listed deposits made to a bank account in Charleston. Oddly enough, the amounts recorded exactly matched the amounts of DeWitt Tanner's payments. The cryptic notation beside each was "Roosevelt House."

Had Miss Lily purchased another house with the money Tanner had given her? Was there a branch location of Miss Lily's School for Social Arts somewhere in Charleston? Annabeth tore a scrap of paper from the back of the journal and grabbed a pen from her bedside table, then scribbled down the account number and the bank. She would call the attorney who handled Miss Lily's estate. Certainly he would know about another property.

Annabeth opened the next journal and the next, but found that each book recorded much the same. Rubbing her eyes, she tried to put all the clues together. Zach's grandfather paid into the business, but as far as she could see, got nothing in return. Why would he invest in an unprofitable venture?

She flipped back through the pages. Where was the payoff? She stared at the page detailing the payments made to Roosevelt House. Suddenly the explanation became clear. DeWitt gave Miss Lily money to invest in another school. And he reaped the profits from that house!

She slapped the book shut, her excitement tempered with apprehension. So much for Zach's theory on his grandfather's involvement with her grandmother. His grandfather hadn't been coerced into giving Miss Lily the house, no more than he had been coerced into giving her money every month for over forty years. They were business partners and as soon as she contacted the attorney in Charleston, she would have proof.

She waited for her excitement to return, but it had been supplanted by niggling uncertainty. With this new information, she had another clue to the past and with a little more searching, she would be able to prove the validity of the deed. But in doing so, she might be forced to present the journals as evidence in court. With Miss Sue Ellen and Miss Blanche covering the legal beat, DeWitt Tanner's reputation would be in tatters before the judge had a chance to say "Court adjourned."

She could win this case and she and the Flowers would keep their home. But she could hurt Zach in the process. With a groan, she threw herself back on the bed and closed her eyes. Why did it all suddenly seem so complicated?

BY DINNER TIME, Annabeth had made her decision. She would approach Zach with her new evidence and try to gauge his reaction. After that, she would figure out how far she could go in court. But to her surprise, Zach didn't make an appearance that evening. She questioned the Flowers but they were vague as to his whereabouts and seemed unconcerned by his absence. As soon as coffee and dessert were served, Annabeth excused herself and ran upstairs to get one of the journals. She would find Zach and they would settle this issue once and for all.

As she stepped out of the kitchen onto the veranda, she saw a light glowing through the window of the servants' quarters. The tiny building, which sat perpendicular to the main house, had once served as a summer kitchen and laundry after the house had been built in the 1800s. A covered walkway connected the building to the main house. When a modern kitchen was built in the main house, the building had been refurbished into a servants' cottage. Annabeth had never been inside and she wasn't sure that she wanted to venture in at this time. But she and Zach had to talk and sort out the past.

She stepped in front of the screen door and peered in. Zach was sitting at a small table, facing away from the door, and dressed only in a pair of khaki shorts. For a long moment, she stood and stared, transfixed by the shimmering play of light across the muscles of his back. Her gaze shifted to his wide shoulders, and then to his neck, where his dark hair curled in the damp heat. A flood of self-consciousness rushed through her, warming her cheeks.

All day long she had tried to banish the memories from her mind, tried to quell the desire to touch him again. Every time she recalled the feel of his mouth on hers, she rationalized his kisses as innocent, a shared moment between new friends. But as she watched him work, she couldn't put Zach Tanner in the role of friend anymore. He was a man who stirred something deep within her, strange impulses that chipped away at her need for absolute control. She was afraid, yet she was powerless to resist him.

Her experience with men hadn't prepared her for the intensity of her feelings toward Zach. She had met David on her eighteenth birthday and they had moved in together three months later. He had provided her with everything she needed: financial security, a nice apartment, constant adulation and a mediocre sex life. Wild and rebellious, no matter what kind of trouble she caused, he had always been there to pick up the pieces, pay for the damages and reassure her of her beauty and talent. She kept him on a string—until one day, he snipped the string and she found herself alone.

But Zach Tanner wasn't the kind of man a woman could control and she didn't want to try. In New York, she had been the center of David's universe and everything revolved around her. She called all the shots. But since her career, and her life, in New York had disintegrated, she knew that absolute control was just an illusion, a comfortable mirage that could vaporize at any instant as it had with David.

Over the past year and a half, she had learned to depend on no one. Everyone she had trusted had let her down—David, the ballet company, her peers and so-called "friends." Even her mother with her refusal to discuss Lily Fontaine. Her life had crumbled before her eyes and she found herself alone, with no one to help her pick up the pieces and put it all back together again.

But since she had arrived in Magnolia Grove, she had sensed a change deep within her. And though she never really wanted to depend on another person again, she had come to realize that, sooner or later, she would have to drop her defenses. She would have to forget her need for control and learn to trust in someone other than herself.

Annabeth cleared her throat and Zach turned around. As soon as his gaze met hers, he smiled.

"You didn't come in for dinner," Annabeth said through the screen door.

"I had work to do. I've got to put together this deal before the end of the week." He raised his arms above his head and stretched sinuously, the muscles in his torso rippling and shifting. "But right now, I need a break. Come in and sit down."

Annabeth shifted nervously, clutching one of the journals in her hands. "Would it be all right if we took a walk in the garden? I have something I'd like to show you."

Zach shrugged. "Sure. Just let me finish up. I'll be right there."

Annabeth turned and sat down on the front step to wait. She didn't have to wait long for he joined her seconds later. He had pulled on a T-shirt, but his feet were still bare.

"Do you want to walk or sit?" he asked.

"Maybe we should just sit here," Annabeth replied.

They sat for a long time, both looking out into the growing shadows of the garden, both silent. He sat close, his shoulder and his thigh grazing hers. Her mind continually focused on the places where their bodies touched, until she felt ready to jump out of her skin and scream in frustration.

As if he could read her mind, he playfully bumped against her. She looked up at him and he grinned. "What did you want to discuss with me?"

Annabeth forced a smile in return then hesitantly handed him the journal. "I found my grandmother's journals in the attic this afternoon. I've gone through them and I found something...interesting."

He slowly turned the pages. "What did you find?"

"I'm pretty certain that my grandmother and your grandfather were..." She paused, still not certain how to broach the subject.

"Tell me, Annabeth. Remember, we promised, no secrets."

"Zach, I think Miss Lily and DeWitt were business partners."

"Business partners? In what?" he asked.

Annabeth's determination wavered. She drew a deep breath. "In Miss Lily's school and possibly another school in Charleston."

Zach turned to her and laughed. "You can't be serious. Annabeth, I know how much you want this house, but trying to destroy my grandfather's reputation won't get it for you."

"I'm not making this up." She grabbed the journal from him and found her evidence. "This is a list of payments your grandfather made to my grandmother."

Zach scanned the column of figures and whistled. "Your grandmother commanded quite a price in her day," he said.

"These aren't payments for services rendered," she snapped. "According to the Flowers, our grandparents weren't—they didn't—you know."

"I do? What do I know?" he teased.

"They weren't on intimate terms."

Zach shook his head. "I find that a little hard to believe."

"So did I. But it's all here. Your grandfather gave money to Miss Lily and she invested it in another house. She noted it as Roosevelt House. It's in Charleston."

"Annabeth, you can't be serious. My grandfather would never invest his money in a bordello. I know him. It would have been political suicide."

"It's true," Annabeth replied stubbornly. "And it may help me to prove that this house is rightfully mine."

"What?" Zach gasped. "You're planning to use this garbage in court?"

"We made a deal," Annabeth said. "Both of us want the truth and this is part of the truth."

"This is bull," Zach countered. "And you know it. If you bring this into court it'll be a matter of public record. If the news media gets a hold of this, my grandfather's reputation won't be worth a plug nickel."

"Zach, I have no choice. If this will help me prove ownership of the house, I have to use it. Besides, this is all in the past. No one cares anymore."

"I care. If you drag his name down in the mud, I swear,

Annabeth, I'll drag your grandmother's name right down alongside his."

"Is that a threat?" Annabeth asked.

"Take it any way you like." He shot back the words.

"I'm not ashamed of my grandmother. I won't bury her memory under some veil of pious secrecy. Your grandfather was as much a part of this as my grandmother and you're just too self-righteous to admit it. You're nothing but a sanctimonious hypocrite, Zach Tanner."

His jaw tensed and his blue eyes iced over. "Then go ahead, Annabeth. Do what you have to do. And I'll do the same."

Annabeth clenched her fists. "I thought we had agreed to be civil about this. I thought we were going to try to be friends."

"Well, now, who messed up that whole plan?"

Annabeth grabbed the journal from his hands and stood up. "Fine. Maybe it's best we remain enemies. I'll see you in court, Zach Tanner." As she strode toward the house, he called out to her.

"Hey, Annie B."

She froze, refusing to turn back to him. Once, he had used that name affectionately, but now he used it as a challenge, a taunt.

"There is another explanation for those payments."

Reluctantly she turned. "What?" she asked.

"Blackmail."

His accusation cut right to her soul and for a time, she couldn't breathe. Or speak. She blinked hard, unable to think of a stinging comeback. Zach stood and yanked open the door to the cottage.

"You better figure out just how far you're willing to go to get what you want," he warned, before he stepped inside and let the screen door slam behind him.

Annabeth let her breath go in one big whoosh. Then she tipped her head back and cursed silently. This was not the way she had hoped he'd take the news. But she had been right about one thing.

Zach Tanner was definitely not the kind of man a woman could control.

Somewhere, deep within the silence of the house, a clock chimed once. Annabeth rubbed her eyes and glanced at her watch. Surprised at the hour, she pushed out of the leather desk chair and stretched. She had closeted herself in the gentlemen's parlor after supper, prepared to comb through Miss Lily's journals for any evidence to refute Zach's accusation. But after reading each and every page, she had found nothing to disprove his theory. She had to admit that, to an objective observer, it might look as if her grandmother were blackmailing DeWitt Tanner.

Still, deep in her heart, she knew it couldn't be so. According to the Flowers, Miss Lily and DeWitt had been friends. Zach was simply grasping at straws, trying to scare her out of bringing the truth to light. The battle lines had been drawn and Annabeth now had to decide whether to step across.

When she thought about leaving Magnolia Grove and the Edisto Street house behind, she felt empty and alone. And when she thought about leaving the Flowers, the pain became more intense and her desperation escalated. She had grown attached to Daisy, Rose and Jasmine. And with their encouragement and love, she had begun to build a new life for herself. A life she was proud of.

"I can't think about this tonight," she murmured. "I'll think about this tomorrow." Maybe after a good night's sleep, the choice would be clearer. And hopefully, her grandmother's attorney would call back soon with news about the Roosevelt House.

Annabeth sluggishly climbed the stairs to her room, undressed and crawled into bed. But after thirty minutes of tossing and turning, she sat up and threw the sheets off her naked body. She felt smothered by the heat and tormented by the images that whirled in her mind. Wrapping herself in a long silk robe, she stepped through the mosquito netting and onto the veranda.

She walked to the rail and leaned over it, drawing a deep breath. A breeze rustled the trees and Annabeth wondered whether the heat wave was about to break. Lightning flashed in the distance and thunder rumbled from far off. She strolled along the veranda, trying to clear her mind and relax her body, feeling a curious anticipation, as if the storm waited somewhere in the dark.

The heady scent of flowers drew her down the stairway and into the backyard. Jasmine's garden was thick with foliage and ran deep into the property. Annabeth wandered along the path, the brick cool against her bare feet, past the magnolias and azaleas, beneath a lacy crape myrtle and around a gurgling fountain. She felt the tension melt away as she put the house and her problems with Zach behind her.

A circle of brightly-colored Japanese lanterns illuminated the weathered white gazebo in the center of the garden. Annabeth climbed the shallow steps and sat down on one of the benches that lined the inside. The lanterns swung in the breeze, the light dancing and fading against the surrounding trees. She turned her face into the fragrant wind and closed her eyes.

"Hello, Annabeth."

Her heart stopped and she held her breath. Had she

imagined his voice? Or was it just the wind singing through the trees or the distant rumble of thunder?

"Annabeth, come on," the deep, rich voice teased. "You can't pretend that I'm not here."

She groaned and put her hands over her face. "Tell me you're just one of those charming Southern ghosts everyone's always talking about." Spreading her fingers slightly, she peered at him. "Go haunt someone else's garden." He stood on the first step of the gazebo, dressed in a pair of faded jeans, and a white shirt, unbuttoned and open to reveal his finely muscled chest. The top button of his jeans was also undone, and she found her eyes drawn to the thin dusting of hair that ran from his flat stomach to somewhere lower.

He patted his hand down his chest and over his stomach. "Sorry. No ghost, just flesh and bone." He stepped into the gazebo and moved to stand before her. "I am charming, however." She felt his fingers around her wrists and he gently pulled her hands away from her eyes and cradled them in his, stroking the soft flesh of her palms with his thumbs. "See, I'm real."

She balled her hands into fists and shook her head. "Go away. I'm tired of fighting with you."

"I've been thinking about what you told me, Annie. And we need to talk about this."

Annabeth pulled out of his grip and clasped her hands in her lap. "Please, can't we just give it a rest? Can't we forget all the accusations and anger and just enjoy the night?"

He sat down beside her, leaned back on his elbows and crossed his legs in front of him. "I can do that," he said softly.

They sat in silence for a long time and listened to the sounds of the night and the approaching storm. The moon appeared from behind a cloud and gilded the garden in a magical silver light. Annabeth held her breath at the sight, then slowly exhaled as the moon disappeared again and the garden faded into shadow. "It's beautiful, isn't it," she murmured.

"Beautiful," he said.

She turned to find him staring at her, his gaze intense. Smiling hesitantly, she turned back to the garden. "When I lived in New York, I never knew what quiet was. I lived above the city in a high rise, and even in the dead of night, the streets hummed beneath me. But here...it's so peaceful."

"Do you miss New York?" Zach asked.

"Yes," she answered automatically. Annabeth paused then realized that she had spoken too soon. "No," she amended. "Now that I think about it, I really don't. There's nothing left for me there. This is my life now."

"Don't you miss your friends?"

Annabeth shook her head. "My career didn't leave much time for real friends. I traveled a lot and when I wasn't touring, I was rehearsing a new ballet or taking class or attending parties. It wasn't much of a life. Besides," she said with a laugh, "I was too self-absorbed for close friends."

"Miss Jasmine says you were very talented. She showed me a picture of you on the cover of a ballet magazine."

"*Swan Lake* with the London Ballet. I worked hard to get to the top. And for a while, I was there. But I didn't really appreciate it at the time. Only after I lost it all, did I realize what I'd had. And then it was too late." Annabeth stood and strolled to the other side of the gazebo. She wrapped her arm around a pillar, her back to him, and watched the garden come alive with movement in the night breeze. "That was a long time ago. A whole different life. I was a different person."

She felt his presence behind her, nearly touching her.

"Who are you now, Annabeth?" he murmured, his breath soft against her ear. He clasped her shoulders in his hands, then ran his palms down her arms. She leaned back against him and closed her eyes, losing herself in the feel of him.

"I'm not sure," she whispered.

Gently he turned her to face him. "Then let me tell you," he murmured, brushing a strand of hair from her eyes. "You're stubborn and opinionated." He stroked her cheek with his thumb. "And you're kind and caring." He bent his head until his lips nearly touched hers. "You're sweet and—"

"Don't." Annabeth interrupted. She stepped out of his grasp and retreated to the other side of the gazebo. Her attraction to him was almost overwhelming, yet deep inside, she knew she should resist. Not more than six hours ago they had been at each other's throats, leveling accusations and insults without remorse. What did he want from her now? Cooperation? Surrender? Her silence about his grandfather?

He leaned back against the rail and studied her, his arms crossed over his chest. "I want you to answer a question, Annabeth."

"If I can," she replied.

"What if there were no court case, no house, no Flowers and no past? What if we could put that all aside? How would you feel then?"

The first drops of rain hit the roof of the gazebo and she listened to the soothing sound and considered his question. "We can't put it aside, Zach. It's right here, standing between us, as big as day. Your grandfather, my grandmother, Rose, Daisy, Jasmine, the whole town for that matter."

He held out his hand to her. "Then maybe we should leave them here," he said, as if it were all so simple. "Just for a little while. Come on, Annabeth. They won't follow us if we don't let them."

How she wanted to indulge in the fantasy, to put aside everything and everyone that stood between them. "How do you know?" she asked.

He stepped toward her and took her hand in his. "Trust me," he said. He gently pulled her down the stairs and out onto the lawn. "Trust me."

Annabeth grinned and shook her head. "My mama didn't raise no fool," she said in a slow, Southern drawl.

With that, Zach scooped her up in his arms and carried her across the lawn, laughing and dodging raindrops, until they reached the canopy of a huge live oak. He lowered her to the ground and wrapped his arms around her waist. Hesitantly she pressed her palms against his warm chest. His skin was satin over steel and she placed her forehead against the broad expanse and drew deeply of his scent.

She felt vulnerable in his embrace, as if all her highly prized control had simply melted away at his touch. But, she didn't want to resist him, she wanted to let their feelings take a natural course. She wanted to discover the real passion between them, without games and artifice and ulterior motives. She wanted to trust him.

His heart thudded beneath her fingers, strong and sure, in a tempo half the speed of hers and she wondered why he wasn't as apprehensive as she. She ran her hand across muscle and flesh, raking her fingers through the soft hair on his chest. Then she turned her face up to his, wanting his kiss, suddenly needing his mouth on hers more that she'd ever needed a man before.

Zach took her face in his hands and covered her mouth in a gentle, but urgent kiss. Clutching the front of his shirt in her fists, she held on, certain that if she let go of him, her knees would buckle beneath her. She was drowning in sensation, yet she wasn't afraid. Zach was holding on to her and she knew he wouldn't let go.

His hands drifted over her shoulders and down her arms and he splayed his fingers until they nearly encircled her waist. Slowly he lifted her and pulled her against his body, wrapping his arms around her waist and burying his face in the soft folds of fabric that covered her breasts. She curled her arms around his head and pressed him closer.

"I remember the first time I saw you," he murmured as he slowly turned her around. "I thought *you* were a spirit, a ghost that haunted the ballroom by night. I was afraid if I touched you, you'd disappear before my eyes. You won't vanish, will you, Annabeth?"

He let her body slide down along his, until she was exquisitely aware of his desire. Her toes found the ground as his lips trailed across her cheek and down her throat. She slipped her fingers beneath his shirt and pushed it over his shoulders. Taking her lead, he yanked it off and tossed it on the ground.

"I won't vanish," Annabeth murmured as he tugged at the collar of her silk robe. His mouth brushed the soft skin above her breast and she moaned softly. "See. Flesh and bone."

The rain fell around them, dripping through the wide leaves of the live oak and making his skin so slick she could feel every contour and muscle she touched. Her robe clung to her like a second skin, heightening the sensation his caress evoked. He slid down along her body, kissing the narrow strip of skin exposed by the open neckline of robe, until he knelt before her on the ground. Catching her waist in his hands, he pulled her down before him, capturing her mouth and tumbling her into the damp grass.

He cradled her head in his hands and kissed her, a deep and soul-shattering kiss she could feel right down to her toes. On and on, his mouth plundered hers, until she wondered whether she would ever breathe again. He stretched out on top of her, pulling her leg up against his hip until she could feel the outline of his erection through the worn denim of his jeans and her silk robe. Drawing back, he traced her jaw with his tongue, his breath quickening, his desire nearly raging out of control.

"Talk to me, Annabeth," he urged. "Tell me what you want. Tell me how you feel."

She didn't want to talk. Instead she wanted to bury her doubts and insecurities so deep that they couldn't jeopardize what she and Zach had begun. But her thoughts cried out to be verbalized until she couldn't ignore them anymore. "I'm confused, Zach," Annabeth whispered, burying her face in the curve of his neck.

"What are you confused about, Annabeth?" She could hear a teasing smile in his voice.

She drew a deep breath. "Zach, you're not doing this—I mean, you're not trying to seduce me so that I'll change my mind about taking the journals into court, are you?"

Zach froze, his shoulders tensing beneath her fingers. Then, in a single instant, he pushed off of her and rolled to a sitting position on the grass, his arms crossed over his knees. "You thought that's what this was all about?" He ground out the words.

Annabeth sat up beside him and grasped his arm. "No...no, I just wanted to be clear on this point."

He turned and fixed her with a sardonic glare, his brow arched and his jaw tense. "Gee, if you're not perfectly clear, I sure am, Annabeth," he replied. "Thank you for bringing this to my attention. But maybe you're the one who had better review your motives."

"Wha—what's that supposed to mean?" she stammered.

"Maybe you've got a little more to gain from a roll in the rain than I do."

"If you think that I—"

Her words were stopped short as he covered her mouth with his in a furious kiss. And then his mouth was gone and he stood before her, thoroughly enraged and ready for battle, his skin gleaming like armor in the soft light from the gazebo.

"Zach, I'm sorry. I didn't mean—"

He shrugged dispassionately. "No need for apologies. You did what you had to do." He snatched his shirt from the ground and wadded it into a ball. "Good night, Annabeth," he said.

She watched him stalk into the shadows. A few moments later, the screen door on the cottage creaked open and slammed shut. She flopped back into the grass and threw her arm over her eyes.

Lord, how had this encounter turned into such a total train wreck? Everything was going so well until she opened her big mouth. But she just couldn't make love to him without knowing for sure. There was too much at stake and her heart was at the top of the list.

She pounded her fists and feet in the grass until her frustration subsided. Maybe she and Zach were just meant to be at odds with each other. Every time they got close, something else would pop up and push them apart. No matter how much they wanted each other, the past would always come back to haunt them.

Annabeth stood up and straightened her robe, then shook her head and raked her fingers through her tangled hair. She looked up into the sky and sighed in frustration. The rain had stopped, the breeze had disappeared and the humidity hung thick in the still air.

The heat wave remained unbroken.

"My heavenly day," Daisy whispered. "That sounds like the Widow Tremaine." She craned her neck to peer into the house from the back veranda. "I suppose she heard about your run-in with the law and decided to check it out for herself. She's got a nose like a preacher for sin and fried chicken."

Annabeth reluctantly turned her attention from the backyard to Daisy. She had been surreptitiously watching Zach dig a hole on the far side of the garden for Miss Jasmine's new dogwood tree. His shirt was off and his sweat-slicked skin was burnished brown by the sun. They hadn't come within one hundred feet of each other all morning and Annabeth was sorely regretting her impetuous behavior of the night before. She should have never let him kiss her, or touch her, or…

"The Widow Tremaine?" Annabeth asked distractedly. "I'm really not in the mood for another interrogation."

"Maybe Jasmine won't answer the door," Rose said.

"Rose!" Daisy scolded. "Our Jasmine would never think of snubbin' a neighbor."

"If Jasmine lets her in, just ignore her, dear," Rose instructed. "She'll go away. Sooner or later."

Annabeth steeled herself for a full frontal assault by one of Miss Blanche's biddies, but when the Widow Tremaine blew through the back door like a Force Nine hurricane, she proved to be the exact opposite of what Annabeth expected. The Widow Tremaine was drop-dead, super-model, trainer-toned gorgeous. And no older than thirty-five if she were a day.

Her raven hair was perfectly coiffed, her salon nails and makeup flawless, and her stunning magenta sundress something out of Bloomingdale's designer department. Annabeth glanced down at the wrinkled silk tank top and batik skirt she wore. Suddenly she felt terribly under-dressed and underdeveloped.

"Darlin's!" the Widow exclaimed, hugging Daisy and Rose. "Here you'all are! I was just passin' by when I realized I hadn't paid a social call in ages and ages. I said to myself, May Belle, stop the Mercedes this very instant! And so I did, and here I am."

"May Belle, please, sit down and join us," Jasmine said.

Rose and Daisy shot Jasmine equally annoyed glares behind May Belle's back, but Jasmine brushed them off and smiled warmly at the widow. "Can I get you an iced tea or perhaps some lemonade?" she offered.

"Darlin', I am positively suffocatin' for moisture," May Belle replied. "Bring me a mint julep. And don't be chintzy with the bourbon. I've had a horrible mornin'." She arranged herself in a wicker chair beside Annabeth, taking great care to smooth her skirt and cross her legs to display herself at her best advantage. When she was settled, she looked up expectantly. "So, dears, aren't you goin' to introduce me?" She turned her eyes in Annabeth's direction and smiled sweetly.

"Of course," Daisy replied. "May Belle Nolton Tremaine Selby Birdwell, may I present Annabeth Dupree. Annabeth, this is May Belle Nolton—"

"Please," May Belle cried, waving her off. "Don't confuse the poor thing." She held out her hand. "May Belle is just fine with me, dear."

"It's a pleasure to meet you," Annabeth said, shaking her hand.

May Belle gave her the once-over and smiled smugly. "Why, aren't you a sweet little thing. Ladies, you are goin' to have to fatten this girl up. Why, a measly-weight like her will never catch a man."

Annabeth felt her self-confidence drain. No longer could she hide behind the untouchable facade of a prima ballerina. Her reed-thin body and pale skin, so highly coveted in the ballet world, now seemed almost childlike next to May Belle's well-tanned voluptuousness. So maybe she needed to eat more of Rose's potato casseroles, but she *had* managed to attract Zach Tanner. For a little while.

"We're surprised to see you out, May Belle," Daisy said. "Your Wendell's funeral was only last month."

"Your husband just died?" Annabeth asked.

May Belle drew a lace-edged black hankie from her purse and dabbed the corners of her perfectly dry eyes. "Yes." She sniffed. "It was a lovely service, wasn't it, ladies? I can hardly believe he's gone." She sighed dramatically then stuffed the hankie back into her purse and smiled. "But you know me. I'm not one to pile on the agony."

"It must be difficult to lose your husband so young," Annabeth said, trying to appear friendly.

"Young?" May Belle cried. "Pooh! Wendell was ninety-three years old, dear. We all have to go sometime. And it was high time for Wendell to go. I must say, it doesn't get any easier, though."

"Easier?" Annabeth asked.

"May Belle's been widowed three times now," Jasmine explained as she passed out drinks from a silver tray.

"I'm sorry," Annabeth said.

May Belle took a long swallow of her mint julep. "Oh,

don't be sorry, hon'," she replied, dabbing at her artfully applied lipstick with a cocktail napkin. "They all left me quite well-off. Why, with what Wendell left me, I'll be lounging in the lap of luxury for at least ten years."

"Three husbands in twelve years," Rose explained to Annabeth. "May Belle prefers...older men."

"You know me," May Belle teased. "I've always been fond of antiques. If it's not over eighty years old, it's not worth havin'." She put on a serious face. "Though I am considerin' changin' my ways. I've decided I might do better to look for a younger, more virile man. Now that I have money, I believe my other *needs* should come first. Don't you'all agree?"

All four of them nodded silently.

May Belle sighed. "Isn't this weather just positively gooey?" She fanned herself with the limp cocktail napkin and surveyed the backyard. "Jasmine, your garden is lookin'—" She stopped short and a sly smile curled the corners of her red lips. "Oh, my. Speakin' of virile, who is that amazin' young man you're hidin' back there in the bushes?"

Like a laser-guided missile, May Belle zeroed in on Zach and watched him with a sultry gaze. A stab of jealousy pierced Annabeth's heart as the widow stood up and sauntered to the edge of the veranda for a better view.

"That's Zachary Tanner," Jasmine offered. "He's the grandson of DeWitt Tanner. He's stayin' here in the servants' cottage while he takes care of some business matters here in town."

"So that's Zachary Tanner," she said breathlessly. "President of Tanner Enterprises. And one of only three unmarried millionaires in Atlanta. The other two are over seventy," she murmured to herself. "Dears, you must introduce me!"

"Zach is busy right now," Annabeth said. "He has to finish planting that tree for Miss Jasmine before—"

May Belle turned to Annabeth and gave her a quelling look. "Certainly meetin' me is more important that plantin' some silly ol' tree." She turned to the Flowers. "Just a simple introduction, then I'll be on my way."

Rose bolted out of her chair and hurried to the railing. "Zachary!" she called. "Zachary, come up here to the house! There's someone who'd like to meet you."

Zach waved at Rose, then wiped his hands on his jeans and started through the garden. Annabeth wriggled uncomfortably in her chair when she realized he wasn't planning to put his shirt on. She busied herself with straightening a deck of cards as he came nearer. Then she grabbed her iced tea and took a slow sip, watching him from over the rim of the glass. At first, his gaze was fixed on her. But as he approached, he noticed May Belle and his attention drifted in her direction.

"Zachary," Rose began. "I'd like to introduce—"

"May Belle," the widow cooed. "May Belle Tremaine. It's a pleasure to make your acquaintance, Mr. Tanner." She held out her hand as if she expected him to kiss it. Who did she think she was, royalty?

To Annabeth's relief, Zach reluctantly took May Belle's fingers in his and shook her hand politely. He glanced in Annabeth's direction and shot her a bemused look. Thank God he could see through that sugarcoated facade to the barracuda beneath, Annabeth thought with satisfaction. But then, to her astonishment, Zach smiled his most devastating smile, drew May Belle's hand to his lips and placed a courtly kiss on her fingertips.

"The pleasure is all mine, Miss Tremaine," he said. "It is *Miss* Tremaine, isn't it?"

"Yes, it is, Mr. Tanner," May Belle replied.

What was wrong with Zach? How could he be stupid enough to fall victim to her overblown charms?

"Well, dears," May Belle said. "I must be goin' now. Mr. Tanner, would you be a gentleman and escort me to my car? This heat does wear on me so."

Zach stepped up onto the veranda and May Belle slipped her arm through his. "It would be my very great pleasure," Zach replied.

"Don't you have some work to do in the garden, Mr. Tanner?" Annabeth asked.

Zach raised a brow and grinned. "I'm sure it will still be there when I get back, Ms. Dupree," he said in a smooth voice.

"You know," May Belle said, as they strolled down the veranda and around the corner of the house, "I've recently come into a rather large sum of money and I was wondering if you might know where I could invest it. I understand real estate development is a profitable option."

May Belle's voice faded away and Annabeth turned back to the Flowers, flabbergasted by Zach's reaction to the woman.

"High-minded alley bat," Rose muttered.

"Trashy little fanfoot," Daisy added.

"Ladies!" Jasmine scolded. "Watch your tongues! And Annabeth, close your mouth. You'll catch a fly!"

"Did you see her?" Rose asked. "She was coverin' him like the dew covers Dixie!"

"Like a duck on a June bug!" Daisy cried.

"Like paper covers rock," Annabeth added indignantly. The Flowers stared at her, puzzled.

"Well, what about him?" Annabeth countered. "I didn't see him putting up much of a fuss."

"Of course not," Daisy explained. "He's a man. Like they say, if you got a rooster, he's goin' to crow."

"Ladies, why don't we forget May Belle's visit and occupy our minds with something more worthwhile," Jasmine urged. "Why don't we teach Annabeth how to play gin rummy?"

Daisy's expression brightened and Rose nodded enthusiastically. Moments later, they had forgotten May Belle the Hussy and were chattering out rules and instructions for Annabeth.

Annabeth numbly took the cards that were dealt and fanned them out in her hand, then stared into the garden. She and Zach had come so close to tearing down the walls between them. She could sense that he needed her, feel that he wanted her in a way he could never want May Belle Tremaine. So why did he go waltzing off with her like she was the most fascinating woman since Madame Curie? Annabeth gripped her cards until they bent in her hands. Maybe he was punishing her. Or was he deliberately trying to make her angry?

"It's your play, dear."

Annabeth looked down at the cards she held, then at the Flowers. "What do I do next?" she asked.

Rose looked at her impatiently. "Either draw a card or take the one Daisy discarded."

She studied the cards on the table. "And what is the point of this game again?"

"At least three of a kind or a straight of three in one suit," Daisy replied. "Take the card I put down. You're collectin' fives."

Annabeth looked down at her cards. Daisy knew more about her hand than she did. She tried to recall if the game required keeping track of everyone else's hand. If it did, she was lost before she had even begun. Her concentration was at an all-time low. Taking Daisy's advice, she picked up the card and discarded another without thinking.

She completed her turn and her thoughts immediately returned to Zach. If he was trying to make her angry, he had certainly succeeded. They had practically made love in the garden the night before. And one silly misunderstanding sent him running into another woman's arms.

"Annabeth, it's your turn again."

Startled, Annabeth snatched up a card and laid another down. Yes, she was angry and— Oh, Lord. Annabeth groaned inwardly. She was...jealous. And she was reacting precisely the way Zach intended. He was exacting his own kind of justice for her mistrust of him, and he was using May Belle Tremaine as the bait. Well, she wouldn't fall for it! She wouldn't let him think she cared. Of all the childish, arrogant, manipulative—

"Annabeth, pay attention to the game!"

She grabbed another card from the stack and placed it in her hand. The Flowers watched her expectantly. "What?" she asked.

"You forgot to discard, dear," Daisy said.

She grabbed a card at random and snapped it down on the discard pile.

"How are you and Zachary gettin' on?" Jasmine asked, picking up the card Annabeth played.

"What?" she said, startled by the sudden shift in conversation.

Daisy studied her cards, then watched as Rose discarded. "I really do think you should try harder to get along with him," Daisy advised. "He may be more...accommodatin'."

"Yes, dear," Rose agreed. "You should be more amiable. He might change his mind about the house."

"I don't think he'll change his mind," Annabeth said. "Whether I'm amiable or not."

"I wouldn't be too sure about that, dear," Daisy remarked. "Look at May Belle. She certainly caught his attention and with very little effort at that. If you'd use your feminine powers, you'd be surprised at what he might do."

"That's right!" Rose said. "A little flirting, a little flattery, and you'll have him wrapped around your little finger. He'll forget this silly little legal problem and *give* you the house."

Annabeth shook her head. She couldn't tell the Flowers that he'd already offered her the house and that she hadn't even batted an eyelash or crooked her little finger. Or that she couldn't imagine Zach wrapped around anyone's little finger, especially hers...though May Belle seemed to have a knack for twisting him around her perfectly painted pinkie. Besides, he wasn't about to repeat his offer, nor would she take it if he did—not after all her talk about independence and making it on her own. "Zach is not going to give me this house."

"Listen to Daisy," Rose said. "If anyone knows how to attract a man's attention, she does."

"Really, ladies," Annabeth protested. "I don't think I'd be able to—"

"It all begins with the walk," Daisy explained. She stood and sashayed across the veranda, waving a lace handkerchief in her hand. "Walk past him as if he wasn't even in the room. Let his gaze follow you. Then, when you're certain you have his attention, turn and glance at him. Not too long, mind you. You don't want to appear too interested. Come here, dear, and try."

Annabeth tried to contain her amusement. Lessons in seduction from three seventy-five-year-old former ladies of the evening. "No, really, Daisy, I don't think that—"

Daisy grabbed Annabeth's hands and pulled her out of

her wicker chair. "Just like this," Daisy said as she demonstrated again, her hips swaying provocatively.

Annabeth imitated her movements, feeling like a clumsy teenager. Even years of ballet lessons couldn't duplicate Daisy's instinctive sensual grace. Jasmine and Rose clapped politely, but Annabeth knew they were being overly generous.

"Well, now, that's a start," Daisy said. "Don't be discouraged. Loosen up a little. Next comes the 'longin' look.' After you're sure you have his attention, you just turn to him and stare right into his eyes. A deep and soulful stare. About four or five seconds should do. Like this."

Daisy demonstrated then waited for Annabeth to reciprocate. Annabeth rolled her eyes and laughed. But a stern look from her teacher was all it took for her to attempt the next lesson in Miss Daisy's Remedial Seduction.

"Annabeth, really, you should try a bit harder," Daisy scolded. "You're not tryin' to frighten him, you're tryin' to entice him."

"I just don't think this is going to work on a man like Zach. Believe me."

"May Belle blew that theory to kingdom come, dear," Daisy countered. "Give that woman a few hours in a dark room and she'll have him thinkin' she hung the moon and the stars. Annabeth, there is nothin' wrong with tryin' to seduce a man. After all, women like May Belle don't hold the franchise on seduction, though they like to think they do."

"Maybe we should begin with conversation," Rose suggested. "Jasmine has always been an expert at the art of social discourse."

Annabeth forced an indulgent smile and tried to appear attentive. After all, they were only trying to help, in their own eccentric way. Annabeth knew nothing about seduction and they did have at least some practical experience in the area.

"It's important to be a good listener," Jasmine explained. "Never offer an opinion, unless it's asked for. And then, be sure it agrees with your gentleman companion. It's never good to appear too intelligent...or too dim-witted. As for subject matter, men enjoy talkin' about themselves. I wouldn't worry about anything beyond that because most of them can rattle on for an entire evening on that particular subject."

"What about Mr. Claude Palmer?" Daisy teased. "I noticed *you* doin' most of the talkin' in Annabeth's dance class."

Jasmine blushed. "Well, now, that's different. Mr. Palmer enjoys intelligent repartee. But he's a bit shy. I was just drawin' him out."

"Jasmine and Mr. Palmer are sweet on each other," Rose explained to Annabeth.

"Rose!" Jasmine cried. "Really. You are such a gossip."

"And you didn't dance with anyone but Mr. Palmer," Daisy accused. "And I heard him ask you to sit next to him on the bus to Atlantic City."

Thankfully the subject turned to Jasmine's new beau and their upcoming jaunt to Atlantic City, though Annabeth was curious to how much further the ladies were prepared to go in their instruction. Sashaying, soulful stares and sweet talk were quite enough for Annabeth.

The card playing resumed and Annabeth struggled to pay attention while the ladies discussed Claude Palmer in great detail. But after fifteen minutes, she was anxious for some time alone. As the three chattered on about their trip, Annabeth rose and quietly excused herself.

She tiptoed across the veranda and had nearly made her escape around the side of the house, when she ran smack into Zach Tanner's naked chest. He leaned one shoulder against the outside wall of the house, his arms crossed in front of him.

"What are you doing here?" she asked.

"I'm..." He frowned. "What was that word you used? Oh, yeah. I'm skulking."

"More like eavesdropping, I'd say."

"Eavesdropping? Now what could you ladies have possibly been discussing that could have been of any interest to me?"

"Nothing," Annabeth replied innocently. "They were teaching me how to play cards."

"I see. And which game did you learn this afternoon, Annie?"

"Gin rummy," Annabeth replied. "And how about you? How was your stroll with *Miss* May Belle? You were gone so long, I was sure she must have parked her car in downtown Charleston."

"Ah, Miss May Belle," Zach said, a satisfied grin curling his lips. "She's got a smile that makes the old feel young and the poor feel rich."

"Oh, please." Annabeth groaned. "Give me a break. That woman is after one thing and that's a new sugar daddy. She's already worn out three husbands and collected a sizable chunk of cash from each. Are you sure you want to be her next victim?"

"It's certainly not a bad way to go," Zach replied. "Besides, why are you so concerned about my sex life?"

"Your sex life?" Annabeth shot back. "I'd be more likely to ponder the pleasures of a root canal than waste a New York minute on your sex life."

"That's not the impression I got in the garden last night," Zach said.

"I was overcome by the heat," Annabeth replied. "I didn't know what I was doing."

"Yeah, it was hot, all right. But for someone who didn't know what she was doing, you were doing it pretty well."

"Obviously not as well as May Belle," Annabeth said.

"That is yet to be determined, but I'll be sure to keep you informed."

"Don't bother. I'd find it all a terrible bore, I'm sure."

"*Are* you sure, Annie? You seem just a touch…jealous."

"Jealous?" she mocked. "In your dreams, Don Juan. Now, if you'll excuse me, I've got to prepare for my next dance class." She pushed past him and strode down the veranda toward the open French doors, her hips swaying provocatively. Well, what could it hurt to use a few of the Flowers' tricks. Zach Tanner deserved as good as he gave.

"And I have to get ready for dinner at May Belle's," Zach called. "I'll be sure to give her your best."

Annabeth stopped and slowly turned around. She looked at him long and hard, then smiled coyly. "You just do that, sugar. And I'm sure May Belle will give you *her* very best, as well."

"AND HOW HAVE YOU and our Annabeth been getting along lately, Zachary?"

Zach hefted the bag of peat moss onto his shoulder and carried it over to where Miss Jasmine kneeled at the edge of her flower garden.

An image of Annabeth, lying in the damp grass under the live oak tree, flashed into his mind, followed by a recollection of her blazing eyes and indomitable temper on the veranda the day before. "Fine," he said in an attempt to sound indifferent.

"Fine," Jasmine repeated. "Now there's a word. Really,

dear, you must learn to be more precise in your self-expression."

"And you, my dear Jasmine, must be more covert in your curiosity," he teased.

She blushed prettily and placed her hand on his arm. "We'd just like to see the two of you getting along. I think that's what your grandparents would have wanted."

Zach opened the plastic bag and dumped the peat moss out. "What makes you say that?"

Jasmine took a handful of the peat moss and worked it into the flower bed with her trowel. "Well, Miss Lily and Senator DeWitt cared about you children and they cared about each other," Jasmine explained. "They'd want you and Annabeth to be friends. I can feel it, as if they were here with us now."

"How do you know that?"

"That they're here? Well, I don't. Not exactly. But it just seems natural that—"

"No. I mean how do you know that they cared about each other?"

Jasmine sat back on her heels and looked off into the distance, as if remembering a long-ago time and place. "Oh, my. That was clear from the start. It was the way they looked at each other, as if there were no one else in the room. When they were together, the whole world stood still for them." Jasmine sighed. "A person would have to be born on Crazy Creek not to see that."

"Annabeth told me they weren't intimate," Zach said.

Jasmine smiled. "So you and Annabeth have been talking. That's a start. Though that's not an appropriate subject for discussion, it's still a start."

"Is it true?"

"What happened behind closed doors was between your grandfather and Miss Lily." She jabbed her trowel into the dirt and frowned. "It truly distresses me that young people today talk about their sex lives to just about anyone who'll listen. All those personal details splashed across the front pages of the supermarket tabloids. Why, they even write books about it. In my day it just wasn't good manners to discuss that sort of thing out loud."

"Weren't you ever curious?" Zach asked.

Jasmine turned to him and slapped his arm with her garden glove. "Young man, you are too impertinent for your own good," she said good-naturedly.

"Zachary!"

Jasmine and Zach looked toward the house. Miss Rose stood on the back veranda, waving at them. "Zachary Tanner, you have a visitor!" she called.

Zach stood and brushed the peat moss off his hands. "It's probably just a messenger delivering some papers for me to sign."

"Or maybe it's May Belle Tremaine," Jasmine teased.

"I hope not." Zach groaned. "I got more than my fill of that woman last night. I wouldn't have accepted her invitation to dinner if I'd have known I was scheduled to be dessert. I'll be back in a bit. Don't try to lift those bags yourself, you hear?"

Jasmine nodded. "Zachary, you will try to smooth things out with Annabeth, won't you?" she said. "It would mean so much to Daisy and Rose and me. And to your grandparents as well."

"I'll try," Zach said. "But don't expect much. Annabeth and I don't see eye to eye on most things."

Zach jogged back to the house, stopping by his room to pick up some signed contracts that needed to be returned to his Atlanta office. He had been running his business from Magnolia Grove for almost three weeks with only one trip back to the city, and he was coming to realize why so many businessmen purchased summer houses in the country.

The slower pace rejuvenated him, cleared his mind of mundane details and allowed his creative side to take over. Since he'd been in Magnolia Grove, he'd mapped out two inventive new development concepts for suburban Atlanta and was toying with an idea for tourist development around Magnolia Grove. The job that had been sapping his energy had now become more interesting and challenging. He felt the way he had during his first year in business, when every day was exciting and full of possibilities.

Strange how that feeling also seemed to apply to Annabeth. Though he had tried to deny it, she was at least part of the reason he didn't want to return to Atlanta. There was something between them, something that compelled him to stay near and wait for more. If he were to believe Miss Jasmine, he'd have to say that the ghosts of the past were hard at work matchmaking.

But he knew his growing feelings for Annabeth had nothing to do with paranormal interference. After their encounter in the garden, he couldn't deny it anymore. He wanted Annabeth Dupree more than he had ever wanted a woman before.

And for the first time in his life, he wanted a woman to want him, to need him in the same overpowering way. He wanted to lose himself inside of her until the past didn't matter. He wanted to hear his name on her lips when the passion between them exploded. He wanted to look into her incredible green eyes and know that she loved him.

Suddenly he felt a desperate need to see her, just for a moment, just to prove to himself that his feelings were real. As he entered the kitchen, he found Miss Daisy sitting at the table with a cup of tea and a guide book to Atlantic City.

"Who's here?" he whispered. "Is it May Belle?"

"No, dear. There's a man waiting in the gentlemen's parlor," Daisy said as she perused the book. "Though he doesn't look like your regular messenger. He's dressed in a three-piece suit."

"Where's Annabeth?" Zach asked.

Daisy looked up. "Annabeth? Why, she's speaking at the Ladies' Auxiliary mother-daughter luncheon down at the Baptist Church. She's speaking on the importance of the arts in a young lady's education. After today, I'd hazard a guess that she'll have some ballet students for her school."

"If you see her come in, would you tell her I'd like to talk to her?"

"Of course, Zachary. Is there something wrong?"

"No," Zach said. "Nothing. Nothing wrong at all."

Zach strode through the back hallway and into the gentlemen's parlor, anxious to take care of business. But when he came face-to-face with the "messenger," he wished he had stayed in the garden with Miss Jasmine.

"Senator Gaines. What are you doing here?"

The senator turned from his examination of Miss Lily's collection of books and smiled widely. "Zach, it's good to see you!" he cried, rushing up to him and holding out his hand.

Zach took the senator's hand. A perfect politician's handshake, he thought. Friendly, firm, but not too aggressive. And a properly plastic smile. What the hell was he doing here?

"How did you know where to find me?" Zach asked.

"We have our ways," the senator joked. "There are

some great perks that come along with this job. When I need to find someone, all it takes is a few phone calls."

Zach made a mental note to call his office and track down the leak. "What can I do for you, Senator?"

"Bill. Call me Bill." He looked around the room. "Can we sit down?"

Zach motioned to a pair of chairs near the window. Once the senator was seated, Zach took his place behind the desk. He wasn't about to give up control of this meeting and keeping the senator off-balance gave him an important advantage.

"How have you been, Zach?"

"Fine," Zach replied. So much for self-expression, Zach thought. Pissed off would have been more precise and to the point.

"Zach, we were disappointed that you didn't make our little get-together a few weeks back. In fact, when your attorney told us why, we were—needless to say—shocked. But after a little investigating, all we can say is, we're downright confused."

"Confused?"

"This business about kickbacks. Zach, we've examined your business dealings under a microscope and we haven't found a hint of impropriety. We don't waste time on a man who can't cut the 'ethical mustard,' if you will. Frankly, my boy, you left me with egg on my face. I'd like an explanation."

"I think I made myself clear the last time we spoke, Senator," Zach replied. "I'm not interested in a political career. Find yourself another boy."

"Zach, I'd caution you not to be too hasty. Your granddaddy was a great politician, but when he was younger, he felt pretty much the way you do. Then he realized the kind of good he could do for his country, and he decided to make a difference. He realized his responsibility to the family."

"Senator, I've made up my mind. The Tanner political legacy stops with me. I'm willing to live with my decision, now I think it's time you and your boys in Atlanta did the same."

The senator shook his head irately. "Is it that Dupree woman?" Gaines asked in an accusing tone. "Has she got you trapped the same way her grandmother trapped your granddaddy? If she has, we can take care of her."

"What?" Zach growled.

"We tried to warn DeWitt about the dangers of associating with her sort. But it was like the man was deaf and blind when it came to Lily Fontaine. She had some kind of power over him and he wouldn't give her up. Shoot, we've got a file on Lily Fontaine an inch thick at the FBI. We tried to talk to her, convince her of the danger she was puttin' him in, but she was as stubborn as he was. Said they were just friends. He never gave her up. It could have ruined him."

"Annabeth Dupree has nothing to do with my decision. I decided this long before I came to Magnolia Grove. I am not interested in your offer. Now, if you don't mind, I have some gardening to do."

The senator's face turned red with anger. "Listen, boy, and listen good. If you have any political aspirations at all, you get yourself out of this house and back to Atlanta. The past has a sneaky way of jumpin' up and bitin' a man in the backside. If the votin' public knew about DeWitt and this Lily Fontaine, the Tanner name wouldn't be worth dirt come election day. Livin' in a sportin' house and associating with a chippy's granddaughter is not smart politics."

Zach stood and rounded the desk. "Get out," he said. "Now, before I throw you out."

The senator approached, holding out his hands in a conciliatory gesture. "I'm sorry, son. Sometimes my temper gets the better of me. I came here to convince you to reconsider your decision, not to argue with you. The party needs a man like you, a man with conviction and vision."

"Maybe I didn't make myself clear," Zach said. "I won't be railroaded and I won't be coerced. I will associate with whomever I please and if that happens to be Annabeth Dupree, so be it. I will live my life the way I want to, *not* the way you want me to. I'm not your boy and I'm not your man. So, if you'll excuse me, I've got a lady waiting for me in the garden. You can find your own way out."

"You're crazy," the senator called as Zach stalked out of the room. "Your granddaddy was crazy and now you're just following in his footsteps. You'll regret the day you ever came back to his town, Zach Tanner. Mark my words, your political future just went up in a puff of smoke."

"Great!" Zach shouted, his voice echoing through the house. "That's the best news I've had in years."

ANNABETH LOOKED UP at the sky through the canopy of live oaks that lined Edisto Street. It was a beautiful Saturday. The hot and humid air was thick with the smell of flowers and she savored it like an exotic perfume. She felt like shouting for joy and skipping down the street, but it wouldn't do to have the town's ballet teacher acting like a child.

The mother-daughter luncheon at the Baptist Church had been a resounding success. She had enchanted ten little girls and their mothers with stories of her ballet career, and by the time she walked out, all ten were begging for lessons. She had invited them all to the house the following Tuesday afternoon for a free ballet lesson. What mother would be able to resist the sight of her daughter twirling around the room like a music-box doll?

With her five gentlemen in the Tuesday night ballroom class and ten little ballerinas twice a week, her weekly income would shoot up to $250. It was still a far cry from what she had made in New York, but it was a future and it was all hers. If she could only find a few ladies for the ballroom class and maybe some housewives in need of a creative outlet for a midday tap class.

As she walked the final block to the house, Annabeth mentally worked out another ad for the *Magnolia Grove Monitor.* Tap aerobics. Fitness made fun. Tap your way to good health. A one-hour class, three times a week, ten dollars a week. She added another five students to her roster and boosted her weekly income by another $50. The future was looking brighter by the minute. Maybe she could again offer to buy the house from Zach.

Annabeth was so absorbed with her plans that she didn't notice the black limousine parked on the street until she turned onto the front walk. A man stepped out of the car and began to walk toward her. She clutched her purse to her side and straightened her posture. A month in Magnolia Grove had not rid her of her New York instincts.

"Miss Dupree?"

"Maybe," she said suspiciously. "Who are you?"

"I'm Senator William Gaines. I'm a friend of Zach Tanner. I was hoping you might have a moment to talk. You are Annabeth Dupree, aren't you?"

She nodded.

"Would you like to step into my car?"

She raised a brow. "Are you crazy," she scoffed. "I'm from New York City. A person steps into a black limo with a strange politician and they end up floating facedown in the Hudson."

"It's air-conditioned," the senator explained.

"We can talk out here. I like the heat."

"All right. I'd like to talk about Zach."

"I'm afraid I can't help you there, Mr. Gaines."

"But I think you can, Miss Dupree. I don't know if you're aware of this, but Zach Tanner has a very promising political future ahead of him. He comes from a long line of respected politicians and the Tanner name carries a great deal of respect and political power in the South."

"So? What does that have to do with me?"

"Respect, Miss Dupree. Voters don't respect a man who gets himself involved in a...questionable situation with less than desirable people."

"What is that supposed to mean?"

"We are aware of your grandmother's profession and of the history of this house. DeWitt Tanner was able to keep his association with your grandmother quiet. But the political climate has changed and our politicians need to be spotlessly clean. If word of DeWitt's unseemly fascination with Lily Fontaine and her ladies got out to the press, it might harm Zach's political chances."

"But that's all in the past," Annabeth said. "No one would hold that against Zach."

"And of course, you're a political expert?" he asked, his voice laced with sarcasm.

"No, but—"

"Zach Tanner wants a career in Washington, Miss Dupree. He's worked his whole life for it. He's made for it. His grandfather could have been president, but Lily Fontaine stood in the way. Don't stand in Zach's way."

"I—I'm not," Annabeth said with a frown.

"Good," the senator said with an impersonal nod. He turned and walked to his car, then stopped before he got in. "One more thing, Miss Dupree."

"What is it?" Annabeth asked.

"Your mother is Camilla Robbilard of Atlanta, isn't that right?"

"Yes," Annabeth answered.

"Lovely lady. I met her once at a charity event. Just lovely. Pity about her father, don't you think?" He stepped into the car and slammed the door.

He didn't need to make the threat out loud. Annabeth knew exactly what he would do if she didn't cooperate. News of Madam Lily and her illegitimate daughter, Camilla, would spread insidiously through the Atlanta social grapevine. Her mother's rung on the social ladder would be cut out from under her. Though Annabeth had often wished for that same thing as a child, as an adult, she knew the news would destroy her mother.

She watched the limo roar off down the street, then shuddered uncontrollably. He would follow through on his threat, of that she had no doubt. Her mother's position in society would be lost and Zach's future compromised if she chose to use the journals in court.

Suddenly, possession of the house didn't seem as important to her in the face of all the pain it could cause.

7

"DANCERS! Pay attention now. Imagine the tiny seed has grown into a flower. The sun is coming out and your petals are slowly opening to drink in the sunshine. Open those petals. Show me how good the sunshine feels."

Zach watched as ten little girls scurried around the floor of the sweltering ballroom, doing their best to interpret Annabeth's instructions. Most raised their faces to the ceiling and spread their arms, whirling like little dervishes in frilly party dresses and huge hair bows. One little girl stood wide-eyed and ramrod stiff, afraid to participate. Another curled into a ball on the floor, still lost in the seed stage of the exercise. And still another sat in a corner and sucked on her thumb.

Annabeth moved gracefully around the room as she smiled her encouragement to each student and demonstrated hand positions to them. She was dressed, from shoulders to toes, in a body-hugging black leotard and pink tights. A filmy black skirt made of a transparent fabric swirled around her waist and thighs, and pink toe shoes covered her feet. Her hair was pulled severely back, away from her face, making her features more pronounced, with only a few damp tendrils at her temples and neck to soften the austere simplicity. She didn't look like Annabeth at all, at least not the Annabeth he knew.

Annabeth of the fiery temper and the sharp tongue and the stubborn bravado was nowhere to be found. He hadn't seen her since their argument on the veranda three days ago. It was as if she were deliberately avoiding him, taking care to be occupied elsewhere whenever he entered the house. Damn his stupidity! Using May Belle to provoke her had seemed like a good idea, and after their confrontation, he was certain it had worked. She was jealous and she hated him for making her feel that way. But behind her anger, he could see that the attraction ran deep. Still, something had scared her away. He was afraid to admit, it might have been him.

She moved closer to the French doors and he stepped back, out of view. Her calm in the midst of near chaos astounded him. Her short-fused temper was absent and she seemed charmed by the creative disorganization of ten energetic little dancers, and their proud mothers, who choreographed their daughters from the sidelines. She glided over to the frightened girl and after a brief whisper and a hug, the little girl joined the others. Then, Annabeth perched the tiny thumb-sucker on her hip and twirled around the room with her, their arms waving and their faces tipped up to the sun.

She was an excellent teacher, Zach thought. Patient and kind and attentive to all. Mothers and daughters were held captive by her elegance and grace. This was a side of Annabeth that he had seen just once—the night he had watched her dance in her underwear by the light of the moon. Self-possessed and focused, slightly detached, and very untouchable. This woman wasn't the Annabeth he knew. This was Annabeth Dupree, prima ballerina, a stranger to him.

As he watched her gather the girls and line them up along a low wooden bar, he suddenly felt an overwhelming need to probe every facet and corner of this beautiful stranger before him. He wanted to know her innermost fears and her hidden fantasies, her wildest dreams and her fondest ambitions. Here was a woman, complex and mysterious, and deep enough to spend a lifetime exploring.

But would he have a lifetime? They stood on such precarious footing, the unstable foundation of their relationship ready to crumble at any instant. From the moment they had met, he had fought her every step of the way, refusing to reconcile his grandfather's memory with her grandmother's profession, until he and Annabeth had become hopelessly tangled in the past. And for what?

To protect an image, not a real man.

His grandfather had made his own choices, knowing the possible consequences of his association with Miss Lily, and he had been prepared to pay the price when the time came. It wasn't Zach's responsibility to cover up his grandfather's indiscretions and to pay that price with his own happiness. He had a life to live and his own mistakes to make. Goading Annabeth into jealousy had been one. He didn't want losing Annabeth to be the next.

The sooner they got this business with the house resolved, the sooner they could leave the past behind and move on with their future. Strange, how easy it was to think of a future with her, and how intolerable it was to consider a future without her. Why had it taken him so long to realize what she meant to him?

He didn't want the house, especially if Annabeth wasn't living in it with him. So he would have to find a way of insuring that it became hers—free and clear. If she didn't win in court, he'd find a way to give her the house—or sell it to her, if she insisted on being stubborn. She would stay in Magnolia Grove if he had anything to say about it.

He watched her arrange her excited students in a semicircle around her with their beaming mothers standing behind them. His decision was made. The house belonged to her. Yet, deep down, he was afraid that without the house standing between them, they'd find themselves with nothing in common. Annabeth would have everything she wanted, a successful dance school, a satisfying career and a stable home. Where would he fit in? Would she want him to share her life or would she leave him behind as part of the past and the bad memories it held?

Zach paced impatiently on the veranda while Annabeth showed her students out. When she finally walked back into the ballroom, he stepped through the French doors. She froze, watching him warily, as if she were ready to bolt.

"Annabeth, I think—"

She held up her hand to silence him. "No," she warned. "I can't do this anymore, Zach. Every time we talk, we just dig ourselves deeper into the mess that our grandparents left behind. I just want this settled so I can go on with my life. And arguing with you won't settle it. Only the judge can decide who belongs here and our fighting about it is not going to make any difference."

"I want this settled, too," Zach said. "Annabeth, I don't care if you use the journals in court. In fact, I want you to use every piece of ammunition you've got. Fire away. I can handle whatever you dish out."

She narrowed her eyes suspiciously. "What is this, reverse psychology? You don't mean that, Zach. I know you don't."

"I'm not trying to pull anything. This is your chance to get what you want. Use the journals, tell the whole story."

"And what about you? What do *you* want?"

"I don't want the house, Annabeth."

"That's not what I mean." She paused, as if she were uncertain whether to speak her mind, then went ahead anyway. "I had a little chat with a lovely gentleman the other day, a Senator Gaines."

"You spoke with Gaines?"

"Yes. Charming man. He gives new meaning to the word *honorable*. He convinced me that leaving the past well buried would be in your best interests. And mine. I got the idea that if I didn't do as he asked, he'd pull the lead galoshes out of his trunk and toss me, feetfirst, into the Edisto River."

Anger shot through him. Damn the man and his meddling cronies! Didn't they understand the meaning of the word *no*? "What did he tell you? Did he threaten you?" Zach clenched his fists and swore under his breath. "So help me, if he said anything to scare you, I'll make him pay."

"I wasn't scared. The river's not that deep and I'm a strong swimmer."

"Don't make light of this. What did he say to you?"

Annabeth cringed slightly at his angry demand. "He told me you have a promising career in politics ahead of you and that I'm standing in your way. He told me not to ruin your future the way my grandmother nearly ruined your grandfather's."

Zach schooled his temper and calmed his voice. "He knows I have no interest in extending the family tradition. He's desperate to save his ass. He promised his cronies a Tanner and he can't deliver. I'm not a politician and I never will be."

"Never is a long time, Zach. When I was at the top of my profession, I told myself that I'd never teach. You know the saying—those who can, do... But look at me now. I'm teaching and I love it. It's given me new respect for the teachers who trained me. You can't predict how you'll feel in the future. What if you change your mind?"

"I won't," he growled.

"I'm still not going to use the journals in court."

"Why the hell not?"

Annabeth lowered her gaze and studied her toe shoe a bit too intently. She was hiding something; he could see it in her downcast eyes. "It's my decision, and I've made it. It's the right thing to do, and nothing you can say is going to change my mind. Your grandfather's reputation is safe with me."

"I don't care about his reputation. What is it, Annabeth? What did Gaines say to you?"

"Exactly what I told you. I have the deed, Zach, and that's all I need. It's handwritten and witnessed by a notary. How much clearer could DeWitt Tanner have made his intentions? Your grandfather wanted Miss Lily to have this house, both you and I know it, and I'll prove it."

"You might not win. The law works in strange ways."

"I'll win," Annabeth stated. "I have to."

"What if you don't? What will you do?"

She shrugged, but deep down, he could tell she was playing hard at indifference. "I'll go on with my life. A dancer friend of mine runs a ballet school in Wichita. After I was injured, she offered me a partnership in her studio, but I turned her down. If she still wants me, I'll go there to teach."

Zach grabbed her by the elbow. "Kansas? Dammit, Annabeth, you can't go to Wichita."

She pulled out of his grasp. "I know it's not the center of the ballet world, but talent doesn't come with geographical boundaries. It's a job and I'll make it work."

"What about the Flowers? And all of your students here?"

And what about us, he added silently. We can't build a future with a thousand miles between us.

"They'll survive."

"No, they won't. If the judge doesn't give you the house, I'll give it to you. It's yours, no strings."

She smiled weakly. "No strings? There are always strings, Zach. Sometimes they're invisible to the naked eye, but they're still there."

"I wouldn't expect anything, Annabeth."

Annabeth walked over to the grand piano and ran her finger idly over the gleaming finish as she spoke. "I stepped into that trap once before. I sold my soul for a glamorous life-style, a fancy apartment and a closet full of furs. Except for my dancing, I felt like I had nothing of my own. Everything that was mine really belonged to David. After a long, long time, I've finally discovered the person I really am. And for the first time in my life, I like her. She wouldn't take the house from you, Zach, and neither will I."

"All right, we'll be partners," Zach said, pacing back and forth in front of her. "I've always wanted to diversify my holdings. A dance school would be a good investment."

"Almost as good as a bordello, right?"

"That's different."

She leaned back into the curve of the piano, her elbows braced on top of it. "Maybe. Maybe not. But in a way, it's like bad history repeating itself. That's all we have, Zach. Bad history. We've tried to get around it, but the simple fact is, it will always be there." She looked up at him hesitantly and forced a smile. "After the court date, I think it would be best if we just got on with our lives." She held out her hand. "What do you say?" she asked softly. "Deal?"

"You're sure about this, Annabeth?" He wanted to shake her until she admitted how she really felt. Damn her stubborn streak and to hell with her need for independence! She cared about him, she wanted him. He knew it as sure as he knew his own desire for her.

"Yes, I'm sure. I'm okay. I'm getting used to handling things on my own and it's not so bad. Gee, I even handled a U.S. senator. I kind of like standing on my own two feet, solving my own problems. Come on, Zach. Let's shake on it and finish this thing with our dignity intact."

Reluctant, he wrapped her fingers in his. "Deal," he replied. *For now.*

"YOU'RE HERE TO APPLY for a loan?"

Hamilton Thompson looked at Annabeth over the top of his reading glasses. She gave him a wavering smile, trying hard to appear self-assured and respectable. She had never applied for a loan in her life and wasn't sure what to expect. It had occurred to her that her appearance might be taken into account, so she had abandoned her rather bohemian wardrobe and searched her closet for the most conservative piece of clothing she owned. She now sat in the president's office of the First Bank of Magnolia Grove wearing a simple, black, long-sleeved, wool jersey dress. In ninety-degree weather.

"Yes, sir," Annabeth said. A bead of perspiration slid from her nape down the middle of her back and she shifted in her chair. "As you are probably aware, Zach Tanner and I have been involved in a dispute over the ownership of the property at 453 Edisto Street. If the court upholds his claim to the property, I will be evicted. If that happens, I'd like to offer to buy the house from him. For that, I'll need a loan."

Hamilton nodded. "So he's agreed to sell you the property?"

"Not exactly," Annabeth replied. "But I'd like to be prepared to make him an offer."

Ham studied her shrewdly. "Why are you so certain the judge is going to rule against you, Miss Dupree?"

"I'm not. I could very well win and the house would be mine."

"Then why would you need a loan?" he asked.

"In case I don't win," Annabeth explained.

"But you haven't gone to court yet," Ham countered, "so how do you know whether you've won or lost?"

Annabeth tried to quell her frustration at the man's obtuse attitude. "I don't. But I want to be prepared, just in case."

Ham leaned back in his chair and clasped his hands behind his head. "Miss Dupree," he began lazily, "our bank is not in the habit of handin' out money for 'just in case' reasons. Either you are going to buy that house or you are not. Until you decide you are, I can't loan you any money."

"But can't you just approve a loan for me as a...contingency plan?"

He shook his head. "Not unless you're willin' to put up earnest money for a preapproved loan. Listen, Miss Dupree, let me give you a little piece of advice. You don't even know whether you'll need a loan. If I were you I'd wait, rather than risk the earnest money."

"Couldn't you at least tell me whether I'd be eligible? Whether you *might* approve a loan for me if I happened to ask for one later on?"

"Well, I suppose I could do that," Ham said. "But of course, this would not be an official approval."

Annabeth sighed in relief. "Thank you, Mr. Thompson. Thank you. I'd appreciate that."

Ham sat forward and pulled out a pen and pad of paper. "How much were you fixin' to borrow?"

She frowned. "I—I'm not sure. Enough to buy the Edisto Street property."

"I 'spect that property's worth near one hundred and fifty thousand, give or take. How much money you plannin' to put down?"

Annabeth gulped convulsively. "Down?"

"Yes, how much money are you prepared to pay up front on the house?"

"Why, nothing," she replied. "That's why I've come to you for a loan."

"Miss Dupree, we can't loan you money for a house unless you are willing to put at least ten percent down. In this case, that would amount to fifteen thousand dollars."

Annabeth gasped. "Fifteen thousand dollars? But I don't have fifteen thousand dollars! If I had fifteen thousand dollars, I wouldn't need to ask you for a loan." She laughed hysterically. "If I had fifteen thousand dollars, I could rent a place for my dance school, I could find an apartment to live in. I could have a life! *I don't have fifteen thousand dollars, Mr. Thompson!*"

Ham waved his hands and tried desperately to calm her down, glancing out the open door of his office to see if anyone had noticed her outburst. "Now, now, hold your tater there, missy. There's no need to get all dithered up about this."

"I am holding my tater!" Annabeth snapped. "Whatever that means!"

"All right, all right. Now, how much money do you have? Cash money."

Annabeth composed herself, taking a few deep breaths and primly folding her hands in her lap. "About five hundred dollars," Annabeth replied.

"In a checking account?"

"Yes."

He scribbled the figure on his notepad. "Any savings?"

"No."

"Any assets? Stocks and bonds, real estate, jewelry, anything that might be used as collateral?"

"I have my car," Annabeth said hopefully.

"That brown foreign model you came into town on?"

"Yes, that's it. It's worth a thousand dollars."

"I hate to say this, Miss Dupree, but that there automobile ain't worth a shovelful of chicken tracks. If you paid a thousand dollars for that car, you got taken. We'll say five hundred to be on the generous side." He added that to her checkbook balance. "Do you have anything else that's of value."

"Yes. I have my talent and my training."

"Your dance school," he muttered. "Well, now that would be more in the line of income, not assets. How much does your school make in a month, before taxes?"

Annabeth straightened in her chair, suddenly more optimistic. "Well, if all ten of the girls sign up for classes twice a week and my five gentlemen all continue with their ballroom lessons, and then if I get some ladies for—"

"Just a ballpark, Miss Dupree."

"Around a thousand a month...give or take. And I get rent from the Flowers."

"What about any outstanding debts. Any loans or credit cards?"

Annabeth winced inwardly and her earlier optimism flagged. "Yes, I do have a credit card that has a...tiny balance. Only three thousand dollars." Credit card debt had been a way of life for her in New York and three thousand dollars had been a blip on the bank card budget. David had always extracted her from the worst of it. But she was on her own now, and this three thousand dollars was not going to go away.

Ham shook his head and clucked his tongue. "Miss Dupree, I'm afraid that you are what we call a bad credit risk. You are self-employed with an unreliable cash flow, your debt-to-income ratio is already paralyzing, and you have no collateral. I can't offer you much hope of a loan from this bank."

"But couldn't you make an exception, Mr. Thompson? I know I can make my school successful. It will just take a little time."

Ham shook his head. "I'm sorry, Miss Dupree, but I have a responsibility to our customers who entrust us with their money. As president of this bank, I'd be no better than a rubber-nosed woodpecker in a petrified forest if I lent money to someone who might not be able to pay it back." He laughed, attempting to lighten the tense mood in his office.

A rubber-nosed woodpecker? More like a tightfisted Scrooge, Annabeth railed silently. She took a calming breath. "Remember when I first met you, Mr. Thompson? You told me to come on down to your bank. You said money's all the same, no matter how it's earned."

Ham turned beet red and squirmed in his chair. "Well, that's when I thought you...you said you were going to...I was under the impression that you planned to reopen Miss Lily's...as it was."

Annabeth stood, her temper threatening to explode. "It seems odd to me that this town would deny an honest, law-abiding, hardworking person a place to build a business and live. I have something valuable to offer this backwater bus stop. But you're not interested. Well, Mr. Hamilton Thompson, bank president, that's your loss now, isn't it?"

Annabeth grabbed her purse and stalked out the door. She didn't need his damn money! Or his pinch-penny condescending attitude! She'd find another way to finance her school and keep the house. After all, there was still a good chance that the eviction notice would be overturned and her claim to the house upheld. A better than even chance if she'd accept Zach's invitation to use the journals in court.

But by the time she reached the street, Annabeth was examining the downside of her situation. She couldn't use the journals without risking her mother's happiness. And without them, proving DeWitt Tanner's intent would be virtually impossible. If the judge ruled in favor of Zach, she had no other choice. All her options had been eliminated.

Annabeth bit her bottom lip, trying to push back the tears of frustration that threatened. There was always a sunny side to every situation, Miss Daisy had told her. One just had to look for it.

All right, maybe Wichita wouldn't be so bad after all.

THUNDER ROLLED THROUGH the thick air, echoing in the distance and fading into the night. Annabeth stared at the horizon. Spears of lightning fractured the black sky and the air was heavy with the smell of the approaching storm. The inhabitants of Jasmine's garden waited, still and silent, for the rain that would finally put an end to the heat wave and the punishing drought it had caused.

Annabeth wrapped her arms around her knees and curled more deeply into the wicker rocker, her feet tucked beneath her oversize T-shirt. Her turbulent thoughts whirled as wildly as the advancing storm and she had abandoned her bed to confront the tempest head-on.

Giselle perched on the wide arm of the chair, sniffing suspiciously at the air and watching Annabeth with curious eyes. Annabeth reached out and stroked the cat's nose with the tip of her finger, resisting the flood of emotion that threatened. Her future was collapsing before her eyes and she could do nothing to stop it.

All that she had built for herself in Magnolia Grove hinged on a single piece of paper and an impartial judge. In one week, her future would be laid out before him. If she won, her life would become her dreams. And if she lost, she would be forced to start again, to build new dreams, the same way she had the day she decided to come to Magnolia Grove.

Though it would be painful, she knew she could do it if she had to. Since she had come to the house on Edisto Street, her inner strength and determination had blossomed like one of Miss Jasmine's well-tended flowers, until she was nearly certain she could face whatever the future held—giving up her plans for her own school, leaving the Flowers, handing the keys for the house over to Zach.

He had offered to give her the property and she had stubbornly refused, steadfast in her determination to stand on her own. Now, in the penetrating solitude of the night, she wondered whether she had made the right decision. Should she have accepted his offer, invisible strings and all? Or had she been right to follow her heart?

It was too late for second-guessing. Zach was gone, a hastily scribbled note left on the kitchen table to greet her on her return from the bank. The Flowers were gone, too, off to Atlantic City for three days along with all the members of her Tuesday night ballroom class.

She had no idea when Zach would return, or if he would return before their court date in another week. Though she had practically pushed him out the door with her stubborn refusal of his offer, she couldn't help but regret his absence. An overpowering loneliness assailed her, draining her emotions until her heart felt hollow and her soul brittle.

She had promised herself she wouldn't second-guess her decision, but she couldn't help but wonder what she had missed with Zach. What if she had let her own desires drive her actions?

Since she had come to Magnolia Grove, an odd restlessness had plagued her, one that she had never experienced during her life with David. At first she had attributed it to the heat wave. Then she realized the affliction intensified whenever Zach Tanner entered the room. Maybe she should consider a quick fling, she thought wryly. Like the Widow Tremaine, she did have needs. Needs that could only be satisfied by a virile, sexy, desirable man. A man like...

"Zach Tanner," she murmured to herself. Annabeth pushed out of the chair, frightening Giselle with her sudden movement. The cat scooted into the bedroom and Annabeth followed her.

Losing herself in some ridiculous fantasy about a man she could never have was a waste of time and energy. Annabeth knotted her T-shirt at her waist, pulled a black dance skirt from the dresser and wrapped it over her black lace underwear. She would use her energy for something more constructive. Dancing would drive all thoughts of Zach from her mind and body, leaving her exhausted and ready to sleep.

The ballroom was stuffy with the heat from the day and Annabeth threw open the French doors to let the growing breeze in. Outside, the lightning and thunder moved closer and Annabeth could feel the approaching rain in the damp wind. She didn't need music. The sounds of nature would be her orchestra.

She laced up her toe shoes, then diligently began to flex and stretch her muscles as she listened to the rhythms of the approaching storm. After a proper warm-up, she slowly began to dance, moving around the room in idle combinations. But as the weather grew in intensity, she pushed herself harder, until her leaps and turns mirrored the wind in the trees. On and on she danced, mixing avant-garde with classical ballet, gathering energy from the turmoil outside and expending it with every movement. Her worries dissolved one by one—Zach, the house, her career, her future—replaced by the burning ache of her muscles and the pounding of her heart, until her mind was empty of all except her body and the space it occupied.

She felt as if she could dance forever, but the sound of the rain stopped her. She froze and listened as sheets of water pelted the roof and the parched ground. A bead of perspiration trickled from her temple down her neck and she brushed it away as she gasped for breath. Tipping her head back, she closed her eyes and let the soothing hiss and patter of raindrops wash over her.

She wasn't sure how long she stood, lost in the storm's embrace. But when she opened her eyes, she knew he would be there, standing inside an open French door, his tall form outlined by intermittent flashes of lightning, the curtains billowing around him. Annabeth stared at him, willing the image to disappear back into the maelstrom of wind and water.

He walked toward her. His clothes were drenched and his hair was slicked back, still dripping water onto his collar. His shirt clung to his shoulders and torso like a second skin and his jeans were muddy around the ankles. He looked as dark and dangerous as the weather that had spawned him and Annabeth held her breath, wanting to flee, yet compelled to stay.

Slowly he reached out and placed his cool, damp palm on her flushed cheek, as if to assure himself that she was real. She turned her face into his touch and covered his hand with hers. There was nothing left to fight him with. It had all been spent on the storm and her dance. She was empty and now she needed to be filled with the raw energy that radiated from this man's caress.

She stepped toward him, until they were just inches apart, inviting his embrace. He waited until the tension between them was nearly unbearable. Then he slipped his arm around her waist and drew their bodies together. The meeting was electric, jolting Annabeth until her nerves sang with the feel of his body, her breasts flattened against his chest, her hips fitted against his thighs, his mouth pressed into the curve of her neck.

"Teach me to dance, Annie," he murmured, his lips soft against her jaw. "Teach me to cha-cha." His voice was smooth and persuasive with a teasing hint of humor.

She wrapped her arms around his neck and rested her head against his chest. His heart thudded a strong beat against her cheek and she moved to the rhythm, leading him in a lazy circle around the floor.

He pulled back and looked down at her face, his eyes hooded with desire. "I watch you dance, Annie, and I see the passion in your movements. You don't know how much I've wanted to hold you and feel that passion in my arms." Suddenly he was leading her, pressing her body into his and mirroring her every movement. It was as if they were one, responding to each other's steps with subtle shifts and sways, until she was molded to him, inseparable.

His gaze was locked on hers as they danced and Annabeth was unable to break the connection. How often had she imagined his face in her dreams, then brushed the image away upon waking? And now, to study him so openly, so freely, she wondered how she would ever be able to turn away. The potent lines and planes of his face, his straight nose and his firm mouth, burned into her memory, and as with an addiction, she craved more.

Her fingers slid to the buttons of his shirt and she worked them open, struggling against the damp fabric and tugging the tails from his jeans. She placed her palms on his chest and pushed his shirt away, skimming her hands over his pebbled nipples. Zach closed his eyes and sucked in his breath, a low moan rumbling in his throat. Emboldened by his reaction, she stripped the shirt from his body and let it drop to the floor.

A feeling of power suffused her as her feminine instincts took over. She had never seduced a man in her life, but somehow she knew what to do, how to make Zach burn for her. And she wanted him to burn, hot and violent and raging out of control, until he had no choice but to take her and feed the fire, or crumble into ashes.

She pressed her forehead to his chest and traced a path with her tongue, circling each nipple and gently biting his taut skin along the way. His breath quickened and he moaned her name over and over again, pulling her hips into his until she could feel his hardening desire.

Then his willpower suddenly shattered. He grasped her face in his hands and pulled her mouth to his. His kiss was urgent and demanding, begging her to stop the torture, yet promising her deeper pleasures. The power of his kiss shook her, penetrating to her very soul, until she was conscious of nothing beyond their embrace.

Reality dissolved around them into the heady sensations of touch and smell and sound and sight. As the fire between them grew, the weather raged outside. The storm was upon them, the sounds of thunder and rain mixed with sighs and moans and whispered needs, the wind whipping through the open door and swirling around them.

Their dance ended in the curve of the grand piano. Zach grasped Annabeth around the waist and effortlessly lifted her onto the piano, then slid her toward him, capturing her legs against his ribs. The balance of control had subtly shifted to him and Annabeth closed her eyes and gave in to his tender exploration of her body. He deftly unknotted her T-shirt and slipped his hands underneath, cupping her breasts in his palms.

"Perfect," he murmured as he lowered his mouth to tease her flesh through the soft fabric of her shirt. A shiver raced through her and Annabeth curled her arms around his head and wove her fingers through his wet hair. It all felt so right, this total abandon to her desires, to him. It gave sudden meaning to a need within her she had too long tried to ignore. Her feelings for Zach ran deep and inhabited places that had been untouched by all others in her life.

He stepped back and drew her legs higher, then bent to place a kiss on her calf, just above the twisted ribbon of her toe shoe. His mouth burned a path across the scar on her knee and along her inner thigh as he gathered the sheer fabric of her dance skirt in his fists. A sigh escaped Annabeth's lips, part moan, part gasp, and she arched her back and braced herself on trembling arms. A tiny knot twisted deep inside her, tightening until she ached with need.

"Let me love you, Annie," he whispered. His lips moved toward the core of her desire and his fingers hooked the damp fabric of her panties. His mouth touched her heat for just a searing instant. A cry tore from Annabeth's throat, and she lost all sense of control at the same moment Zach did.

She pushed herself up and reached for the top button of his jeans as he tugged at her silk underwear. The delicate fabric ripped in his fierce urgency. "Please," she pleaded breathlessly. She fumbled with his zipper, then finally freed him from the faded denim and silk boxer shorts. Her hand skimmed along his erection, magnetically drawn to the hot, silken hardness. Sucking in his breath, he grabbed her wrist, stilling her touch.

"Tell me you love me, Annie," he whispered. "Even if you don't mean it, I want to hear you say it, just once."

"Please, Zach," she pleaded, poised on the edge of her release.

It took him only a moment to pull protection from his wallet and sheath himself. A moment that seemed like hours. He probed gently at her moist entrance. "Say it, Annie."

"I—I love you," she cried, willing to say anything to have him inside of her. He filled her in one swift, sure movement, drawing her into his arms and locking her legs around his waist. "I love you," she murmured into the tensed muscles of his neck and shoulder, realizing that she truly meant the words.

Later, twisted in the sheets of her bed, they made love again, until they fell back into the pillows, their desire spent and their sweat-slicked bodies exhausted. As the thunder and lightning echoed in the far reaches of the night, Annabeth watched him sleep. She reached out and smoothed his rumpled hair, then drew her finger along his beard-roughened jaw.

She did love Zach Tanner. The realization changed everything...yet it changed nothing.

8

ANNABETH AWOKE with a start, the sharp rapping at her bedroom door snatching her from a deep and dreamless sleep. She pushed her disheveled hair from her eyes and glanced around the room. Something wasn't right, something was out of place. Blinking hard, she tried to sweep the cobwebs from her sleep-muddled mind. Awareness slowly seeped into her thoughts and she realized what was wrong.

Zach was gone.

Jasmine called from the other side of the door. "Annabeth, are you awake? Dear, it's nearly ten o'clock. Can I come in? I've brought you some breakfast."

Annabeth tossed the covers away and jumped out of bed, then noticed she was stark naked. Frantically she searched for something to put on, but found only her dance attire scattered around the floor. She found her robe draped over a chair and pulled it on, then made another search for Zach. In the bathroom, outside on the veranda, in the armoire, under the bed. Where was he?

"Annabeth? Are you all right? You aren't sick, are you?"

Sick? She shook her head then pressed her palm to her forehead. She did feel a bit feverish. But she certainly couldn't have dreamed last night, could she? It had all seemed so real, so vivid and intense. The storm, their dance, Zach's body joined with hers. She searched the room again, looking for some clue that he had been with her in her bedroom, but there was nothing. Nothing, except...

Touching her lips with her fingertips, she detected a slight puffiness, as if she'd been kissed...many times. Her hand fluttered to her cheek and there, an almost imperceptible roughness where his beard had chafed her skin. She lowered herself to the bed and felt a warm, aching dampness between her legs.

Oh, God, she hadn't been dreaming. She had spent the night making love to Zach Tanner. Suddenly she *did* feel a little sick.

Grabbing a pillow, she pressed her face into it and smothered a groan. The scent of his cologne lingered on the pillowcase and she squeezed her eyes shut and held her breath. How could she have let this happen? In less than a week, she might have to leave this house and she had slept with the man who was prepared to take it all away from her. Now was no time to let her hormones rule her behavior.

"Annabeth?" The soft rapping continued on the door.

"Yes?" she croaked.

"Can I come in, dear?"

Annabeth pushed from the bed and walked to the door. After one more anxious look around the room, she opened it. Jasmine bustled into the bedroom, a rosewood tray in her hands.

"Darlin', what is wrong with you? You were sleeping like the dead! I've been knockin' for the longest time."

"I—I'm sorry," Annabeth replied.

Jasmine set the tray on the bed and turned to her, concern etched across her smooth, lovely features. "Are you feelin' all right, Annabeth? You look a little flushed."

"No—no, I'm fine. Just a little groggy. I just woke up."

"You don't look yourself at all. Your cheeks are pink and your eyes look a bit glazed. Why don't you lie down and rest? I brought you coffee and some warm biscuits and fresh sliced peaches."

Annabeth stared at her in confusion. "What are you doing here? You're supposed to be in Atlantic City. You left yesterday morning."

"I decided not to go to Atlantic City."

"You decided not to— You were here? Last night? In this house?" Had she heard them? Jasmine's room was right next door. And if Annabeth recalled anything from the previous evening, it was that they hadn't bothered to be quiet.

"No," Jasmine replied, straightening the bedclothes. "I was in Charleston. With Mr. Palmer. His sister fell ill and he had to cancel out of the trip to Atlantic City. I didn't feel like going without him, so I offered to accompany him to Charleston to see her. Rose and Daisy were scandalized, of course. And his sister wasn't as ill as all that. She's a bit complainy. So rather than turn 'round and drive back, we decided to have dinner. And after dinner, we went dancin', and then it was too late to drive back, so we stayed in Charleston."

"Jasmine! You and Mr. Palmer stayed in a hotel, in the—"

"In separate rooms," Jasmine said. She turned to Annabeth with a worried look. "You don't think I was too forward, do you? I mean, askin' to accompany him to Charleston. It felt like the right thing to do."

"No, I don't think it was too forward. You're a nineties woman, Jasmine. Trust your feelings. Go for it."

Jasmine sighed. "Good. I'm just not always sure how to proceed. I've never been courted before. Now, why don't you lie back and eat your breakfast?" Jasmine reached over and fluffed the pillows, then frowned. "What's this?"

Annabeth swallowed convulsively. "What's what?"

Jasmine held up a delicate white gardenia. "This. It was

nestled between your pillows. It looks like a gardenia from the garden. How did that get up here?"

"I—I—I picked it, last night," Annabeth said.

"Last night? But look, the dew is still fresh on it." She held it out to Annabeth and the sweet scent touched her nose. Zach must have picked it for her and placed it on her pillow before he left.

Annabeth took the flower from Jasmine and dropped it on the bedside table. "Rain. It was raining hard last night. It's just wet. Lord, I am famished. Did you bring some honey with those biscuits?"

"Yes, dear. Settle back while I pour you a cup of coffee. Now that the heat wave has broken, we can enjoy a hot cup of coffee in the morning without wilting."

"The heat wave," Annabeth murmured. A cool breeze blew through the open windows, billowing the lace curtains and the mosquito netting. She hadn't noticed. Though she had slept soundly for the first time since she arrived, she suspected it was from sheer exhaustion and not because of the change in weather. She leaned back against the pillows and closed her eyes, feeling a sudden headache coming on.

"Well, I'll just leave you to your breakfast, dear," Jasmine said as she hurried to the door. "Mr. Claude Palmer and I are having lunch today and I need to get ready. Oh, by the way, there's an envelope for you on the tray," she added. "It looks like it's from Zachary."

Annabeth's eyes snapped open. "Zachary?"

"Yes, it's in a Tanner Enterprises envelope. It was on the kitchen table." She stood in the doorway, studying Annabeth with discerning eyes. "Dear, would you mind if I gave you a bit of advice?"

Annabeth felt her face warm. "Advice? What kind of advice?"

"I know you're a nineties woman, dear, but be sure to

wear a scarf today. You've got a love bite on your neck and I wouldn't want anyone to get the idea that your virtue has been compromised."

Annabeth slapped her hand to her neck. Jasmine smiled coyly then slowly closed the door. Groaning, Annabeth flopped back against the pillows.

There were no secrets in Magnolia Grove. "Even my ingrowed toenails is on the outside of my shoes," Annabeth muttered, repeating a saying she had heard more than once since she arrived. She rolled her eyes. Oh Lord, now she was starting to sound like them, too.

She reached out and snatched the letter from the tray. Her name was scrawled across the envelope in an urgent hand. She opened the flap and removed the single sheet, wondering if the missive contained an excuse for Zach's disappearance from her bed. Maybe he was having second thoughts as well. Maybe, he, too, had realized that last night had been a mistake.

Annie B.
Court appearance moved up to 3:30 p.m. today! See you there.

Zach

Annabeth stared at the note, shocked. What was he trying to pull? Their court date was still a week away. Damn him! He'd pulled some strings, wielded his family's considerable political power and probably bribed Judge Clemmons to hear their case early. He couldn't do that, could he? Not without her permission. But he had.

She wasn't ready! Though she had decided not to use the journals, she had hoped she would be able to devise a way to prove DeWitt Tanner's intent without dragging all the details out into plain view in front of the entire town. And she'd heard nothing from her grandmother's lawyer about Roosevelt House, though she probably wouldn't use the information even if she had it. Still, she needed more time.

She had no doubt that her day in court would be as well attended by the populace of Magnolia Grove as Sunday service at the Baptist Church. Miss Blanche and her biddies probably had a box social and quilting bee planned for afterward so they would have ample opportunity to cluck over the scandal. The town had remained quiet for this long, but all it would take would be one greedy onlooker, a phone call to the tabloids and a thorough examination of the public records, and the story would be headline news. DeWitt's reputation and Zach's future would be in pieces.

And after that, a well-placed comment from Senator Gaines at a high-society Atlanta cocktail party and her mother would be the one made to suffer. The best she could hope for was an empty courtroom and a sympathetic judge, because she had little more to present than a forty-year-old deed that had never been registered.

Another week wouldn't have made much of a difference, Annabeth admitted to herself. It was time to plead her case. In a way, she was glad it would happen today. No matter what the outcome, one way or another, Zach, and the feelings of confusion he caused, would be out of her life by sundown. Obviously Zach felt the same way. He wanted their dispute settled so he could go on with his life as well.

A sharp pain pierced her heart at the thought of losing Zach. Why couldn't he have come along at a different time in her life, a time when she was stronger, when she had more to offer...after she had proved everything she needed to prove to herself? She could have loved him then, opened herself to the wild and intense feelings he brought forth in her. She could have shared her life with him.

She would forget last night and the strange feelings Zach

Tanner aroused in her. She would determine her own destiny. And no matter what the judge decided today, she would find happiness.

"I WANT ANNABETH DUPREE to have the house," Zach said.

John Crawford looked at him in bewilderment. "But the house is yours. You've got a perfected deed, Zach. Under race notice law, you hold the title. And unless she can convince the judge of your grandfather's intentions, her deed is not valid."

"I know that," Zach replied. He slouched in the vinyl booth, his gaze drifting distractedly over the patrons at the Hide-A-Way Café. John Crawford, in his tailored suit and polished wing tips, looked absurdly out of place among the faded denim and farm caps. He would have to advise his attorney on the proper dress code for brunch at Magnolia Grove's truck-stop diner. Zach took a gulp of his lukewarm coffee and turned his attention back to Crawford. "There has to be a way we can lose this case without it appearing that we've taken a legal dive. What about adverse possession? Couldn't she claim the house on those grounds?"

Crawford shook his head. "It wouldn't work. DeWitt was well aware that Lily Fontaine was inhabiting the house. I don't understand, why would you want to lose this case?"

"I have my reasons," Zach said. "I can't allow Annabeth Dupree to leave Magnolia Grove."

"If she's got a sharp attorney who knows real estate law, he might be able to prove intent. She's got a handwritten deed and that's a pretty powerful indication right there. The court usually tries to determine the true intentions of the parties involved, rather than following the letter of the law. The moral argument is often stronger than the legal argument. The deed was registered in your name as part of the closing of your grandfather's estate, without your grandfather's knowledge. For some reason, Lily Fontaine or your grandfather never perfected that first deed. A good attorney will have an explanation for that."

Zach shook his head. "She doesn't have an attorney. I don't think she can afford one. She barely has any money. But she does have some solid evidence regarding our grandparents' relationship. Journals detailing their financial entanglement."

"All right," Crawford said. "That would help her case. When she presents them in court, we won't raise any objections."

"She won't present them in court, John. She thinks that revealing them might damage my political future."

Crawford frowned. "What political future? I thought you told Senator Gaines—"

"I did. And I told her the same, but she wouldn't believe me. Besides, I think she's just using that as an excuse. Gaines threatened her or scared her in some way and she's trying to cover that up. I just can't figure out what he might have said to frighten her. Annabeth isn't the type to frighten easily."

"Maybe I have some insight into that," John said. He pulled a file folder from his briefcase and handed it to Zach.

"What's this?"

"I had a private investigator do a background check on Annabeth Dupree. I thought it might be helpful to know a little more about the person we're dealing with."

Zach tossed the folder onto the table. "I don't need to look at this. I know all I need to know about Annabeth."

Crawford shook his head. "She led a pretty wild life in New York. Night clubs, trendy parties and a taste for expensive things—clothes, furs, jewelry. Zach, this is not the kind of woman you want to get involved with."

He shoved the folder back at Crawford. "She's not like that anymore."

"Zach, listen to—"

Zach leaned forward and slammed his palms on the Formica tabletop. "No! You listen. I know Annabeth and she's left that life behind. Besides, she's already admitted those things to me."

The room went silent as all eyes turned in their direction. Relaxing back into his seat, Zach smiled apologetically. "Sorry. I didn't mean to bark at you like that." He raked his fingers through his hair. "I didn't get much sleep last night."

Crawford accepted his explanation with his usual discretion. He reached for the folder. "There is one other thing that Gaines might be holding over her head. Her mother."

Zach frowned. "Her mother? Annabeth has a mother?"

"Most of us do," Crawford quipped acerbically, breaking the tension that hung over the table.

"What I meant was, I just assumed her mother was dead. She never speaks of her."

Crawford handed him a newspaper clipping. "Camilla Fontaine Dupree Robbilard."

Zach stared at the photo that accompanied the article on a recent Atlanta symphony benefit. "Camilla Robbilard is Annabeth's mother? But why would Annabeth want to keep that a secret?" He had met Camilla on several occasions and faced with the photo, he had to admit that Annabeth and Camilla bore a remarkable resemblance to each other. She and her current husband were prominent figures on the Atlanta social scene.

"Maybe Camilla is the one who'd rather keep her daughter a secret," Crawford suggested. "Annabeth has a reputation for being rebellious. Her mother put her in East Coast boarding schools at a young age and then in ballet school in

New York. Maybe she wanted to keep her out of trouble in her high-society backyard."

Zach grinned in satisfaction. "Or maybe Camilla wanted to keep her own parentage a secret. From her daughter *and* the public. She's the illegitimate daughter of a madam. And Miss Lily obviously tried to contact Annabeth. Why else would she have named her as her heir? Put grandmother and granddaughter together and the resulting gossip would not be welcome in Camilla's very proper social circle. I'll bet that's what Gaines is using."

"Sounds logical. So what do we do about it?"

"Remember that questionable development deal we passed on with Q.C. Construction? Gaines invested heavily in that venture and when it fell through, he came out of the rubble without a scratch, and quite a bit richer. I'm sure the news media might be interested in how those poor senior citizens lost their life savings, and Senator Gaines didn't lose a penny. But before you call the papers, make sure you call Senator Gaines first and give him an opportunity to confirm or deny. If he's open to negotiation, make a trade."

"Done. But what about Annabeth Dupree?"

"Let me handle that. Now that I know what's stopping her, I think I've got a way around her."

"CASE NUMBER 9-4-6-7. Tanner versus Dupree in the matter of eviction. Will the parties please step forward?"

Annabeth glanced around the courtroom as she stood and made her way to the front. Though the court date had been rescheduled just that morning, news had spread quickly and the entire town had turned out. Attendance rivaled that of the Magnolia Grove Volunteer Fire Department's annual tractor pull and demolition derby, which until this day, was the town's social event of the year.

She felt Zach's gaze follow her as she came forward and a

shiver shot through her body. He was dressed in an expensive business suit, with a pristine white shirt and a red paisley tie. An image of him, naked, his long legs tangled in the sheets of her bed, flashed through her mind, and a flush of heat crept from her toes to her cheeks. She blinked hard and deliberately avoided Zach's eyes as she stepped in front of Judge Clemmons's bench.

The judge waited for a long moment, then looked around the courtroom. "Where is your attorney, Miss Dupree?" he asked.

"I don't have one, Your Honor. Like Mr. Tanner, I'll be representing myself."

The judge sat back and eyed her critically. "But Mr. Tanner is himself a lawyer. He understands real estate law. You don't and though this may seem like a simple eviction case, the circumstances surrounding it are quite complex." The judge turned to Zach. "I thought you told me Miss Dupree was prepared to present her case. That's the only reason I agreed to reschedule."

"I am, Your Honor," Annabeth interrupted. "I want to settle this. Today."

"All right. Miss Dupree, let's start with you. Present your case."

Annabeth handed him her copy of the deed. "This is all I have to present. This is a handwritten copy of a deed giving Lily Fontaine title to the house at 453 Edisto Street."

The judge picked up the deed and scanned it through squinting eyes. "As I explained to you before, Miss Dupree, this deed has not been perfected. It wasn't registered, so it is invalid. Mr. Tanner, on the other hand, holds a registered deed. In a race notice state, in the instance of two deeds, the first to register is granted title."

"I object, Your Honor," Zach said.

Judge Clemmons turned an imperious gaze in Zach's direction. "You what?"

Annabeth followed his lead and stared at Zach, but hers was a look of confusion. What was he up to now?

"I object," Zach repeated.

"Just what might you be objectin' to, Mr. Tanner?"

"I think Miss Dupree should know that the first to register isn't always granted title to the house. There are extenuating circumstances that may prevent that...as I'm sure you know."

"I know my real estate law, Mr. Tanner, and you are arguin' against your own case. Objection overruled. Miss Dupree, please continue."

"Lily Fontaine and DeWitt Tanner were friends, Your Honor," Annabeth explained. "I believe that Senator Tanner deeded the house to my grandmother as a gift for all their years of friendship. He wrote out this deed and gave it to her, but for some reason it was never registered. Maybe they both thought the other was taking care of it. My grandmother lived in the house for over twenty-five years after the deed was dated. There is no evidence that she ever paid Mr. Tanner rent. Why would she? She believed she owned the house and so did he."

"Do you have some kind of proof that she never paid rent?" the judge asked.

"No, Your Honor—"

"Yes, Your Honor, she does," Zach interrupted.

Annabeth spun around and glared at Zach.

"Mr. Tanner!" the judge scolded. "As you are a qualified attorney, I'm sure you're aware of courtroom procedure. It is Miss Dupree's turn to talk. You'll get your turn later, when she's done. Now, Miss Dupree, is this true? Do you have proof?"

"No, Your Honor, I—"

Zach jumped in again. "Your Honor, may I have a word with Miss Dupree?"

The judge stiffened in his chair, his aggravation with Zach growing and his patience waning. "No! You are not allowed a word with her!" the judge shouted, shaking his finger. "She's not your client and you're not her lawyer!"

Zach remained unfazed, his expression cool and competent. "But, sir, I believe I have some information that is crucial to Miss Dupree's case."

Annabeth's breath caught in her throat and her heart twisted in fear. What was he doing? He couldn't really mean to bring up the journals himself, could he?

The judge cleared his throat and schooled his temper. "Mr. Tanner, tell me. Did you attend any of your law school classes or were you absent the entire year in which your class studied courtroom procedure? For a case to come to court, we must have two opposing parties. If the parties are not in opposition, we don't have a court case. Now, I want you to go over there and sit down and I don't want to hear another word from you until I call you forward."

"But—"

"Not another word, Mr. Tanner, or I'll hold you in contempt."

Zach glanced over at Annabeth. *Tell him*, his gaze urged. Annabeth averted her eyes.

When Zach was seated, the judge straightened the sleeves of his robe and began again. "Miss Dupree, continue."

"That's all I have to say, Judge Clemmons," she said.

The judge fixed her with an irritated frown. "Mr. Tanner," he said through clenched teeth, "you may *now* come forward and state your case."

Zach strode forward, as sure and confident in the courtroom as he had been in her bedroom. Annabeth held her breath as she watched him, unable to keep from admiring his smooth gait and handsome profile. Her admiration stopped when she saw what he held in his hands.

"Your Honor, I'd like to present these journals as evidence. These journals will prove that Lily Fontaine lived in the Edisto Street house for nearly thirty-five years and never paid rent."

"I object!" Annabeth shouted, attempting to snatch the journals from his hands. "You took those journals out of my room! Your Honor, I object!"

Zach held the journals above his head, just out of her reach. "Overruled," Zach said to Annabeth. "It's my turn to talk now. You had your turn."

The judge frowned. "Wait a second here! I'm the one who's supposed to do the overruling."

Zach turned to the judge and nodded apologetically. "Sorry, Your Honor."

"Overruled, Miss Dupree." The judge studied them both. "Now let me get this straight. Mr. Tanner, you are presentin' this evidence to prove Miss Dupree's case? And Miss Dupree, you are objectin' to this evidence?"

"Yes, Your Honor," they said in tandem.

The judge's gaze shifted back and forth between the two of them. He clenched his fists and pushed himself out of his leather chair. "Both of you, approach the bench!"

Zach stepped forward, then turned and waited for Annabeth. Hesitantly she joined him as Judge Clemmons, now thoroughly incensed, bent over his bench. "I have the sneakin' suspicion you two are wastin' the court's time with this case," he whispered.

"Your Honor, if I could just have a word with Miss Dupree, I think we could clear this whole matter up."

"I object, Your Honor!" Annabeth cried.

"Overruled. Miss Dupree, I order you to talk to Mr. Tanner. Now, before I boot you both out of my courtroom."

Zach grabbed Annabeth by the arm and pulled her down the center aisle. As they walked out the swinging doors, the courtroom observers buzzed with speculation. Annabeth almost expected a reporter with a microphone and a television camera to jump out in front of her and question her.

"What are you doing?" Annabeth snapped as she yanked out of his grasp.

Zach grabbed her arm again and steered her down the hallway into an empty courtroom. He firmly pushed her down into a chair, twisted it to face him and stood bending over her, a hand on each armrest. "I'm trying to help you!"

She tried to stand, but she was trapped and she bumped back down into the chair. "I don't need your help!" she shouted, crossing her arms and scowling at him belligerently. "And I don't *want* your help!"

"That's right," Zach shouted in return, trying to capture her gaze. "You don't need anyone, do you? Well, I've got a news flash for you, Annie B. You need me. You're just too contrary to admit it."

"I don't need you," she shot back, turning her head away.

"You think by needing me you're admitting some kind of failure or weakness. What about last night? Didn't that mean anything to you?"

"Last night was a mistake," she murmured. "It never should have happened."

"It wasn't a mistake. You wanted it as much as I did."

She drew a shaky breath and tried to stand. He stepped away from the chair and she rose, then met his gaze without faltering. "Not as much as I wanted the house," she lied. Her heart twisted in her chest as his expression froze.

"You're lying. I offered you the house once before and

you wouldn't take it. Last night had nothing to do with the house. It had everything to do with you and me."

"There is no you and me, Zach."

His icy expression barely hid his scorn. "Is that what you believe?"

She nodded.

He laughed bitterly. "Fine," he said. "There is no you and me. There never was. So why don't we go back into the courtroom and put an official end to our acquaintance?"

"Fine," Annabeth muttered, pushing past him.

"Annabeth," he called.

She stopped, her palms pressed flat on the door. She didn't turn to look at him, just waited for him to continue.

"Don't worry about Senator Gaines. He won't say a word about your mother. I've made sure of that."

Annabeth spun around, her mouth open, dumbfounded by his disclosure. He knew! How could he? She'd kept the threat to herself, determined not to involve him in her family's problems.

Zach sauntered up to her and placed his finger under her chin. "Close your mouth, Annie B. You'll catch a fly." He flipped his finger up, then turned and walked out the door.

She watched it swing shut behind him. He knew about Gaines, about her mother, about everything. She could have used the journals; he had tried to get her to use them, and she had refused. Annabeth groaned.

He won't say a word about your mother. I've made sure of that. Annabeth tried to sort out the jumble of feelings that raced through her. Zach had learned of her problem and he'd helped her. He'd protected her. And as a result, he had made it possible for her to argue her case. Maybe he was right. Maybe she did need him after all.

Annabeth pushed the door open and hurried back into the courtroom. The judge, Zach and the entire gallery were waiting patiently for her return. The judge cleared his throat and started where they had left off.

"Mr. Tanner, do you have anything more to present?"

Zach's voice was cold and distant, his expression indifferent. "No, Your Honor."

Annabeth looked at him, then at the judge. The journals were perched on the corner of his bench. "Your Hon—"

The judge picked up his gavel and struck it down once. The sound echoed through the now silent courtroom. "In the matter of Tanner versus Dupree, the eviction notice stands. All parties living in the house at 453 Edisto Street are ordered to vacate the premises within the next thirty days."

"But, Your Honor," Annabeth pleaded. "I'd like to explain the journals."

"You had your chance, Miss Dupree," the judge replied. "And I've made my decision. Next case," he called.

The courtroom exploded into noisy bedlam as everyone moved to leave and chattered over the outcome. Annabeth stood numbly in the front of the room, unable to believe that she had lost. She and the Flowers were being evicted, thrown out on the street. How could she have let this happen? She was supposed to take care of Daisy and Rose and Jasmine, and instead, she had let them down.

"Annabeth?"

She looked dazedly up to find Zach standing before her, his cool expression softening into one of concern.

"Annabeth, can we talk?"

Still stunned, she nodded and followed him out of the courtroom. He took her elbow and gently guided her to a quiet corner in the hall.

"I'm sorry it had to turn out this way," he said. "I didn't want you to get hurt."

"I'm fine," Annabeth replied in an involuntary response.

"Annie, I want to make this right," he said, skimming his

hands along her upper arms. "I want you to be happy. If you won't take the house from me, then I'll sell it to you. Go ahead, make me an offer."

She looked up at him and shook her head. "I don't have any money. I—I went to the bank and they won't loan me any. I can't take the Flowers' money, and I certainly can't take yours. How can I possibly buy the house from you?"

"We'll work something out. We'll—"

Annabeth grabbed his arms and dug her fingertips into his biceps. "Do you really want to work this out?" she asked, her voice betraying her desperation.

Zach nodded.

"Then let the Flowers stay in the house for as long as they want. They pay me rent. It's not much, and if you need more, I think they might be able to pay a little more. Just don't put them out in the street, Zach, please. They've lived there for so long. It's their home. Having to leave would devastate them. Promise me, Zach. Please."

"I promise," Zach said. "They can stay for as long as they want."

A flood of emotion choked her voice and she could only nod. "Thank you," she whispered.

"And what about you?" Zach asked. "Will you stay?"

She snapped her head up and looked directly into his eyes for the first time that day. "No," she said.

He stiffened, his features regaining some of their iciness. "What if I said the Flowers couldn't stay unless you did?"

"You wouldn't do that to them. You care about them as much as I do."

Zach softly brushed her cheek with his knuckles. "Stay, Annabeth. Please."

She lowered her gaze and stared at her feet, then shook her head. "No. I can't. I have to go. I have to make a new start, away from all this."

He shook her once in frustration, then tipped her face up until her gaze met his. "There's nothing wrong with needing someone, Annabeth. It doesn't make you weak, it makes you human."

"I know that." She swallowed hard. "And in a way, I do need you, Zach. But you need a woman with something to offer and I've got nothing. This is all I am, Zach. This and a rusty old car and a Himalayan cat. You deserve better."

"Dammit, Annabeth, don't say that." He yanked her against him, and covered her mouth with his, kissing her deeply. For a moment, she let herself respond to the kiss, but then reality returned and she pulled out of his grasp.

"Goodbye, Zach," she said as she backed away from him. "Take good care of the Flowers." Annabeth spun on her heel and ran down the hall, bursting through the front door. She felt as if she were running away from everything she had come to know and love, running toward a huge black void. She didn't stop running until she was out of breath and a painful stitch knotted her side.

"I will be happy," she murmured between gasps for breath. "I will be happy."

9

SHE DECIDED TO SPEND her last hour in Magnolia Grove in Jasmine's garden. The sun had risen two hours before, yet the flowers and leaves still shimmered with tiny droplets of dew. Annabeth inhaled deeply of the fragrance and closed her eyes. The South. The latitudes of lovely languor, Daisy had called it. No matter where she lived she would always remember the sweet, exotic scent of the soft breeze, the sun-drenched days and sultry evenings, the morning cries of the blue jays in the oaks and the gentle song of crickets at night.

Annabeth had decided to wait a few days until Daisy and Rose returned from Atlantic City before she said goodbye to the Edisto Street house and Magnolia Grove. Jasmine had spent the time in between trying to persuade Annabeth to stay. True to his word, Zach had agreed to rent the house to the Flowers for as long as they wanted to stay—at twenty-five dollars a month. Jasmine was quite pleased with her bargaining power and Annabeth was grateful to Zach for his generosity. He had specifically included Annabeth in the offer, Jasmine explained. But Annabeth refused to change her plans.

She would remember it all. And intricately woven into those memories would be memories of Zach. His smooth, deep voice. His mesmerizing blue eyes. His sculpted body and arresting features. How would she manage to extract him from those things that she wanted to remember, without losing it all?

He had left immediately after the judge had ruled, packing his bags and kissing Jasmine goodbye before Annabeth had even realized he was gone. Maybe that was for the best, she thought. A clean, quick break with no arguments or anger. Over the past two days, she had tried to drive him from her mind, but he had become as much a part of her as the Flowers and the house and the garden. She had grown used to having him near, as if his quiet strength was somehow a necessary element in her life, like water or food or sleep.

She loved him. Or at least she thought she did. Though she had tried to resist him, he had carved out a place in her heart and in her life. But how could she trust such an emotion? She had no experience to draw upon, nothing to hold up as a comparison. Once, she had tried to convince herself that she had loved David and she had almost accomplished that. But what she felt with Zach was different, more powerful and intense. But was it a true, everlasting love?

His feelings for her were just as mystifying. How could he possibly love her? He barely knew her—who she was and who she had been. A man like Zach didn't fall in love easily, especially not with a jobless, homeless, penniless ex-dancer. No, he couldn't love her. He just wanted her, desired her. She had been wrong about David's feelings for her. She wasn't going to make that mistake twice.

Annabeth took one long last look at the garden, then turned and walked to the house. She had planned to leave for Wichita after lunch, but the car was already packed. There was no reason to wait any longer, to bear through an emotional farewell lunch with the Flowers, to listen to their pleas and their reasoning. Yes, it would be better to leave now.

Though she tried to keep from looking, she couldn't help but stop in front of the servants' cottage. The door was closed and the curtains drawn, the cottage as empty and dark as her heart. Zach was gone, she was leaving and their lives would never cross again. She would survive, she told herself, and she would be happy again. Someday.

Annabeth pushed open the screen door to the house. The Flowers sat gathered around the kitchen table, the *Magnolia Grove Monitor* spread in front of them. They looked up at her as she entered, their expressions sad, but at the same time hopeful.

She forced a smile and a warm greeting. Leaving the Flowers would be the hardest farewell of all. They were her family, more than her mother and stepfather had ever been. They had loved her unconditionally, supported her dreams, and worried over her happiness. And they had served as role models of feminine strength and resiliency, three women who had put their pasts behind them to build new lives for themselves.

Good mornin', dear," Jasmine said. Daisy and Rose gave her wavering smiles. "We were just discussin' somethin' that might be of interest to you. There's a lovely storefront for rent downtown with an apartment above it. It would be the perfect place for your school. And the rent is very reasonable. Here's the advertisement." She held out the paper to Annabeth.

"We wish you'd reconsider your decision to leave," Daisy said.

Annabeth looked at the ad and shook her head. "This looks like a wonderful place. And the rent is reasonable. But it would have to be less than fifty dollars a month for it to be reasonable for me. I'm sorry, but I can't afford this."

"We could lend you the money, just until you get started," Rose offered. The offer had been made many times before, and each time she had refused.

"I appreciate your generosity," Annabeth said. "And I love you all for making the offer. But I've decided to go to Wichita. I can't change my mind. And I can't take your money."

"Can't or won't?" Jasmine asked.

"Both," Annabeth replied. "You have to trust me on this. This is something I have to do."

Jasmine stood and hugged her. "I do understand," she whispered. "You have to find your own place in this world."

Annabeth stepped back and looked into her misty eyes. "Thank you," she murmured. She looked up at the others. "I've decided that it might be best if I left now. It's nearly nine and I've got quite a drive ahead of me. And I'm not one for long goodbyes."

Daisy shook her head and looked frantically at Jasmine, then at Rose, then back to Annabeth. "But I thought you were going to stay for lunch, dear. You can't leave."

"You have to stay," Jasmine urged. "Just for a little while longer."

"Just stay until ten," Rose blurted out. "Then you can leave."

Annabeth looked at the trio suspiciously. "Why? What's happening at ten o'clock?"

The three went silent, nervously studying their teacups.

"Tell me," Annabeth said.

Jasmine was the first to crack. "Zachary called earlier. He's on his way from Atlanta and he wanted to speak to you before he left. He made us promise that we wouldn't let you leave until he got here."

Annabeth gnawed at her lower lip and shook her head,

trying to still her rapidly rising pulse. "We've said everything we could possibly say to each other. There's nothing more to discuss."

"Couldn't you stay and find out what he wants?" Daisy asked. "He said it was very important."

She drew a deep breath and let it out slowly. "No, I have to leave. And you have to let me go. Tell Zach I'm sorry, but I couldn't wait."

Jasmine wiped at her teary eyes. "We have some gifts for you," she said. "Gifts that will help you remember your time with us." She drew Annabeth toward the table and pushed her down into a chair.

Rose left the room and reappeared with a huge gift-wrapped box in her outstretched arms. Annabeth tugged at the ribbon and carefully tore away the foil paper. Inside the box, nestled in shredded paper, was Rose's antique china tea set with the red rose pattern. "It was your grandmother's favorite," she explained. "She left it to me and now I want you to have it."

Annabeth stood and threw her arms around the tall, reserved woman and hugged her fiercely. "Thank you," she said. "I'll treasure it always."

Rose brushed a tear from her cheek. "No proper Southern lady should ever be without her tea set."

Daisy handed her a long, narrow box made of worn leather. Annabeth flipped it open to find an exquisite lace-and-ivory fan. "For those warm summer evenings in Wichita," Daisy explained.

Annabeth kissed her soft, wrinkled cheek. "Thank you."

Jasmine's gift was last, wrapped in burlap and tied with a short piece of twine. A thorny stalk and a ball of dirt. Annabeth frowned.

"The rosebushes in the garden were planted here before the War Between The States, right after this house was built. Plant that cutting wherever you live, tend it carefully and it will bloom for you. And if you leave, take a cutting with you. That way you'll always have a piece of Magnolia Grove in your garden."

Annabeth gathered them together in a group hug. "Thank you all. You've given me more than you'll ever know and I'll never forget you."

"You'll visit?" Daisy asked.

"Yes," Annabeth assured her.

"And you'll write?" Rose asked.

"And call?" Jasmine added.

Annabeth laughed. "All of those. This isn't goodbye for good, I promise. Now why don't you help me carry these things out to the car? I have to collect Giselle and then I'll be ready to leave."

Fifteen minutes later, after a flurry of kisses and promises, she waved to the Flowers from her car as she pulled away from the front walk. She watched them in the rearview mirror, the three of them staring forlornly after her. It was only when she turned onto Palmetto Street that she allowed a sob to wrench from her throat and a tear to escape from the corner of her eye. She brushed it away, determined to master her emotions. Her new life started now, this moment, and she *would* be happy.

Annabeth turned to poke her finger into Giselle's cat carrier. "You'll like Wichita," she said, more for her own benefit than the cat's. "We'll find a nice apartment and I'll have a real job with a paycheck. It will be good. I promise."

She swung the car onto Main Street and took one last look at the town that had become so familiar to her. Past the phone company and Ben Early's General Store, the library and newspaper office. She had almost reached the edge of town when her car began to sputter.

"No," Annabeth cried, pumping the gas pedal furiously. "You can't quit on me now! Please, don't do this." But her cries had no effect. The car coughed once, then died. It rolled to a stop past the "Welcome to Magnolia Grove" sign.

Annabeth lowered her forehead to the steering wheel and cursed Elmore Turnbull, the mechanic who had given her car a tune-up just yesterday. He had told her that he was "certain-sure" that the car would get her to Wichita.

Well, Elmore was about to get her opinion on his "certain-sure" notion of quality control. The gas station was only a few blocks away. She'd walk there and give him a piece of her mind, before she ordered him to fix her car free. Annabeth rolled up the windows, grabbed Giselle's carrier and stepped out of the car, locking it behind her.

The filling station was deserted when Annabeth arrived. "Stand By Your Man" blared from an old radio inside and the chest-style soda machine out front hummed and rumbled in the heat. She walked into the garage and found Elmore, his two feet sticking out from beneath an old Cadillac convertible. She placed Giselle's carrier on the garage floor and peeked under the car. "Elmore Turnbull, I have a bone to pick with you! Come out from under that car right now."

Elmore slowly slid from beneath the Cadillac, revealing his huge body inch by inch. His face appeared and he grinned. "Howdy, Miz Du-pray. What ken I do fer ya?"

She braced her fists on her hips. "My car broke down just outside town. It won't start. I thought you told me you'd fixed it!"

Scowling, he sat up and rubbed his greasy hands on his coveralls. He pondered her statement for a long moment. Elmore, though supposedly brilliant with a socket wrench, operated in an entirely different time zone than the rest of the town. "Well, I thought I did," he drawled lazily. "But them foreign jobs got a way of kerflummixin' me. I ain't worked on a car like that since the dog et grandma. You got to know that fixin' that thing was tougher than puttin' socks on a rooster, Miz Du-pray."

"Spare me your excuses, Elmore. I want you to take your tow truck, go get my car and fix it, right now." She handed him her car keys.

"I guess I kin do that," he said, struggling to his feet.

Annabeth nodded her satisfaction, then watched impatiently as Elmore spent the next five minutes searching for his cap and another fifteen searching for the keys to the tow truck. By the time he returned, her car in tow, it was nearly ten-thirty. He crawled out of the truck and plodded back into the station.

"Well?" Annabeth asked, following him into the garage. "What's wrong with it?"

Elmore made a long ceremony of removing his hat and hanging it on a nail in the garage. "Cain't rightly say. It don't start, fer one."

"I know that," Annabeth replied. "How long will it take to fix?"

He shook his head lethargically and pushed his bottom lip out. "Cain't rightly say."

"What *cain* you rightly say, Elmore?"

He scratched his chin. "Might be best if you went on home and I'll call ya when I got 'er all sorted out."

"I'll wait here," Annabeth said.

"Suit yerself," Elmore said with a shrug. He walked back to the tow truck, lowered her car and opened the hood. Two hours, three Cokes, and one half-melted, vending machine Hershey bar later, Elmore lumbered back into the front room of the garage, a greasy component in his hand.

"What's that?"

"Fuel pump," Elmore said.

"That's what's wrong with my car? But, I just had that fixed a month ago!"

"'Spect you did. This here's a rebuilt model. Looks like it weren't rebuilt very well."

Annabeth ground her teeth. "How long will it take to fix?"

"A few hours."

"Great," Annabeth said. "Go ahead and fix it."

Elmore frowned. "I would, but I ain't got the part."

Annabeth's hopes fell, all her frustration and impatience dissolving with the realization that she wouldn't be leaving Magnolia Grove anytime soon. "How long will it take to get the part?"

"Cain't rightly say."

"Guess, Elmore," she pleaded. "Give me your best educated guess."

"Maybe a day or two."

Annabeth closed her eyes and rubbed her temples with her fingers. "I don't even want to know what it will cost," she said. "Just fix it and call me when it's done." She grabbed her overnight bag from the car, then headed for the front room of the garage and Giselle's cat carrier.

"You want I should drive you home, Miz Du-pray?" he asked.

"No," she replied, waving over her shoulder. "I'll walk."

Friday afternoon in downtown Magnolia Grove was about as busy as the small town got. Annabeth strode purposefully down Main Street, hoping she wouldn't run into anyone she knew. She glanced at her watch.

It was nearly one o'clock. If Zach had arrived at the house at ten, he had certainly left by now. The Flowers usually spent Friday afternoons playing cards with their senior citizens' group. She could sneak into the house without notice and surprise the Flowers when they came home. And if she was lucky, she would say another round of fast farewells tomorrow.

"Hey there, Annabeth Dupree!"

Annabeth turned and watched Sue Ellen hurry down the sidewalk toward her.

"Hello, Sue Ellen. How are you?"

"I'm fine," she answered. She looked down at Giselle's carrier. "Is your cat sick?"

"No, I'm just...taking her out for a stroll." Annabeth had kept her departure a secret from everyone but the Flowers. She had mailed out letters to all her students that morning, explaining her departure, which would arrive in their mailboxes the following day.

"I wanted to talk to you about startin' my mother in your ballroom class. She and her sister have been tearin' up the pea patch wantin' me to talk to you. They're both real nice ladies, widows for years, and I'd appreciate it if you would consider takin' them into your class."

Annabeth didn't know what to say. If she told Sue Ellen she was leaving, it would be all over town in ten minutes. It would be best to keep quiet; she'd learn soon enough. "I'll look at my class schedule," Annabeth said, "and I'll give you a call in a few days."

Sue Ellen grabbed her hand and shook it gratefully, before she hurried back to the phone company. "Thank you," she called. "I'll tell them. They'll be real excited."

Annabeth continued down the street and had taken no more than ten steps before Ben Early stopped her. "Hey there, Miss Annabeth," he greeted. "What's wrong with yer cat?"

"Nothing," Annabeth said. "I'm taking her out for a walk."

He peeked into the cage and nodded, then straightened. "I got that new faucet you ordered for your kitchen sink. If it's all right by you, I'll stop by tomorrow and put it in fer you."

"That would be fine, Mr. Early. I'm sure the Flowers will be glad to lose that dripping sound."

"See ya tomorrow, then," he said before he tipped his cap and continued down the street.

Catherine Jacobs, the librarian, was the next to stop Annabeth. She smiled tightly and approached in her supremely efficient stride. "Good afternoon, Miss Dupree," she said. She glanced down at Giselle, then looked up at Annabeth, her eyebrow raised.

"I'm taking her for a walk," Annabeth explained. "She's not sick."

"Hmm," Catherine replied. "If she ever gets sick, there's a fine veterinarian in Newton. He takes care of my three cats and he's very kindhearted to felines. If you need his name, please don't hesitate to call me."

"I won't," Annabeth said.

"Oh, by the way," Catherine added. "The girls from your ballet class have been in asking for books on classical dance. I've ordered ten new titles and they should be in circulation in a few weeks. I'd appreciate your advice in selecting some titles for the adult patrons. The girls' mothers seem to be as anxious to read about the ballet as their daughters. Could you stop in tomorrow and look through some catalogs?"

"Could I call you about that, Miss Jacobs?" Annabeth asked. "My schedule is a bit unclear right now."

"Of course." Catherine nodded.

By the time Annabeth turned onto Palmetto Street, three more people had stopped her to talk. In all her years in New York City, she had never spoken to her neighbors, never said hello to a stranger on the street, never had more than a handful of nonprofessional acquaintances. But here in Magnolia Grove, she had friends, real friends, people who were genuinely happy to run into her and chat for a spell.

As she strolled down Edisto Street, she wondered whether she had made a mistake in deciding to leave. Maybe her broken fuel pump was a sign, a warning for her to stop and reconsider what she was leaving behind. She had made a place for herself in this community and her students were counting on her. She had something to offer, something of value.

Annabeth stopped short on the sidewalk and turned slowly around in a circle, looking up to the canopy of live oaks that had so enthralled her on her first day in Magnolia Grove. Had her pride gotten in the way of common sense? Had she been so stubborn in her quest for independence that she had ignored the value of good friends?

She turned and gazed down the street, toward the large white house that stood at the end of the block, then took a deep breath. What would be the crime in accepting the Flowers' offer of help? And Zach's offer of a place to stay? It wasn't a matter of pride at all, she realized. She needed these people as much as they needed her. She had just been too stubborn to admit it.

Suddenly the walk home took on a magical quality. The air was sweeter than she'd remembered and the sounds of the birds in the trees more musical. She'd once thought the house seemed run-down, but now, as she approached, it looked like a fairy castle, perfect in every way.

The house was silent as she opened the front door and walked in. The Flowers never locked the house, a habit Annabeth had never been able to get used to. Now she was glad that they had refused to change their attitude. She set down Giselle's cage and opened the door to let her out. Giselle stepped daintily from the cage and strolled around the foyer, as if she'd never left.

Parched from her long walk, Annabeth headed toward the kitchen for a glass of iced tea. She would find a quiet place on the veranda, relax for a long while and reconsider her decision. And then, when the Flowers returned, she would discuss it with them.

A tall glass of cold tea in her hand, she pushed the screen door open and stopped in her tracks, clutching the edge of the door. Slowly she let the door close behind her, taking care to make no sound.

He was sprawled in a wicker chair, his hands folded across his chest. She waited for him to turn toward her, certain that he must have heard her footsteps. But he didn't move. She tiptoed across the veranda and looked cautiously over at him, trying to read his expression. She expected a cool frown or a sexy, challenging grin. But he appeared to be asleep. Bending down, she stared at his face, then listened to his breathing.

He looked utterly exhausted, as if he'd just dropped into the chair and fallen asleep instantly. His clothes were wrinkled and he hadn't shaved for a couple of days, and there were dark circles under his eyes. Even his shirt was buttoned crookedly. She looked out over the backyard and saw his car parked in front of the carriage house. She hadn't expected him to be here and wasn't sure why he still was. Once he had learned she was gone, he should have returned to Atlanta immediately.

But he didn't. Annabeth smiled and looked down at Zach. He was incredibly handsome when he was awake, but in sleep, his strong features softened until he looked almost vulnerable. Annabeth's fingers tingled as she remembered the feel of him beneath her palms.

Her memories drifted to the passion that his touch had aroused in her. If she hadn't been so pigheaded, they may have been able to find happiness together. Instead she had pushed him away at every opportunity. Annabeth frowned. But he had come back. Every time. Until he finally found her gone. And even then, he hadn't left. Had he somehow sensed she would come back?

Was there still time? Annabeth wondered. Could they try to work through their differences? She reached out to touch his cheek, then stopped and clenched her fingers into a fist. No, she would let him sleep. She wasn't sure what to say to him when he awoke and she needed more time to figure that out.

As Annabeth tiptoed past him, she noticed a battered shoe box at his feet. Taking care not to disturb him, she bent over and picked it up, then peeked inside. The box was filled with old letters, tied into packets with red ribbons. Annabeth withdrew one of the packets and stared at it. The letter on the top was addressed to DeWitt Tanner...in her grandmother's tidy, precise script.

Slowly she walked along the veranda and turned the corner, seeking some private place to examine the letters. Sinking into a wicker rocker, she placed the box in her lap and stared at it. Is this why Zach had returned? To bring her these letters?

She took the first packet from the box and untied the faded ribbon. The envelope was yellowed with age but she could still read the date on the postmark. October 17, 1946. She slipped the letter from the envelope, carefully unfolded it and began to read.

My dearest DeWitt,
Though it has been just an hour since you left me, I already feel the loneliness invading my heart. I'm sorry

that we had to part with angry words between us, but please know that no matter what troubles we may encounter, I will always love you. You must understand why I had to refuse your proposal of marriage. I've dreamed of the day when we might live together as man and wife, but my past and your future will always deny us that chance. This will never change the way I feel about you, my darling, for my love for you will last through eternity and it is there that we will find true happiness together...

A tear trickled down her cheek, and before she realized she was crying, she wiped it away. The letter, so short, but so revealing, was a revelation. In between the lines, she could read the pain in her grandmother's heart at having to deny a future with the man she loved. And she could sense DeWitt's frustration at having to hide his love for Miss Lily in order to continue the work he found so important.

She opened another letter from the packet, this one addressed to Miss Lily from DeWitt. One after another, she read each letter, from beginning to end, each piece of correspondence adding another chapter to the chronicle of a love that refused to die. In good times and bad, the letters continued, yet through it all, an unshakable faith in love and trust.

...you are always in my thoughts and in my heart, dear. Until we are together again I remain...

Your devoted Lily

Two hours later, Annabeth tied the ribbon around the last packet of letters. It was all there, in the letters, every detail of her grandmother's life and her love affair with

DeWitt Tanner. Even the Roosevelt House was no longer a mystery. Her grandmother had used DeWitt's money to fund a house for unwed mothers. The thought that she had ever considered her grandmother capable of blackmail now seemed just as preposterous as DeWitt Tanner profiting from Miss Lily's school.

As she returned the last packet to the box, she found one more letter awaiting her, separated from the other packets. She pulled it out, noting there was no address or stamp on the plain envelope. As she unfolded it, she noticed how smooth and unwrinkled it was, as if, unlike the others, it had never been read and reread. Her eyes scanned down the page to the salutation.

Dearest Annabeth,

She grabbed the envelope and examined both sides, then looked at the letter again. She recognized the handwriting immediately. It wasn't the perfect writing of her grandmother, or the ragged script of DeWitt. She was reading the strong, determined hand of Zach Tanner.

Dearest Annabeth,
By now you have read these letters and know the truth. Our grandparents shared a very special relationship, one that transcended society's bounds and grew ever stronger through the years. I found these letters in a box of my grandfather's things and thought you should have them. I am sorry I ever doubted your grandmother and her motives. I should have known that the unwavering honor and fierce independence you possess in abundance, you inherited from her. There is one other truth that you must know and believe above all. I love you and my feelings will

not change. I will wait for you as my grandfather waited for his Miss Lily, forever if I have to. Please learn from these letters, Annabeth. Don't keep me waiting a lifetime.

Zach

Annabeth tipped her head back and let the tears flow freely. She had almost lost him, running away from the love and security he offered, as if it might destroy the woman she was trying to become. But his love wouldn't undermine what she had built, it could only make her stronger.

Clutching Zach's letter in her hand, she stood and looked into the garden. For a fleeting moment she could almost see her grandmother there, strolling along the path, hand in hand with the man she loved. Lily and DeWitt had been denied a real life together, but she and Zach had a chance for much more. No, she wouldn't keep Zach waiting a lifetime. Their future together would begin now.

"Thank you, Grandmother," she whispered. "Thank you."

ZACH OPENED ONE EYE, then closed it with a groan. How long had he been asleep? However long it was, it wasn't long enough. He was still exhausted and felt like he had a hell of a hangover, though he hadn't touched a drop of liquor in days. He just hadn't slept for more than two or three hours each night since he had left Magnolia Grove.

At first he had tried to put Annabeth out of his mind, angry with her stubborn refusal to meet him halfway. But his attempts to forget Annabeth fell flat and before long he was trying to piece together a solution. He had less than forty-eight hours to find a way to keep Annabeth in his life. After a search through every box of his grandfather's belongings and papers, he found the letters at seven the previous night and spent an hour reading them. Then he composed his letter to Annabeth, suddenly wanting, needing, to put his feelings into words as his grandfather had so many years before.

He wasn't sure when she intended to leave, or if she had already left, but a late-night call to the Flowers gained him Annabeth's departure time. There was still a chance, still time to make this work. After a few hours sleep, he had hopped into his car and headed for Magnolia Grove, knowing that he had the key to his future with Annabeth in a battered shoe box. If she refused to see him, at least he had a chance with the letters. He knew she would be compelled to read them.

But he had been too late. Suddenly the adrenaline that had kept him awake for the previous two days drained from his body and he had found himself exhausted and utterly defeated.

How could he have let her go? He loved her, for God's sake! She was the most important thing in his life and he had let her get away. Somewhere along the line he had failed to make her see what they could be together. He had neglected her fears and insecurities and tried to force her to recognize her feelings for him.

Zach rubbed his eyes with the heels of his hands. As he shifted in his chair to work a kink out of his neck, he felt something tug on his shoelace. He straightened and looked down at his feet. A huge white cat with a gray face and paws and big blue eyes stared up at him.

"Hey there, Giselle." He leaned over and scratched the cat under her chin. "What are you—" Zach stared at the cat. Giselle. What was Annabeth's cat doing here? He frowned, searching the veranda around his feet. The box of letters was gone. Zach pushed himself out of the chair, so quickly he sent Giselle running for cover under a bush.

Footsteps sounded on the veranda and Zach turned and watched Annabeth come around the corner. Their gazes locked and Annabeth stopped. They stood in silence for a long time, neither one believing the other was real.

"Hello, Annie B."

"Hello, Zach," she said softly. A smile broke out on her face. "What are you doing here?"

"I came back to see you. I was sort of thinking I might sign up for some of those cha-cha lessons you give."

Annabeth's smile widened. "Is that all you came back for? Dance lessons?"

"You underestimate your abilities as a teacher, Annabeth. The last time we danced was pretty incredible. But practice does make perfect, isn't that right?"

Zach slowly walked along the veranda, his eyes never leaving her beautiful face. When he reached her, he grasped her hand and yanked her into his arms, burying his face in the curve of her neck. "God, Annabeth, I thought I'd lost you. I thought you were gone."

"And I thought I'd lost you. I was so blind, Zach. I had everything right here, everything I've ever dreamed about, only I was too stubborn to see it. I was too stubborn to reach out and grab it."

"But you're here now, Annabeth. That's all that matters. You've got me now and I don't ever want you to let go again."

"I won't make the same mistakes my grandmother made," Annabeth said.

"You read the letters?" he asked.

She nodded. "I need you, Zach, and I want you to be a part of my life. I love you."

Zach stepped back and cupped her face in his hands,

looking deeply into her wide eyes. "I love you, Annie B. And I'm never going to let you go." He kissed her long and hard, until his face was damp with her tears of happiness. Then he picked her up and spun her around and around, until she laughed out loud, a sweet, musical sound he wanted to listen to for the rest of his life.

He put her down and kissed her again. Then she stepped out of his embrace, grabbed his hand and dragged him into the house. "Where are we going?" he asked, grabbing her around the waist and pulling her up against his body. He nuzzled her neck and she giggled.

"Cha-cha lessons," she said.

"Umm. Can't that wait?"

She pushed him away playfully and took his hand. But as they passed the ballroom and started up the stairs, he pulled her to a stop. "Aren't we going to the ballroom?" he teased.

She shook her head. "I give some students cha-cha lessons in my bedroom."

He raised a brow dubiously. "*Some* students?"

"Well, only one student. Only *you*," she added with a laugh.

Zach growled and scooped her up into his arms, then carried her up the stairs. "That's right. Only me. And after the cha-cha, I thought maybe I'd like to learn the tango."

Annabeth gently nipped his earlobe. "That could be arranged."

"And after the tango, how about the rumba."

"Good choice," she whispered, outlining his ear with her tongue.

"And after that, how about—"

"Zach," she murmured, her breath warm in his ear.

"Yes, Annabeth?"

"Let's just start with the cha-cha and see where we go

from there. You wouldn't want to wear your teacher out after just one lesson, would you?"

Zach stopped in front of Annabeth's bedroom and kissed her thoroughly. Then he kicked the door open and carried her inside. They had the rest of their lives to dance, and he planned to spend every single minute with Annabeth in his arms.

"HEARD TELL there's goin' to be a weddin' back of Miss Lily's place next month." Ham Thompson pulled his fine Panama hat lower over his eyes and yawned, then hooked his thumbs under his suspenders. "Miss Lily's granddaughter and DeWitt Tanner's grandson?" he asked.

"Yep," Claude Palmer answered.

Ham watched the traffic pass by Ben Early's General Store from beneath the brim of his hat. "Don't that beat all," he said.

Claude stretched his legs out in front of him and crossed his arms over his chest. "I 'spect Miss Lily and Senator DeWitt would be happier than two ducks in a roomful of June bugs to see their kin livin' happily ever after," Claude drawled. "Makes a body believe in the power of love, don't it?"

"Shoot," Ham said. "You're startin' to sound as serious as a jackass in a graveyard. What kind of clabberheaded nonsense you got stuck in your craw now?"

"Nothin'," Claude replied. "I've just been thinkin' I might want to cut the cake myself. Zach Tanner's got hisself a real sweet lady there. I could use some of that kind of sugar in my life."

"You invited to the nuptials?" Ham asked.

Claude nodded lazily. "Yep. I'm escortin' Miss Jasmine."

"Humph. I bet Zach Tanner gets cold feet and gives her

the go-by," Ham predicted. "He'll be buckin' at the halter before the next full moon."

"How much?" Claude asked.

"Fifty?"

"Make it a hundred and I'll take that bet."

Ham studied his friend's expression for a long moment, then shook his head. "You ol' cheese-eater! I swear, you're as crooked as a barrel of snakes. I ain't bettin' with you no more!"

"And you didn't have no more chance than a dog in a pig race of winnin' that there bet, Ham."

Ham yawned and closed his eyes. "Truth to tell," he murmured, "I figured I was bein' foxed."

Claude leaned his chair back on two legs and closed his eyes. "Yep, love's a fine and powerful thing," he said. "A fine and powerful thing."

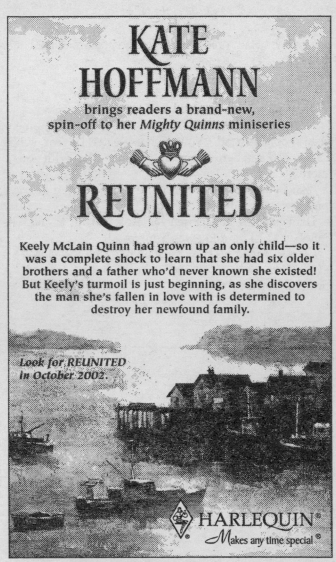

KATE HOFFMANN

brings readers a brand-new,
spin-off to her *Mighty Quinns* miniseries

REUNITED

Keely McLain Quinn had grown up an only child—so it
was a complete shock to learn that she had six older
brothers and a father who'd never known she existed!
But Keely's turmoil is just beginning, as she discovers
the man she's fallen in love with is determined to
destroy her newfound family.

*Look for REUNITED
in October 2002.*

HARLEQUIN®
Makes any time special®

HARLEQUIN®
Temptation.

Receive 75¢ off your next Harlequin Temptation® book purchase.

75¢ OFF!

Your next Harlequin Temptation® book purchase.

RETAILER: Harlequin Enterprises Ltd. will pay the face value of this coupon plus 8¢ if submitted by customer for this product only. Any other use constitutes fraud. Coupon is nonassignable. Void if taxed, prohibited or restricted by law. Void if copied. Consumer must pay any government taxes. For reimbursement submit coupons and proof of sales to: Harlequin Enterprises Ltd., P.O. Box 880478, El Paso, TX 88588-0478, U.S.A. Cash value 1/100¢. Valid in the U.S. only.

Coupon expires March 31, 2003.
Redeemable at participating retail outlets in the U.S. only.
Limit one coupon per purchase.

109910

5 65373 00075 5 (8100) 0 10991

HARLEQUIN®
Makes any time special ®

HARLEQUIN®

Temptation.

Receive 75¢ off your next Harlequin Temptation® book purchase.

75¢ OFF!

Your next Harlequin Temptation® book purchase.

52603860

Visit us at www.eHarlequin.com
NCP02HT-CANCOUPON
© 2002 Harlequin Enterprises Ltd.

HARLEQUIN®
Makes any time special ®

The holidays have descended on

COOPER'S CORNER

providing a touch of seasonal magic!

Coming in November 2002...
MY CHRISTMAS COWBOY
by Kate Hoffmann

Check-in: Bah humbug! That's what single mom Grace Penrose felt about Christmas this year All her plans for the Cooper's Corner Christmas Festival are going wrong— and now she finds out she has an unexpected houseguest!

Checkout: But sexy cowboy Tucker McCabe is no ordinary houseguest, and Grace feels her spirits start to lift. Suddenly she has the craziest urge to stand under the mistletoe...forever!

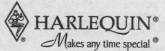

Receive
MOULIN ROUGE™
on VHS video

with two proofs of purchase
from any four specially marked
Harlequin® collector's editions.

Special Limited Time Offer

YES! Please send me my *MOULIN ROUGE*™ VHS
video without cost or obligation, except for shipping
and handling. Enclosed are two proofs of purchase from
specially marked Harlequin® collector's editions and a
check or money order for $3.50* shipping and handling
fee made payable to Harlequin Books.

*New York State residents please add applicable sales tax.
*Canadian residents please add 7% GST.

_____
Name (PLEASE PRINT)

_____
Address   Apt. #

_____
City   State/Prov.   Zip/Postal Code
                                    097 KJL DNC9

IN U.S. mail to: **IN CANADA mail to:**
MOULIN ROUGE Offer   MOULIN ROUGE Offer
3010 Walden Ave.   P.O. Box 608
P.O. Box 9023   Fort Erie, Ontario
Buffalo, NY 14269-9023   L2A 5X3

MOULIN ROUGE VIDEO OFFER TERMS
To receive your *MOULIN ROUGE*™ VHS video, complete the above order form. Mail it to us with
two proofs of purchase (one of which can be found in the upper right-hand corner of this page)
from any four specially marked Harlequin® collector's editions. Requests must be received no later
than March 31, 2003. Your *MOULIN ROUGE*™ video costs you only $3.50 for shipping and
handling (plus applicable taxes for Canadian and N.Y. State residents). It has a retail value of
$14.98 U.S. All orders subject to approval. Terms and prices subject to change without notice.
Please allow 6-8 weeks for delivery. Offer good in Canada and the U.S. only. Offer good only
while quantities last. Offer limited to one per household.

© 2002 Harlequin Enterprises Limited

Visit us at www.eHarlequin.com   PHNCP02-OFFER